I0778843

Keeper of the Hearth

The Three Sisters MacBeith
Book Two

Laura Strickland

© Copyright 2024 by Laura Strickland
Text by Laura Strickland
Cover by Kim Killion Designs

Dragonblade Publishing, Inc. is an imprint of Kathryn Le Veque Novels, Inc.
P.O. Box 23
Moreno Valley, CA 92556
ceo@dragonbladepublishing.com

Produced in the United States of America

First Edition January 2024
Trade Paperback Edition

Reproduction of any kind except where it pertains to short quotes in relation to advertising or promotion is strictly prohibited.

All Rights Reserved.

The characters and events portrayed in this book are fictitious. Any similarity to real persons, living or dead, is purely coincidental and not intended by the author.

ARE YOU SIGNED UP FOR DRAGONBLADE'S BLOG?

You'll get the latest news and information on exclusive giveaways, exclusive excerpts, coming releases, sales, free books, cover reveals and more.

Check out our complete list of authors, too!

No spam, no junk. That's a promise!

Sign Up Here

www.dragonbladepublishing.com

Dearest Reader;

Thank you for your support of a small press. At Dragonblade Publishing, we strive to bring you the highest quality Historical Romance from some of the best authors in the business. Without your support, there is no 'us', so we sincerely hope you adore these stories and find some new favorite authors along the way.

Happy Reading!

CEO, Dragonblade Publishing

Additional Dragonblade books by
Author Laura Strickland

The Three Sisters MacBeith Series
Keeper of the Gate (Book 1)
Keeper of the Hearth (Book 2)

Chapter One

Northwest Scotland, June 1620

RHIAN MACBEITH RAISED her gaze and scanned the battlefield. The fighting here, fierce and desperate, had lasted most the afternoon. She'd watched from her father's keep just behind her, aching because she could do nothing to help the people she loved—those who bled and suffered and, aye, all too often fell beneath the swords of their rivals and enemies, the MacLeods from across the glen.

Fear, anger, and frustration made her sweat. As a healer, she found it tortuous to stand by and watch, unable to act while others suffered. She'd wept and prayed for their MacBeith warriors to turn back their enemies, chase them back to the loch that separated the MacLeod from MacBeith lands.

The warriors of Clan MacBeith included two women, for both Rhian's sisters fought in this battle. Moira had, since their father's death early this summer, set herself up as chief of Clan MacBeith, and took her duties most seriously. Saerla, Rhian's dreamy-eyed, fey younger sister, who made a surprisingly fearsome warrior, had long since trained for the field.

The battle had turned just before nightfall when members of the MacLeod vanguard fell, and the others withdrew. Pursued by Rhian's sisters, their war chief Alasdair, and the rest of the howling MacBeith hosts, the enemy had not paused even to pick up all their dead. Everyone Rhian loved was still out there, in danger.

Now, in the rapidly gathering gloaming, she stood heartsick and surveyed the carnage.

She'd come stealing out of the keep past the forecourt and the main gate, which now stood open, with her basket of simples over her arm. No one had ordered her to stay inside, mainly because no one remained who had the authority to do so. Dead and dying—members of both clans—lay everywhere. Her heart told her it was her duty to alleviate suffering where she could.

But standing here, it seemed pure folly to think she and her basket of cures could do much good. The smell of blood arose and assaulted her nostrils. It mingled with that of sweat and mud trampled underfoot, for it had rained earlier. The air felt soft, and mist had begun to claw its way down the surrounding hillsides, mingling with the dusk to obscure what she did not want to see.

By God, what could she do here in this sea of suffering? Where to begin?

"Mistress Rhian!" One of their men, Hector, ran up beside her. He'd been defending at the gate for most the day and bore a number of garish wounds. One, which coursed down the side of his face, still dripped blood. "Ye should no' be here."

He was right—she likely should not. Moira would have a fit if she knew Rhian had ventured out. But her sister yet risked her life somewhere off in the gathering darkness.

Could she, Rhian, do any less?

"There are wounded," she began to Hector, but he had already left her. She could hear him still, calling to his fellows who had begun moving out into the field. "Bring in our wounded. Any MacLeods who are no' dead—finish them!"

Finish them. End their lives. Let whatever blood they had left after contributing to the morass that lay at Rhian's feet flow.

Murder accomplished here in the soft dark. *Madness.*

She went sick inside, and aye, she nearly turned back. Her

skills would be needed when they began bringing in their wounded. She should retreat.

But—what she heard coming out of the gloaming would not allow her to turn away. Men calling out. Groaning, crying, one screaming from a wound he could not bear.

How could she turn back when these men needed succor?

She tightened her grip on the basket. She could not think of her own safety. She must put her feelings of horror aside, as she had so often in the past. When her ma, whom she adored, had died. When her brother, Arran, had fallen in a battle not long after, and with him the hope of the clan. And Da—cut down only weeks ago in a battle against these same opponents. She had learned to bear the unbearable, to present a serene front, to think always of others.

She headed for the man she could hear screaming, who lay to her left. Most of the rescuers-cum-murderers had moved out straight ahead, where lay the thickest numbers of casualties.

Here, here had been the flank. She found her man lying among other wounded and dead. She could tell which were which because the living moaned or cried out. This man's shrieks were wordless and tortured.

She went down on her knees in the soaking turf next to him. Blood wet the ground all around him. As soon as she laid eyes on him, she saw there was nothing she could do.

She knew him, of course, as she knew most everyone. His name was Brann, and he was less than a score and five years old. He'd been partially disemboweled, his clothing rent along with the flesh beneath. His guts spilled from his body, and he stared in shock. He still held his sword in his right hand.

Rhian seized his left in both of hers and spoke his name. "Brann." She added a lie: "'Twill be all right."

"Mistress? It hurts. It hurts."

If she were truly bent on alleviating suffering as she so often claimed, she would open a wound just beneath his ear and, aye, let his life's blood flow. She had a *sgian-dubh*—no one went about without a knife, ever. And she could do naught else for him.

His gaze clung to hers in the dim light of the gloaming.

"Am I dying?"

"Aye."

"Tell my wife—"

He got no farther. A spasm racked him, and a gout of blood gushed from his mouth. He went still.

Thank God. Thank God!

Rhian got to her feet shaking in every limb and fought down sickness by drawing in great gulps of air. She should be accustomed to the smell of blood. But not like this.

The name of his wife, so Rhian remembered, was Aisla. She tucked that away in her head for later. She would tell Aisla her husband's last thoughts were of her.

Struggling to tuck her emotions away also, she moved to aid the other men nearby, homing in on the sounds of the moaning, the gasping, the desperate cries. She dressed the wounds of one man who then got to his feet and moved off under his own power. Another bore a grievous wound to the leg. From what Rhian could see, he might well lose it, and it was more than she could treat here. She called to two men who came with a litter, and she moved on.

Dead, dead, and dead. Fighting must have been fierce just here on the flank. MacBeith and MacLeod warriors lay together, sometimes entangled in their death throes. It did not matter what they wore, in the end. They all stared at her sightlessly.

She did not at realize at first how far she had moved off into the gloom. Above her, here, stretched the wall of the stronghold. Had these men tried to scale that wall? For MacLeod tartans lay thickly.

And someone just ahead cried out for mercy.

It could be one of her own who'd been battling these would-be invaders. She could not let him lie alone.

"Mercy! Och, please, God!"

She found him lying half beneath the body of another dead

man, whom she rolled off him. A big fellow, from what she could see in the gloom. Fair-haired, sprawled on his back, and awash with blood.

Och, by heaven, this must be bad.

She crouched down as she had beside all the others and set her basket on the ground. She could not immediately tell if the blood was his own or that of the man who'd been lying atop him. There was too much of it.

"Where are ye hurt?"

"Lady?"

He reached for her, closing a powerful hand stained with blood on her wrist. Desperate eyes reached for hers also, and as he moved, a groan tore from his lips.

She did not know him, and aye, she knew at least by sight, if not name, nearly everyone of MacBeith blood. But she could see and feel his pain just as if it came to her through his fingers that touched her. The hold that she kept so fiercely upon her emotions threatened to crack. Her compassion rushed forth.

"Hush. 'Twill be all right," she told him just as she had Brann. "Tell me where ye be hurt so I can help."

"Merciful lady." He gasped the words. "My right arm. I canna move it. The wound is deep."

"Your right arm, ye say?"

"Here." He let go of her in order to clutch at the arm just below the shoulder that gushed blood. By God, she thought, his arm might be half off, judging by all that blood. How was she to treat such a wound?

"Hush," she repeated. "Lie still. I will tie it up."

She began to work there in the poor light, tore away the soaking remnants of his clothing, and surveyed the wound beneath. The wound, as he said, was deep, the flesh torn in a gaping, ragged hole that exposed the tendons and bone beneath. Despite the horrific appearance of the injury, her hands steadied with the familiarity of the task.

She kept hoping she would recognize him. He might be one

of the men come in from outlying MacBeith lands to join the fight against their neighbors. Or, far worse, he could be a stranger.

He had a broad, strong chest and a massive build that included brawny arms, one of which was now chewed to shreds. A wound such as this, he might not survive.

"Ye be lucky," she told him as she rifled through her basket for enough bandaging to make a pad, and tied it on.

"Ye think so?" he asked through gritted teeth.

"Aye, so. Had ye taken this selfsame wound in your chest, ye would likely be dead."

"I might die, still."

Their eyes met, there in the gloom. A curious expression twisted his features. "Ye do no' ken who I am, d'ye, mistress?"

"I am afraid I do no'." She hoped, *hoped* he was one of their own. Yet her heart told her otherwise, and his expression confirmed it. She did not know him because nay, he was not a member of Clan MacBeith.

She blinked and moved her gaze over him, trying to peer beneath the blood. A big man, aye, with something compelling about him even though under all that blood—

He wore MacLeod tartan.

Chapter Two

SHE LOOKED LIKE an angel, this woman who hovered over him. But no ordinary angel with golden hair and feathered wings, all in white. Nay. She had an oval face, wide, steady eyes, and a lot of hair, all braided. He could not tell its color in the poor light, but it was not fair.

She was beautiful, and 'twas her compassion that made her so.

Now she sprang to her feet and backed away from him, having just realized she'd spent the last moments tending a mortal enemy.

Leith sat up in her wake, a gasp of agony tearing from him. What would she do now? The dead—his and hers alike—lay all around them, but the living remained not far off. He could quite clearly hear them, the members of Clan MacBeith. Carrying their wounded from the battlefield. Dispatching their enemies.

Men like him.

All this woman needed to do was call out. Those men who so efficiently dispatched his fellow MacLeod warriors would come. A quick blade to the throat and his life would end.

He drew a breath, which served to intensify his agony. His wound was bad—he'd known that from the instant he'd taken it. Lying there with the body of his fellow warrior, Carr, weighing him down, he'd been as good as dead.

Then he'd heard her. Moving closer, and closer. She'd appeared above him and knelt down, mercy in her gaze. Gentleness in her hands.

Neither could last.

If he could escape her, he might be able to get away through the dark. If he could stand, that was. At the moment, he doubted it. To reach home, he'd have to swim across the loch or make the long trek around by the burn, away up the glen.

Neither of those things was going to happen, given his present condition. Curse it all, he could not even get to his feet.

What he should do—what he truly should do—was silence this woman before she called out. His sword must be here in the grass, somewhere beside him.

He groped for it with his left hand, since the right refused to obey him. That fact drenched him with horror and sweat. His right hand—the right hand of a warrior—would not serve.

Even as he searched for the weapon, he knew he could not use it on her. Not even to save his life.

Abandoning the search for his blade, he attempted to scramble to his feet and failed. Aye, she would call out now. Realizing who, what he was, she would abandon all mercy and betray him.

Only it would not be a betrayal, would it? She was MacBeith and he MacLeod.

There did all mercy end.

He could hear the others getting closer, her clansmen. She had only to open her lips.

For the span of twenty heartbeats, she remained silent. Forty heartbeats. She must call out. And him, without the strength to rise.

Then, quite suddenly, she bent toward him. "Here."

Her arms came around him, tight. One slender shoulder lodged at his armpit. Even then it took Leith a moment to grasp her intentions, to accept that she meant to help him up.

They managed it, but not without difficulty, and stood swaying together while he fought back the agony and tried to catch his breath.

Despite his being soaked with blood, she kept hold of him, unwilling to let him fall. He could feel the warmth of her there in the rapidly cooling evening. He could smell her, by heaven, even over the heavy scent of the blood. She smelled like herbs. Like woman.

Leith had known his share of women in the past. Women liked to banter with him. To laugh and tease. To seduce.

None had ever looked at him this way, with her very soul in her eyes.

"Lady, wha' be yer name?"

"Rhian. I am Rhian MacBeith."

As beautiful as she was.

"I am Leith. Leith MacLeod. Wha' d'ye mean to do wi' me?"

Her gaze moved over his face and, incredibly, lingered on his lips. "Do wi' ye?"

"Will ye call your guards? Let them finish me off like the others?"

"Nay." She shook her head.

She still held him, which meant her breasts were pressed into the side of his chest, her mouth a mere whisper from his. No lightness here, no banter or teasing. What he felt was serious as life itself.

"Can ye stand on yer feet? Can ye walk on yer own?"

"I do no' ken."

"Go, if ye are able." She released her hold on him. He stumbled and nearly fell.

Go, she said. Out into the darkness where, aye, lay still another barrier to home. The broad expanse of the loch, which he could not cross in his condition. He might not make it.

Yet her mercy allowed her to offer him the chance.

He took one last, long look at her as she stood there, watching him. He memorized her features and wondered again at the color of all that hair.

"Thank ye, merciful angel," he whispered, the last words to

pass between them.

SHE SHOULD NOT have done that. Rhian knew at once she should never have let the man go. Yet she stood quite still and watched him stumble off into the gloaming. She should have called her men. Because he—he was the enemy.

Leith MacLeod.

She hadn't known that when she first found him, and him so soaked with blood she could not see the pattern on his tartan. Once she'd tended him, bandaged his wound, looked into his eyes—how could she let the men even now searching through the dark come and snatch his life?

Yet he was dangerous. A MacLeod warrior. One who could go off and lick his wounds, grow strong again, and return to harm what she loved. And och, aye, she loved. She loved the very stones of this place and those who lived in it. She might not express it often, she being a woman who looked after her emotions the way she looked after her duties. No one would ever accuse Rhian MacBeith of being exuberant. Calm, aye. Practical. Even serene at times. She remained devoted to this place, however, and those in it.

As she watched Leith MacLeod disappear through the gathering dark, however, she *felt*. Not calm nor practical. Definitely not serene. Shaken. Moved beyond all reason.

Aware of him as a man.

Which was pure foolishness. She had tended him because he'd been in need, nothing more. She would do the same for most anyone, be it man, woman, child, or animal. She rarely revealed the depth of compassion in her heart. That did not mean it failed to exist.

She would not, though, knowingly extend care to a MacLeod. That thought came to her, strong. Not if she knew. How could she provide succor to a member of the clan who had cost her brother, Arran, his life? Stolen her da from her, and harmed so many others?

Och, what had she done?

She turned back toward the keep, away from the darkness, thinking about her sister Moira. Of the three sisters MacBeith, Moira was the eldest, strong and valiant. A woman who had, herself, only recently lost her heart to a MacLeod.

Aye, so, it was the talk of the clan. Moira had assumed leadership after Da's death and, with the help of their war chief, Alasdair, done a braw job of leading them. But she'd fallen in love with a MacLeod prisoner seized during a raid—the very man who had struck their father down.

Rhian could not comprehend it. She understood love, aye. Or perhaps she did not, for she'd never yet fallen into that state. It seemed to her a woman should be able to put such feelings aside for the greater good.

Moira had not done that. Instead she'd brought the man, called Farlan, to live with her, and planned to wed with him. Even though he'd renounced his name and his place as a MacLeod for Moira's sake, and sacrificed his birthright, the MacBeith clansfolk knew him for the man who had killed their beloved chief. They'd near beaten him to death for it.

They did not want to accept him here at Moira's side. In fact, 'twas still to be decided whether she would be allowed to keep her place as chief if she did not part ways with him.

Rhian had heard it argued that Alasdair should take the place of chief, even though he was not a member of the chief's house. She'd even heard it whispered, by God, that *she* should take the place.

A worse prospect she could not imagine. She was a woman who worked in the background. She did her best to fill the place of her mother, who in a way had kept them all united till her death. Not her da's place.

"Mistress Rhian, come! Come awa' in."

One of their warriors called to her and, when she came near enough, caught her by the arm.

He had blood flowing freely from his jaw and his sword in his hand. He stared into her face earnestly.

"Any more o' our wounded out there?" He jerked his head toward the battle's flank, where she'd been. "Be they all dead?"

She could still betray the man who'd called her merciful angel, if she chose. He wouldn't have got far yet, and they might well run him down. He was the enemy.

She parted her lips and hesitated. "They be all dead."

"'Tis no' safe for ye out here, Mistress Rhian. Come wi' me."

She went. The horrors of the dark fell away behind her, but the man with the broad chest and the winsome, desperate face—he remained in her mind.

Chapter Three

RHIAN LOST HERSELF for a time after that in tending the wounded, of which there was no lack. They came to her in a steady stream, reeking of sweat, blood, and the remnants of fear. If they could not come to her, she went to them and forgot everything else in spending herself on those who needed her.

The clan had other healers, two of them, both male. Indeed, though Rhian performed the duties, she was not a healer as such. She ran the household, moving behind the scenes to accomplish all that must be done.

And yet she could not miss the fact that some of their wounded seemed to prefer her care to that of the other healers. Och, Timor and Preslan were competent, but folk would wait patiently for Rhian to see them instead.

Even now, as she cared for them, she wondered why. She never gushed or exclaimed over her patients, though she felt deeply for their hurts. One could not show such sympathies and attend competently to what must be done. Was it possible they picked up on her underlying compassion?

She did have a definite sense for what others were feeling. Not as her younger sister, Saerla, did. Saerla possessed a measure of clairvoyance. More than that, she carried a nearly visible aura of magic.

Yet those Rhian tended seemed to relax beneath her touch.

They steadied and went away feeling better than they had, despite their wounds.

The injuries she saw were terrible ones. She soon emptied her basket and had to fetch more supplies. On her way to her next patient, she paused abruptly, assailed by the memory of the man she'd encountered out in the gloaming.

His had been a dire wound indeed. Would it prevent him getting away? Would she ever see him again?

Did she want to?

Nay, to be sure, she did not. No woman of sound mind wanted to encounter a MacLeod warrior, however compelling he might be.

She pushed the thought of him away again and returned to the great hall, where many of the wounded had gathered. She had not seen either of her sisters since the end of the battle. She hoped both had returned safely. She could only imagine they would have collected injuries.

Indeed, she'd no sooner resumed tending the wounded than she looked up and beheld Saerla. Rhian made a swift assessment even as she readied the next set of bandages.

A curious and amazing woman was her sister. Though the youngest of Iain MacBeith's daughters appeared fragile and carried a wealth of dreaming in her misty blue eyes, she never hesitated to march out and face the worst of MacLeod's warriors with a sword in her hand.

Rhian's first impulse was always to try to protect her. She'd learned better, however. Saerla often had reasons beyond the ordinary for doing the things she did, and it was better not to question those reasons.

"Sister, how badly hurt are ye?"

For Rhian could see that, aye, Saerla was injured. Pain glinted in her eyes, and she had blood on her chin. Her leather armor bore slash marks across the breast.

Rhian caught her breath. A near thing, that must have been. The thickness of the leather had saved her.

Saerla held out her hand. It bore a slash across the palm that still oozed blood.

Horror and sympathy rose inside Rhian. As always, she tried to push it away. No place here for personal feelings.

"Och! Can ye move your fingers?"

"Aye." Saerla did so, and caught her breath against the pain.

"'Tis a blessing, that."

"I caught a slash from a MacLeod sword."

The cut was filthy. "I will need to clean this. 'Twill sting more than a bit. Here, sit down."

They sat facing one another, heads almost touching. Saerla laid her hand on Rhian's knee with perfect trust.

No one, seeing them so, would ever doubt they were sisters. Both had red hair, wild with curls when it went unbraided, and blue eyes. The MacBeiths bred true. If Saerla's mane shone a little brighter than her sister's, it could not be told in the torchlight. Rhian's profile might be a hint stronger—Moira's was stronger still. In a curious way, Rhian resembled their mother even as Moira resembled their da. Saerla had always followed her own path.

"Have ye seen Moira?" Rhian asked. "Is she safe? Wounded?"

"I ha' seen her, aye. Not hurt, so's I could see. She was speaking wi' Alasdair, who's no' hurt either."

"That is good."

Rhian thought again of the MacLeod warrior, out in the dark. "And Farlan MacLeod?"

Saerla's gaze came up and met Rhian's. "Moira says ye can no longer call him that. He's no' a MacLeod anymore."

"Then wha' am I to call him?" Their enemy? Moira's husband? But they were not yet wed. Her lover? Because aye, Farlan lodged with Moira and shared her bed. An interloper who would undoubtedly affect the leadership of the clan? Aye, he was that.

Rhian did not dislike the man. There was little enough to dislike in his self. He seemed a steady, patient sort, and he had sacrificed everything for Moira.

But he was—whatever Moira tried to claim—a MacLeod. He'd been Rory MacLeod's closest friend. And he'd struck the blow that ended her da's life.

Rhian still was not certain how Moira dealt with that.

"He was there. With Moira," Saerla said.

"Och." Rhian half grunted the word. "The MacLeods did no' kill him, then."

She had wondered about that. Since he'd been injured when he came to Moira, Farlan had not marched out to fight in the previous battles for their land—not until now.

"Curse MacLeod anyway," she muttered as she cleaned Saerla's wound. The old MacLeod chief, Camraith, had held his hand from destroying Clan MacBeith, considered the weaker of the two clans. But like her own da, Camraith was now in his grave, and his son, Rory, had sworn to claim all of Glen Bronach for the MacLeods.

By all accounts, Rory MacLeod was a most determined man. But he'd lost his closest friend, Farlan, to his enemies. To *love.*

"I am surprised yon Rory MacLeod did no' take the opportunity to murder Farlan there on the field, out o' revenge."

"Mayhap they did no' encounter one another. I ken Moira was worried about it." Saerla met Rhian's gaze again. "I ken fine folks are no' yet certain about Farlan. Perhaps even ye ha' doubts."

Rhian bit her lip and chose her words carefully. "I sympathize wi' Moira. And I can see she truly loves Farlan." An unusual enough circumstance when it came to Rhian's serious, focused sister. Moira rarely lost her head. And she lived to defend the clan.

Until now.

"And," she went on, even less steadily as she tied the bandage on Saerla's hand, "I ken fine that hate is a poison which will do none o' us any good." She raised her gaze to Saerla's face. "Those I treat who keep a sunny, hopeful mien tend to heal faster and more surely. 'Tis no' imagining, that, but something I ha' witnessed."

Saerla nodded.

"At the same time—" Rhian broke off.

"He is the man who killed Da," Saerla finished for her. "Aye, I ken."

"I fear he will cost Moira her place at the head o' the clan. And I struggle wi' finding any reason Moira would risk losing our MacBeith lands."

"Aye," Saerla agreed. "When it comes to love, there maun be some magic in it."

Chapter Four

THREE TIMES, LEITH nearly went down there in the dark. Once he tripped over something he could not see and kept going, stumbling forward. After that, with his blundering and trying desperately to find his way, increasing weakness hampered him, twice almost taking him to his knees.

That, and the pain.

He was a strong man, renowned for it. His cousin Rory often joked that Leith was a kitten in the body of a bull. *If ye had the will for it, man, ye'd be dangerous.*

Leith did not have the will to savage, to attack or slaughter. He'd much rather laugh, sing songs, and court women.

But others, looking at the size of him, took him as formidable.

And he thought, as he stumbled away through the gloom following his encounter with the MacBeith angel, perhaps he'd taken his own strength for granted. Relied upon his stamina and the muscles that sustained his great frame.

For now, when that strength deserted him, he was ill prepared.

The wound in his upper arm was a bad one. He'd known that the moment his opponent, a MacBeith warrior screaming his head off, plunged the blade into his arm. It had been Leith's own weight, or so he figured, that did much of the damage. He'd fallen toward the man onto the blade. When the fellow stepped back and wrested the sword away, it had twisted and ripped, gouging the flesh. Leith had fallen where he stood—the very place the angel had found him—and others had died atop him.

He'd been fighting on the flank when it happened, where Rory usually assigned him. So it went—Leith on one flank, their aging war chief, Murgor, on the other, Rory at center with his close friend Farlan at his side. The way it had always been.

Until now. Leith, staggering, trying to locate the rest of the MacLeod forces by sound as much as sight, grimaced. Farlan had lately defected, renounced his place in Clan MacLeod, and abandoned Rory. All for the sake of a woman.

Leith's thoughts flickered back to the merciful lass who'd tended him there on the field. Was Farlan's woman equal to her? If so, Leith could almost understand it.

Rory, however, could not. He'd denounced Farlan as a traitor and declared he'd strike him down if they ever met in combat.

Leith did not quite believe that. The two of them had been near inseparable since boyhood. But Rory was very angry. And hurt.

More to the point, Farlan's abandonment of his clan had put Rory in a vile mood, a persistent one. Which was good for no one.

And Rory'd had to march out without Farlan at his side. Was that why they'd lost this battle that they should have won?

Leith stumbled to a halt, gasping for breath. He could hear that the bulk of his company even now retreated, moving steadily away from him. He might follow, but he would have a vast distance to cover, a loch to cross, before he reached home.

If he failed to make it back to the MacLeod stronghold, Rory would not know what had happened to him. He would have a pretty good idea when no one who had been assigned to the right flank with Leith returned, for his companions had all perished.

Rory would not know if he'd been captured, or lay dead.

He had to make it home. Since Farlan had renounced his birthright, Rory had relied even more heavily than usual upon him. Aye, the three of them had always been close, in friendship and in strife. In war and in mischief. Rory needed him.

That conviction allowed him to get moving once more despite the great pain of his wound. His right arm hung limp as a hunk of meat, and he could feel that blood had soaked through the bandaging placed by the merciful woman.

Perhaps he would die here, out in the center of the glen. He did not particularly want to die alone, but he could tell he trailed the main part of the retreating army.

If he went down here, he would not get up again.

At least he would perish out under the sky in the glen he loved. He glanced at the firmament above him, spangled with stars that looked like bright eyes gazing down. The gloaming had faded as much as it ever did at this time of year, and he found himself gazing at eternity.

Ah, and who had thought it would end this way for him? It did so, aye, for many a warrior. But he'd wanted much more from his life. He'd always thought he'd stop playing and settle down someday. Have a family, a crop of laughing children and a wife who cared for him. That, *that* was why he'd fought—to secure this glen for MacLeod and make an enduring home.

Now the blood—his life's blood—seeped from him as steady as his heartbeat, and his life with it.

Ahead of him something stirred in the shadows, and hope leaped within him. Perhaps after all he'd caught up with their retreating men.

It allowed him to force his body back into motion.

"There!" cried someone up ahead. "'Tis one o' the bastards!"

Not his men, then. A cleanup crew of MacBeiths.

He drew a hard breath that expanded his broad chest and increased his agony. He lifted his sword in his left hand, since the right no longer served him. One last battle, then. He'd rather die out here beneath the stars than as a captive.

There were three of them, and they loomed before him like something from a bad dream. Splashed with blood they were, hard-eyed and well-armed. Aye, when he was whole, he might be able to take on three of them. Especially with his back to the wall. He was not whole now.

"Kill him!" one of the MacBeith warriors howled, and they all fell upon him.

His sword did not work as well as it should in his left hand. His muscles did not respond as well as they should either. But he fought with the desperation half choking him, till they beat him down to his knees.

He glimpsed one face coming closer, and felt a blow to the head before everything went dark.

He could not see. He could not see, but he could still hear, so that must mean he was still alive.

"Bring him," said one of his opponents. "And his sword. 'Tis a fine sword, that."

The others guffawed. "He's awfy big to carry. Can we no' just put a dirk through his brain?"

"Nay. Alasdair said bring any prisoners. He's no' dead—yet— and that makes him a prisoner."

I canna see. That fact frightened Leith badly, and he tried to express it even as the MacBeith men hoisted him up. It came out as a croak, and they ignored him.

He wished they'd plunge a dirk into his brain, because he did not want to be taken prisoner. Rory would never forgive him.

And he certainly did not want to live as a man blinded.

Chapter Five

"THERE IS A prisoner ye maun see." It was Alasdair who dropped the words in Rhian's ear. She raised an inquiring gaze to him and groaned inwardly.

Morning had come, bringing light that displayed all too clearly the scars of last night's battle. The blood, the broken and butchered bodies. The scattered weapons.

Not that Rhian had found time to look outside. She'd been kept busy tending the wounded since she came back into the stronghold.

She glanced up at Alasdair with impatience. He'd clearly had no respite either and had come from the field in his current condition—blood splashed on one side of his face and spattered over his leather armor. Rhian assumed that last was not his own.

Alasdair, a big man with an ironlike disposition, seemed indestructible. Though he fought always in the vanguard, frequently beside Moira, he rarely took other than minor wounds.

"I do no' ha' time for prisoners." Not that she failed to care. Suffering was suffering. She thought briefly of the MacLeod warrior she'd tended out in the dark. "I ha' enough o' our own men to tend." She indicated the man, lad, really, who now suffered beneath her hands.

Alasdair scowled at her.

"Is Moira whole?" she asked. He would know, since he

looked after Moira as an overgrown hound might.

"She is inside," Alasdair confirmed. "With that man o' hers beside her."

"Ah, then the MacLeods did no' kill him?"

"They did no'." Alasdair snorted.

The lad beneath Rhian's hands echoed the snort and got to his feet. "Thank ye, Mistress Rhian." He glanced at Alasdair. "As for that MacLeod bastard, if his own folk do no' kill him, someone here soon will."

He stalked off, and Alasdair frowned after him.

Rhian cleaned her hands carefully. "I ha' others o' our men waiting. I tell ye, Alasdair, I ha' no time for prisoners."

"This man is important. Farlan says so."

"Farlan does?" That surprised her.

"Aye. Farlan caught a glimpse o' him as he was carried in."

"Ah." Rhian wondered at it. Did Farlan speak up for the man's benefit? Or the benefit of Clan MacBeith? Despite Farlan's obvious love for Moira and the near-visible bonds between them, Rhian still found it difficult believing he would work against his own clan.

Something that might be spite flickered in Alasdair's dark eyes. "This man is close to Rory MacLeod. His cousin, so Farlan says."

Not that again. Farlan had been a prisoner, aye, and also valuable to Rory MacLeod. Rhian had tended him in turn.

"I ha' several more o' our men to care for. Then I will come."

To her discomfiture, Alasdair lingered and watched her care for said men. She could not help believing he must have more important things needing his attention.

She took her time giving the care, keeping her hands steady and gentle. They remained so until she gathered her bandages and salves back into her basket, and allowed Alasdair to lead her away.

"Where is he, this prisoner?"

"In yon cattle shed."

Rhian grimaced. The very same place Farlan had been housed when first he came to them. Could this be happening all over again?

"What is wrong wi' him?"

"A bad wound to the upper arm."

For an instant, only an instant, Rhian wondered. But nay, that man had either escaped or, given the state of his injury, perished out there in the dark.

"Blinded," Alasdair added.

"What?" Then it could not be him. For the man she'd tended had stared into her face, marking her features as if he wanted to memorize them.

She found Moira at the door outside the cattle pen when they arrived. Farlan stood at her side.

Rhian still found it impossible not to think of him as Farlan MacLeod, even though Moira insisted that name had been stripped from him along with his right to wear the MacLeod tartan. He was a big man, broad of chest and long of limb, with a cap of rich brown hair and a pair of earnest brown eyes. They fastened upon Rhian now, full of honest concern.

"His name is Leith, mistress. He is Rory's cousin and as close to him as—as I used to be."

For an instant, Rhian's world spun. *Leith MacLeod.* No, it could not be! What were the chances? And—blinded?

She shot Moira a look before returning her gaze to Farlan, holding hard to her scattered emotions. "A friend of yours, then, also?"

"Aye, mistress."

"Does he ken ye be here?"

"Nay. He has no' seen me yet." Farlan's features twisted with distress. "It appears he canna see."

"'Twould be well to keep him alive, if ye can," Moira put in. "He might be traded for some o' our men. They've taken two o' our own."

Rhian sighed. Nay, this could not be happening—could not

be happening again. Only weeks ago, Moira had made a hostage of Farlan before turning around and falling in love with him.

But Leith MacLeod…

Farlan said, "I do no' ken whether he can be saved. It looks verra bad. If anyone can save him, Mistress Rhian, 'tis yoursel'."

"Let us see what we have, then." Rhian raised a hand. "All o' ye stay out here. I will no' be crowded."

"I am coming," Moira replied, since she so seldom listened to suggestions.

A torch burned inside the shed, casting some light. The man had been laid on a pile of sacks at the center of the place, so covered in blood that Rhian could not immediately get a good look at him.

Was it indeed him? The same man she'd bandaged out on the killing ground? A big man, this. Fair hair all tumbled and half drenched in red. Powerful arms were flung to either side.

She went closer, and conviction crept over her. He lay with his head turned and one cheek upward. But she knew that face. She'd seen it just last night out in the gloaming. And aye, there was the rent leather meant to cover his arm, all torn padding, and the sundered flesh beneath. And her own bandaging, now soaked through with blood.

Dismay gripped her. She muttered a curse and set her basket down so she would not drop it and soil everything inside.

Moira glanced at her. "What is it, sister?"

Rhian did not want to say. Those moments out in the dark had been apart from the ordinary. Almost magical. She need not share them, not when it would achieve nothing.

"Farlan is right. This looks verra bad."

"Is he dying? Losing him would damage Rory MacLeod a great deal, or so Farlan says."

"Aye?" And did they *not* want to damage Rory MacLeod? Was it not the goal of their every choice and action? Mayhap she would do best to let Leith MacLeod die.

Could she, though? Could she, having once looked into his

eyes?

Merciful angel.

She swore she heard the words again, tumbling into her ear. The effect of them poured through her, triggering a storm of emotions. All the compassion she'd been keeping pent up this whole night long, so it would not get in her way and spoil her intentions.

To be sure, she could not let him die.

She bent over him, performing a swift assessment, not liking what she saw. He lay senseless, most likely having passed out from pain. He might, aye, have great strength and vitality, but she had no doubt most of it had drained away with his blood. If ever a man lay close to death, it was this one.

"Sister," she whispered, "I can hold out little hope for his life."

"Are ye sure ye can no' save him? I ken fine there is magic in your hands."

Rhian shook her head slowly. "It is Saerla who possesses all the magic."

A commotion at the door heralded Alasdair, who came pushing in to the tiny place. So tall was he, his head nearly brushed the roof. He brought with him a heavy smell of sweat and blood.

"Well? Will he live?"

"I canna tell yet, Alasdair."

His expression stark, Alasdair pulled a dirk from his side. "I ha' been thinking about it. I am no' sure, Moira, we want all this nonsense over again. Let me but finish him and save Mistress Rhian a deal o' work. He is better dead."

"Nay." Moira imposed her body between Alasdair and the prone man.

Alasdair's dark eyes glowed with wrath. "We will, mistress, ha' no repeat o' what took place last time."

Last time. A MacLeod prisoner. A MacBeith sister who fell in love with him.

Nay, Rhian thought. They could not allow that to happen again.

She turned and faced Alasdair. "No need to employ your dirk. He has already lost most of the blood in his body."

Alasdair swept the fallen warrior with a disparaging look. "Then let him lie, mistress, and finish bleeding out. Ye were right in what ye said before—there is no need for ye to waste yer time and yer mercy upon him."

"Aye," Rhian agreed. It was perhaps the kindest thing to do. Why claw the man back from the brink of death only to have him endure blindness, imprisonment, and perhaps questioning by ordeal? Farlan still recovered from the beating their men had given him. Because he was a MacLeod.

But the word *mercy* echoed in her head.

She remembered the man's gaze clinging to hers out there in the dark. His spirit reaching out to her in a manner she could not comprehend.

Should her compassion be bound by who was MacBeith, and who MacLeod?

"Go, Alasdair," said Moira after a swift glance at Rhian. "Ye do no' belong here, and ye tak' up too much space."

He rumbled in protest. The dirk still rested in his fingers.

Rhian turned to face him. "Go, and let me do my work."

Few men chose to defy her when she had a certain glint in her eye. Alasdair backed down now, though he did not look happy about it.

When he'd gone, Moira puffed out a breath. "Aye, sister, do your work."

It would not be Rhian's hands that saved this man, if he lived. His life, as she felt quite clearly, lay in the hands of a far higher power.

Chapter Six

LEITH WANDERED IN a dark place, far different from the gloaming where the MacBeith war party had caught him and driven him to his knees. That had contained pricks of light. Flares from torches carried by his enemies. The vast field of stars overhead. Glints of their reflections in the far-off loch waters.

When he was young, he used to love standing and gazing up at the heavens. Back in the old days this was, when he, Rory, and Farlan were lads, after the old chief, Camraith, took Farlan in to raise alongside Rory. The three of them would sneak out long after they were meant to be abed and lie on their backs in the green sod. He would let his mind wander, wondering how it would be to have a boat that could sail through the firmament. Rory would talk about how he would one day own the whole glen, be the monarch of Glen Bronach. Leith barely listened to him.

He invariably became lost in the beauty of that sky.

Now, however, he existed in complete darkness. Lost. He could not tell up from down or forward from back. He did not know where safety might lie.

Perhaps there was no safety. Mayhap this was death.

Och, and he'd hoped for better of it. A warrior thought about death, to be sure he did. No man, lest he be a fool, could take to battle with a sword in his hand and fail to wonder if he would come back home again.

But aye, he'd expected something better from the brink of heaven. Hillsides full of flowers, perhaps, or streams of light. Rich beauty spread before him. The singing of angels.

There had been an angel.

She'd bent over him there in the field, before he'd come to this dark place. He summoned her up before his mind's eye once again. An oval face, a pair of eyes filled with somber compassion. A vulnerable mouth and a wealth of hair, the color of which he could not tell. Soft, gentle hands with caring in their touch.

Ah, and if he lay now in the very clutches of death, there was much he would grieve at losing. Sunlit days with friends. Evenings drinking ale by a warm fire. The laughter.

He would grieve losing the chance to see her again, most of all.

What would his mother say when he failed to come home? She was born sister to Rory's father, and in a way had mothered them all. His da was gone—gone on ahead of him, as it now seemed. Would he meet his da again when he crossed to—

Where? Where was this plane of death?

Perhaps all the dark around him argued he headed not to heaven. Quite possibly he did not deserve that place. He'd never done any man deliberate harm, save with a sword in his hand. As a warrior, he'd killed a few. Aye, more than a few. He'd never hurt the women with whom he dallied. They had been happy in his company, had enjoyed sharing laughter and occasionally other pleasures.

He'd never left them weeping. But nor had he ever found that one who would take ownership of his heart. Keep the fire on his hearth and give him the bairns he desired.

Och, he did not want to die alone. No one in sight for good or ill. Cold and forsaken.

"Here now," a woman's voice crooned from out of the dark. "Do no' greet."

Had he been greeting? A fine thing if so, for he'd not shed a tear since childhood. But surely he knew that voice. Why could he not open his eyes and see her? Mayhap his eyes *were* open. Yet still he could not see.

He could not see, no, yet the terror of the darkness eased. It eased because she was beside him. He knew her, surely he did.

Hands touched him. Gentle hands. One brushed at his cheeks—aye, he must be weeping. Another pressed against his upper arm.

Pain exploded there.

It erupted from out of the darkness, from all around him, and latched on to his right arm with sharp teeth. So severe was it, it drove the breath from him.

He wanted the pain to stop. By God, he wanted to live.

He wanted to see her still more.

But aye, he could feel her, and that was almost enough. She leaned close above him, her hand still on his arm. He could smell the sweetness of her even above the reek of blood. He felt her breath course across his cheek, so close was she.

If only he could see her.

"Can ye save him?" someone asked. A woman. Not *his* woman.

Nay, for she still bent over him, mercy, kindness, and warmth flowing from her, into him.

He reached up with his good hand and seized her wrist. Immediately, sensation rushed in upon him. It was like she consisted of a tingling force that spread through him, combating his weakness and his panic.

She had not answered the other woman's question. *Can ye save me?* He echoed it in his mind.

She did not move, there in his grasp. He said low, in an appeal meant for her ears alone, "Merciful angel?"

The breath rushed from her. He heard it, he felt it, but still he could not see her, save in his mind. The oval face he'd glimpsed out in the dark. Eyes of deep, bottomless blue trapped between thick, dark lashes. A mouth held tight, as if she shared his agony.

Mayhap she did.

"Be still," she bade him. Her voice flowed over him like warm honey. He clung to it with his entire being.

"I canna see."

"You have taken a terrible blow to the head. Your sight may yet return. I canna tell yet."

"Merciful lady," he muttered. If he lay under her care, all hope could not be lost for him.

She drew away slightly, though she still did not pull her wrist from his grasp. She spoke to someone else. "Perhaps I can save him after all, sister."

She could. This woman could drag him back from the very brink of death with but her presence.

He tightened his grasp on her wrist.

Her voice full of warmth, she told him, "Ye will need to leave go o' me if I am to tend this great wound o' yours."

He did not know if he could leave go of her. What would happen to him if he did? Would he slip away into the vast darkness?

Gently, she drew away. Reluctantly, he let her. It did not matter because he could feel her still, even as she stepped from him. He lay struggling to draw breaths against the pain that racked him.

The darkness in which he lay, aye, terrified him. But he could endure it and all the pain that accompanied it, so long as she remained near him.

"I SAID PERHAPS I can save him." Outside the door of the stock pen, Rhian spoke with her sister. "He is very weak and may not rally. I can make no promises."

She had dressed the great wound in the man's shoulder—again—a gaping maw of rent flesh where she glimpsed bone.

Together, she and Moira had stripped the sodden clothing from him. Without his MacLeod tartan, he was just a man.

But och, what a man! Long of limb, with a great, deep chest covered with sandy hair, liberally marked by old scars. A warrior he was, and with a body like that, he should be naught else.

She'd washed what blood she could from him and tended the wound at the back of his head where he'd been struck down. She'd covered him with a blanket, all the while wondering at the emotions that filled her in the doing.

Och, why did this man—this one man—have the ability to affect her so profoundly? She could not tell, but that moment he'd seized hold of her by the wrist and held her to him had shaken her to the bone.

"Is he blinded?" Moira asked. "Will he regain his sight?"

"Who can tell? That blow to the head was a vicious one." He could not see, nay, but he knew her. Beyond question, he did.

"So ye be certain he is blind?"

"Certain, aye." He had opened his eyes—pale gray-blue they were, wild with pain and desperation. With appeal. But he had seen nothing.

Aye well, she could supply him the aid he so clearly needed. Out of common decency, she could. She could seek to mend his torn flesh and even hold his hand.

Moira nodded. "Do your best, sister." She smiled briefly. "Your best is verra good."

"Aye." Rhian would call upon all the healing she possessed and do her best for—*Leith*. Aye, out on the field he'd told her his name was Leith. The one thing she could not do was forget that, even stripped of his tartan, he remained a MacLeod, and her enemy.

Chapter Seven

RHIAN HAD OTHER wounded to visit and her own clansmen to tend. It was afternoon by the time she'd seen the last of them, and she ached with weariness. She gave much more than simple care and bandages while healing. She gave a measure of herself to each patient, and it drained her in ways she did not completely understand.

She longed to retreat to her bedchamber, to be alone for a time. Change her soiled clothing and wash down properly. Sit beside the fire, perhaps with a restorative brew.

There was a magic, or so she'd discovered, in a hearth fire. Her mother had been a peaceable sort of woman who had tended their hearth with calm serenity. Her fire had been the center of their home, their family and the greater family that occupied their part of Glen Bronach.

A quiet strength, it had been, and aye, an almost magical presence in their lives.

Rhian could not comprehend the loss when Ma passed. The very heart of them all passed with her. She remembered quite clearly the morning after Ma's death when she'd come down to find the hearth in the small chamber where they'd always gathered as a family cold.

The shock of it had reverberated through her and she could barely breathe for panic. For an instant, she'd faced a darkness too powerful to overcome.

She'd gathered up the makings for a fire, laid it carefully in the hearth, and struck the spark. As the fire took hold and grew, it beat back the darkness just enough.

No one seemed to notice that she took over the duty from that morning on. When they greeted a new day, or ended one, when they faced their duties, they gathered still around a fire.

Her fire.

Someone had to step into that place. Yet her life had changed immeasurably on that morning she performed her ma's duty. She was not the young woman she'd been. She used to have hope for a future of her own. She'd lost that along with the laughter that once brightened her days.

She rarely laughed anymore.

Sitting beside a fire still restored her, though. That and the man lying back in the cowshed were all she could think about.

She would not go to him. She would not, though the fact that he lay blind and alone haunted her. She must take it on faith that she had done her best for him. He would live or die, and she was removed from it. There came a time when the fate of a patient rested in hands other than her own.

Still, she did not want him to die.

She was on her way to her quarters when she met Saerla. The younger of her two sisters had found time to change out of her leathers, but she looked nearly as weary as Rhian felt.

"Sister, please come."

"Why? And where? I am for my chamber and a spell o' time on my own."

"But ye maun come!" Saerla's misty blue gaze met Rhian's. Rhian sometimes thought Saerla did not focus completely on anything in their world. A part of her always peered into some other, more mystical realm. She now appeared rational, though, and troubled.

"They are besetting Moira. Threatening to strip from her the title o' chief."

"Who is doing this?"

"Ewan, and some other members o' the council."

Aye well, it had to come. Moira seizing the place of chief had been a dubious proposition at best. She was loved for her own sake as well as Da's, respected as a warrior who took the field. But as soon as she'd taken up with Farlan MacLeod, support for her had begun to erode. When he'd defected and returned to MacBeith, and when it became known she spent her nights with him and meant to wed him, a faction of clan members withdrew their support completely.

They were led by a man called Ewan, who'd been close to Da. No doubt the pain of grief drove some of his actions now.

God knew, it drove them all.

"Ye maun come and speak for her," Saerla urged. "Else the place o' chief will slip through her fingers."

Rhian sighed. "Mayhap it should."

Saerla looked shocked. "How can ye say so? Wha' would Da say if that happened? This has been the chief's house for generations."

"Sister, I am tired o' fighting. Let the council bestow the place o' chief where they may. Let them gi' it to Alasdair. Wha'ever will unite us."

"I, too, am tired o' fighting. God knows. But I canna quit. Rhian, when I look ahead, I See visions o' a resolution. O' peace, aye, here in the glen. But there are many battles still before us e'er we reach that place. Many dangers."

"Saerla, I canna."

"Ye be weary to the heart, aye. We are all so. But we canna surrender this fight."

"Tell that to Moira," Rhian snapped, waspishly for her. "She insists on lying down wi' a MacLeod though she surely knows the harm it maun do."

Saerla lifted her chin. "Da does no' blame her for it. He has told me so."

"Och! Da is no' here, is he, to wade through this morass o'

trouble."

"He is. They all are, our ancestors. Ye merely canna see them."

Sudden love for her young, fey sister wrang Rhian's heart. Her anger died away, leaving her twice as tired. "Wha' can I say, Saerla, that will change the council's minds?"

"Just speak for her. Say what is in your heart."

Rhian no longer *knew* what was in her heart. "Let me change into some clean clothing, and I will come."

"Hurry. They are in the great hall. They beset Moira and Farlan like a pack o' hounds."

Moira and Farlan? Was he with her? Could their elder sister not see that there lay the trouble?

Rhian hurried off to her chamber with a knot of bitterness in her gut. She loved Moira, indeed she did. And she believed in what Saerla tended to call *true love*. More or less. Her ma and her da had loved each other that way. But they'd never had to weigh it against their loyalty to the clan.

She had sympathy for Moira, aye. She also had sympathy for the members of the council and for Alasdair, who she knew full well had long harbored feelings for Moira.

Why could Moira not have wanted to wed Alasdair? It would have made things so simple. They could have led the clan together, and not one voice raised against it.

Instead, Moira had to choose a man with MacLeod blood in his veins. Even if Farlan's chief, Rory MacLeod, had cast him off, that blood remained.

And would besmirch any children they had together.

Her thoughts flicked again to the man lying in the cowshed. Och, aye, she understood the temptation. Only a fool of a woman, though, would give in to it.

She scrubbed the last of the blood from her hands and from beneath her fingernails, donned fresh clothing, and went out. She heard those gathered in the great hall before she reached the door. Shouting. Tempers were high.

She could not imagine where they got the energy.

The first person she saw when she passed through the door was Moira, front and center. And aye, the others did gather around her like a pack of hounds. Snapping.

She had to hand it to Moira for courage. Moira had fought in the battle just past and must be every bit as tired as Rhian. Yet she stood strong, head up, still clad in her battle leathers.

Da would be so proud of her. That thought pierced the last of Rhian's anger, and softened her when she went in.

She took in the others who made up the party. Alasdair, of course, standing nearly a head above everyone else save Farlan, who was a tall man. Alasdair too still wore his battle armor, and a goodly measure of blood. He should have come to her for tending, she thought, though was unsurprised he had not.

The council was made up of a mix of men who had been on the field and those too aged for that duty. All had been close to Da, and he'd heard advice from them. But then, Da had been willing to listen kindly and patiently to everyone who came to him.

Saerla stood to one side, trouble in her face. Poor Saerla picked up the emotions of others quite easily. This turmoil must cause her great anxiety.

Lastly, Farlan stood at Moira's side. He did so quietly, seeking to draw no attention to himself. It did not matter. The man had a presence, and anyway, he offended these others merely by existing.

It was he who engaged Rhian's gaze when she went in. He had a fine pair of brown eyes, did Farlan, and she could tell what he was thinking. *Say somewhat to aid your sister.* No question that Farlan loved Moira. He had given up everything for her.

Too bad he had not loved her enough to keep away.

Chapter Eight

FARLAN HAD QUIT wearing the MacLeod tartan. Indeed, were the stories to be believed, he no longer had a right to wear it. He had no right to wear the MacBeith tartan either. No one would tolerate that. So he stood clad mostly in gray and white, as the wool had come from the sheep.

Gray, white, and blood red. He too had come straight from battle, his first since he'd healed up after the beating given him by these very clansmen.

He now wore a sword and a knife Moira had doubtless given him, and stood with his hands hanging loosely at his sides. Listening, listening to the venom being spat at the woman he loved.

Ewan stood at the forefront of the council. He'd also been on the battlefield.

"Ye had to ken this would come, Mistress Moira," he shouted as Rhian came in. "We canna let ye stand at our head wi' that—that *traitor* at yer side."

Moira flinched visibly. Rhian could have told these men they might push her sister, but only so far. "This is no' time for a change o' leadership," Moira whipped back. "We are in the midst o' a spate o' battles. And in case ye ha' overlooked it"—she pointed at the door—"we are winning those battles!"

"For now," Ewan shouted back. "Rory MacLeod may only be

getting started. Why no' ask that great lump at yer side?"

"Rory is just getting started," Farlan confirmed quietly. "That does no' mean we canna win."

"We?" screeched another of the council members, outraged. "Who is *we*, then? The MacBeiths or the MacLeods?"

"MacBeith," Moira snapped. "Farlan stands wi' me now. Wi' us."

They all sneered.

An older man spoke up. "We ha' heard, Mistress Moira, ye mean to wed wi' this man."

Moira's hand crept out and clasped Farlan's, which hung at his side. A telling gesture. "I do."

"Then how, tell me," Ewan said, "can we leave ye in the place o' chief? Ye'll soon be birthing MacLeod bairns."

Moira flushed. "Any bairn I birth will be born o' the chief's house—"

"And MacLeod's."

"'Tis an outrage," yet another elder, Brechan, chimed in. "'Tis bad enough ye maun keep him by ye. But for us to stand and watch a MacLeod lead this clan at yer side—"

Saerla stepped forward. "I, for one, support my sister. She already has the place o' chief and has led us well in it. She has a firm hand, and I see my father's strength in her."

That knocked them silent. No one there disrespected Saerla's ability as a Seer. They exchanged glances.

"Alasdair?" Saerla appealed to the big man.

Alasdair's expression betrayed that he did not want to speak. His feelings for Moira and his animosity toward Farlan must sorely tangle with his loyalty to the clan.

He had stepped out and defended Farlan, though, when Farlan defected and came to Moira's side. Did that mean he'd do the same now?

He scowled. "I no more like a MacLeod lodged in the chief's house than ye do. But—"

Moira began hotly now, "He is no'—"

"He sleeps in Chief Iain's verra bed wi' ye!" another council member howled. "D'ye think we do no' know that?"

Moira lit up in defense of her lover. "And where would ye ha' me lodge him? Back in his own quarters, so ye lot can beat him near to death once again?"

"Moira," Farlan said, and squeezed her hand.

"Big, brave MacLeod warrior," sneered Calan, who, much to Rhian's dismay, was also in attendance. "Who canna do aught but hide behind a woman's skirts."

This was getting them nowhere. Rhian stepped forward. "Moira does ha' a point about Farlan's safety." She had tended Farlan following his battering, and it had been bad.

Ewan turned on her. "Wi' all respect, Mistress Rhian, I would expect ye to tak' your sister's part here. The daughters o' Iain MacBeith ha' always, aye, stuck together. But I want to hear wha' Alasdair has to say. Because we"—he gestured to himself and the other men—"think Alasdair is the proper man to take the place o' chief."

Everyone stared at Alasdair, who looked intensely unhappy.

"I think," Saerla said, "my father would want one o' his own offspring at the head o' this clan."

With that, Rhian could only agree. "I, too, believe that."

"And would he want a MacLeod standing there also?" Ewan challenged. "In the place that should ha' been occupied by his son, who was killed by those selfsame MacLeod bastards? 'Tis an abomination."

True enough, Rhian acknowledged. Da had been heartbroken by Arran's death. He had, in fact, never really recovered from it.

Saerla lifted her chin a notch. "My father has expressed his approval of Moira's joining with Farlan. I ha' been told so."

Dead silence met this pronouncement. Everyone there stared at Saerla. They all knew she had the Sight. Would they argue it with her?

"Aye, well," one of the older council members said, "her bein' wi' him—even takin' him to her bed or wedding wi' him—is no' the same as her leading wi' him at her elbow. Mistress," he said to Moira directly, "if the man means so much to ye, then gi' up your place as chief to another. God knows, he has given enough up for ye, in turn."

True, that was. And everyone, including Farlan, might look upon it as a test of Moira's devotion. He had surrendered all, including his right to his name. Would she not step down from leadership for him?

Her lips parted and her eyes went wide with dismay. She did not speak.

A deep rumble sounded as Alasdair cleared his throat. "I ha' no yet stated my opinion." Moira and Farlan still held hands. Alasdair's gaze touched there before he went on, "I ha' heard many o' ye talking of me taking the place o' chief. 'Tis true, I was long Chief Iain's right-hand man, as well as his war chief, even before Master Arran died. 'Tis true also I would do aught I could for this clan. But I believe the place o' chief should remain wi' Iain's house."

Everyone began speaking at once, mostly expressing loud objections.

Alasdair spoke over them. Looking at Saerla, he said, "I ken naught o' signs or portents. I possess nae magic and canna say what our chief has expressed to Mistress Saerla. I believe wha' she says, though. Perhaps"—now he turned his dark stare on Rhian—"Mistress Rhian might take the name o' chief."

"Me?" Rhian pressed her hand to her chest. "I cannot possibly. I am no warrior, and I ha' duties enough to occupy me."

"Mistress Saerla, then."

Saerla appeared stricken, as did the members of the council. While Saerla's abilities were respected and while she was well-loved, she was Iain MacBeith's youngest daughter. Someone to be protected, even though she regularly took the field.

She said merely, "I canna. 'Tis no' my place."

"Mayhap ye might consider on it," Ewan told her gently. "Speak to the powers that guide ye, mistress."

Saerla nodded woodenly.

"Meanwhile, Alasdair?" Ewan turned back to the big man.

Alasdair shook his head. "I say we leave Mistress Moira in charge for the time. The defense is going well, and she is no' yet wed wi' the MacLeod. So long as they remain unwed—"

Moira glared at him but said nothing.

"And if the battles begin to go badly?"

"Then," Alasdair said, "I will step up and lead wi' her jointly—or wi' Mistress Saerla. I do no' think leadership should leave the chief's house."

"Aye, well," Ewan declared, "it seems we shall ha' to be satisfied wi' that for the time being. But mistress"—he shook a finger at Moira—"if any hint comes to our ears that ye ha' let this rogue influence your decisions as befits his clan—"

"I would no'," Moira snapped. "He would no'."

An older council member said, "There are ways a woman may be influenced." He shot a stare sharp as a dagger at Farlan.

That made Moira straighten. "If I find anyone has raised a hand to Farlan again, there will be an answer, swift and hard. D'ye hear me?"

They heard, and they did not like it. Nor did Farlan, if Rhian could judge by the sudden flash in his eyes. It could not be easy for him to stand by while his lover defended him. Very little of what Farlan had done lately, so Rhian had to acknowledge, could have been easy.

The council members filed out of the hall, their faces like stone. Only the three sisters, Farlan, and Alasdair remained.

Moira broke the silence by turning to Alasdair. "So I am forbidden from marrying him, am I? I am to live in sin?"

"Nay." Alasdair's gaze, when it rested on Moira, became enigmatic. "Nay. Ye might gi' up sleeping wi' him."

Moira bit down hard on what she wanted to say in reply.

"They are right," Alasdair told her. "It is an abomination having him"—he jerked his head at Farlan—"standing at the head o' the clan when we are fighting his own folk for survival."

Tears came to Moira's eyes.

Farlan said quietly, "My loyalty is all Moira's now."

"Aye, well." A grimace twisted Alasdair's lips. "I might believe ye. Try convincing the rest o' them."

Chapter Nine

"MISTRESS RHIAN, I would like to see your patient, Leith MacLeod."

Rhian stared at Farlan in consternation. Alasdair had stepped out, leaving MacBeith's three sisters and Farlan alone in the hall.

She met Farlan's steady brown gaze, wondering despite herself how he managed to keep his composure while being spat upon by some of the men who had taken part recently in beating him senseless. If it was indeed the power of love that sustained him, then he made a wondrous testimony to it.

"The man is sorely injured," she told him.

"So I do understand. Blinded, so Moira says."

"Aye. I do no' ken that he will survive his wound."

Sorrow twisted Farlan's features. "All the more reason I need to see him. We were the closest of friends, once."

But no longer, since he'd defected? Rhian could but ask herself.

"Why do we no' give it a day and a night to see whether he lives?"

Moira stepped up into the conversation. "Ye are holding him under guard, sister?"

"He is in no' condition to escape us."

"I'm thinking for his protection."

"Aye, there be guards." Of course, those guards could themselves decide to enter the pen and kill Leith. His life did not hang by much. "I mean to go soon and check on him."

"Let us come," Moira requested.

Rhian faced her. "Sister, ye be weary enough to drop, as I can tell merely by looking at ye. I suggest ye go get some rest and worry about the prisoner tomorrow."

Farlan said, "My presence may make a difference to Leith."

Rhian eyed him. "If he is your friend, this Leith MacLeod, ye might do better to leave him be. If he comes awake, he will be in agony."

Farlan and Moira exchanged speaking looks. "Come, love." Moira tugged at his hand. "We will tak' my sister's advice and seek our rest."

They went out, leaving Rhian and Saerla alone. Saerla, or so Rhian felt, had acted strangely throughout. She continued to do so now, standing with her head down and her gaze averted from Rhian.

Aye, and all this might well overset the best of them—which Saerla undoubtedly was. The youngest of the three sisters had long been cherished for her sweetness, her beauty, and her ability to contact the other world. Rhian remembered Ma saying to her once, when Saerla was still quite small, "Rhian, ye maun look after your sister. She has a rare gift."

It had evolved to where Rhian looked after not only Saerla but everyone else besides. She supposed when she'd stepped into Ma's place, she'd inherited all that. She was a mother without having birthed a child.

"What is it, Saerla?" she asked now, softly. She half expected Saerla to go on about the council and their ill feelings, because Saerla hated discord. Or about Moira and her difficult situation.

Instead she came and stepped up to Rhian. Raising both hands, she laid them on either side of Rhian's face.

"Sister, ye will go carefully."

"Wha' ha' ye Seen?" No question that Saerla had Seen something. She rarely spoke in this tone unless conveying messages from beyond her.

Gazing into Saerla's wide eyes, Rhian felt herself falling. Into deep waters and through a patterned field of stars. It knocked the breath from her precisely as if she'd been thumped hard in the chest.

Fire and heat. Scorching kisses, a sense of belonging so strong it stole what remained of her breath. And laughter, deep and wide and comforting.

When she returned to herself, she still gazed into Saerla's eyes, which were now filled with sorrow.

"Go carefully," Saerla whispered again.

What was that? But Rhian did not say those words aloud. She could not speak. She drew in ragged breaths even as Saerla released her.

Swiftly, swiftly Saerla went out, leaving Rhian alone.

IT TOOK HER several more moments to gain control of her emotions and depart the hall in turn. She meant to go straight back to the cowshed but was delayed by two more requests for her to recheck wounds.

By the time she managed to free herself from those obligations, it was late and anxiety filled her mind. What would she find when she returned to the MacLeod? By now, he might well have slipped away.

Would it matter if he did? He was just another MacLeod prisoner, if one said to be of worth, and they'd certainly had enough of that with Farlan.

Bad it was, fighting a war—worse when the stakes became complicated. Moira's feelings for Farlan had certainly complicated this fight. Besides, it was true what she'd told Farlan. If and when Leith MacLeod awakened, it would be to pitiless agony.

Those thoughts so occupied Rhian's mind that as she approached the makeshift prison, it took an instant for the truth to penetrate.

No guards stood at their posts outside the door.

Moreover, the area lay otherwise deserted. Granted, it was located in an area somewhat off the beaten track, but in the past when Farlan had been held there, folks had found excuses to walk by, if only to glower. Rhian, who did not possess a touch of her sister's sensitivity, had been able to feel the hate.

Now, it echoed to her step, in emptiness.

Her heart began to pound and her feet quickened. She'd left the men, both of Alasdair's choosing, on guard. She'd also left a light burning. Now she could glimpse no light seeping around the ill-fitting door.

"By God," she whispered as she barged in. She had to fumble for the rushlight beside the door, striking the flint no less than three times.

When the light bloomed, she was sure Leith MacLeod was dead. She'd left him on a pallet stretched across the floor. Now he sprawled half on his side, most of him no longer located on the straw. His arm had been flung up, and a filthy bolster lay covering his face.

It took her a moment to accept what she was seeing. When she did, her hands began to shake. A bolster, a heavy one. Someone must have come in here and held that over his face. Tried to smother him. Attacked him while he lay defenseless. Tried to kill him? Or succeeded?

She fell to her knees on the filthy floor at his side and tossed the bolster aside. The rushlight beside the door did not lend as much radiance as she might wish. But as she turned Leith over onto his back, she could see the angry red marks across his face.

By God! By God, he was gone.

The fact that she consistently kept a rein on her compassion did not render it lacking. It flooded through her now, off the lead and strong. What a dreadful way to die—alone and at the hands of hatred. Unable even to see his attacker. A senseless, terrible thing. A waste of a strong, vital life.

He had struggled, even if whoever had done this deed had fallen upon him while he was unaware. That struggle had tumbled him from the pallet and opened up the wound she'd bandaged carefully so it bled anew.

It bled.

She caught her breath and laid her fingers against the side of his neck. A pulse, if a faint one. Faint and slow. She could count to ten between the beats.

Still, he was not yet gone.

"Leith. Leith!"

No response. His lashes, thick and brown, lay unmoving. The place to which he had retreated was far away.

She dragged him back onto the pallet, no easy task, since he was a big man and shifting him was very nearly beyond her. She got up and lit a torch from the rushlight with hands that shook so badly, she could barely accomplish it. She'd left the door ajar, yet still no one passed outside—suspicious in itself. Usually, the clansfolk had an instinct for any untoward happening.

People were keeping away.

She went back down on her knees beside Leith once again. At that moment, he was just a man in need. MacBeith or MacLeod did not matter. She laid aside the bolster—it belonged to someone, but she would worry about that later.

She whispered a prayer. Or perhaps it was a charm.

She did not possess her sister's talent for magic, nay. But a healer often had to reach beyond herself. And any woman keeping a hearth might speak simple charms for the safety of all she held dear.

She wanted this man to live. She could not say why, save no one should die hated and alone.

He was not alone now.

Her basket lay nearly empty of supplies. She pawed through it, looting it mercilessly, peeled off the bloodied bandages, and replaced them.

He still bled.

While her hands worked, her mind wandered. Why had someone tried to smother him? A sharp dirk to the throat would have been more efficient and would have done the job far more easily.

And had Saerla Seen this? She'd Seen something without a doubt, and had warned Rhian to be careful. She had not told her to go and save Leith MacLeod's life.

Perhaps she had not needed to. Because Rhian was here, her hands were stained red with the man's blood.

And her compassion had been utterly and completely engaged.

Chapter Ten

IT MUST BE a dream. It had to be, because the next time Leith opened his eyes, filtered green light shone down upon him, and he was able to see. See his surroundings. He stood in a forest with trees stretching so high over his head that he could not glimpse their crowns. Birds flickered like jewels among the branches, which very nearly blotted out the sky.

A pleasant, enchanted place it seemed, but one where he felt dwarfed and altogether strange in himself. Aye, he'd had some odd dreams in the past, but none where he—

Was a young lad once more.

Bemused, he looked down at himself. Small, grubby hands, the nails rimmed with dirt. Bare, equally grubby knees and deer hide boots he'd nearly outgrown. Clothing messed and torn. How many times had his ma scolded him for ruining his clothing?

What if it wasn't a dream? How had he come here? He struggled to remember, and concluded he'd been playing with his cousin Rory and their friend, Farlan. The three of them could most often be found together and usually had a braw time of it, save that Rory always had to be in charge. He made the decisions as to what games they would play—hunt the bloody MacBeiths being a favorite—and who would do what.

But Leith had never played here before, had never beheld such trees as these. And where were his companions?

"Rory!" he called out, and his voice held none of the deepness of the present day. It piped like that of a bird. Had he ever sounded like that?

Were Rory and Farlan playing a trick on him? Even Rory was never so cruel as to lead him out somewhere and then abandon him. How was he going to get home?

He must have got separated from his companions by accident. Many of the exploits into which Rory led them went bad. They frequently ventured into mischief and all got in trouble for it. Rory, along with Farlan, since he had no parents of his own, would have to answer to Leith's Uncle Camraith, who at least was always, always fair.

Leith would answer to his own da, who Ma complained never took his transgressions seriously enough. Da would attempt to appear stern while he listened to an account of the misdeeds. In the end he would grin in sympathy and give Leith a wink Ma did not see.

He needed to find his fellow culprits now.

He stopped walking and spun slowly, searching for—well, anything. He saw naught but trees stretching endlessly in every direction, the light between the trunks turning milky green.

Fear struck him. He did not know how to leave this place. To get home.

Home. The hearth in the small house his family shared, his parents and sisters gathered around it. His ma dishing out pottage and her oatcakes—or better yet, some bannock, of which he could never get enough. A feeling of warmth and belonging.

He had strayed so far from that now.

If he called out again, would Rory come? Rory might well have his own path to follow, from which he would not stray. Better to call Farlan, who had a kind heart.

Something niggled at his mind. Farlan had gone, given up his place in the clan. Rory was beyond furious with him.

Was that how Leith had come here? Searching for Farlan? No matter what, Farlan was his friend. He would never leave Leith abandoned here. Alone.

"Farlan?" he called, and then listened to the silence.

RHIAN SMOOTHED THE bandages in place and let her hands linger on Leith MacLeod's skin, slide across his chest and his shoulders. Down his arms. She caught his hands in her own.

"Can ye hear me?" Was he there? No flicker, no glimpse of spirit animated him. Rhian squeezed his fingers and felt—*something*. A tingle. A stirring.

But she could not tell quite whether that tingle came from him or from inside her.

She needed to fetch help. She must find someone to set a new guard. She had to notify Alasdair that an intruder had tried to commit murder here.

If she left, though, whoever had done this might return and finish the job. Might use a dirk this time.

If she let go of this man, he might perish.

Why should she think that, though? She did not hold the man here. Did she? Indeed, he did not even know she was with him. His hands—large, strong hands—lay limp in hers.

"Leith MacLeod?" She received no response. Yet she could still feel something. She could feel his spirit. Trapped somewhere alone.

Bending her head over their joined hands, she again whispered a prayer. Then she spoke a charm, a summoning, employing what small measure of magic she did possess.

"Leith MacLeod, hear me."

His head stirred on the pallet and his lips moved. A breath of a sound escaped them.

Rhian bent closer in an effort to hear him.

"Help me. I am lost."

Rhian's heart thudded in her breast. Before she could react, his left hand moved in hers, writhed, and clutched her fingers tight.

His voice rose in an eerie wail, crying like that of a child in the dark. "Farlan. Farlan!"

"Aye. Quiet, now."

"Farlan, help me."

Och, by all that was holy, what should she do? Leave hold of him? Abandon him here, to go and fetch his friend?

"Farlan?" Leith did not see her, that was plain. He saw nothing at all.

"Hold tight," she told him, and folded his hands on his chest. "I will bring your friend."

She shut the door of the pen after her and whispered another charm, one of protection this time. She could not say what the man inside meant to her, save that she'd taken on his protection. Without her permission, her heart had done so.

Where would she find Farlan? With Moira, no doubt. But where was she? Not in the great hall, since they'd left there not long since. And not in council. Making arrangements to bury their dead, mayhap.

Rhian decided to try Moira's quarters, located behind the great hall. She did not find her sister there, but when she banged on the door and called frantically, Farlan came out.

"Ye maun come wi' me."

"Why?"

"Someone has tried to murder yon Leith MacLeod. He is asking for ye."

Farlan did not argue it. He came away with her, pausing only to seize his weapons. "Where?"

"The pen. The same one where ye were held."

He said no more, but his features twisted in disgust. They went swiftly, and aye, now they did attract attention. One of those they passed was Alasdair, and Rhian reached out for him.

"Ye maun come. The guards ha' forsaken their posts, and someone half murdered the MacLeod."

He grunted and joined them. Others, their interest caught, followed. They had a small train when they reached the pen.

"Wha' happened?" Alasdair demanded. "I had twa men here."

"I do no' ken. 'Twas dark and deserted when I came."

He grunted. "Go ye in. I will stand guard mysel'."

They went into the guttering torchlight, Rhian with Farlan at her heels.

"By God!" Farlan sank to Leith's side. "Leith? I am here, man."

He clasped Leith's hands as Rhian had before him. The big man shuddered and gasped.

"Farlan? Wha' is this place?"

"Ye be still at MacBeith, man. Prisoner."

"Nay. All these trees."

Farlan shot a look at Rhian. "Nay trees here, Leith."

"I canna find my way home."

"Ye are no' for home, for the time being."

"Did Rory lead us here?"

In a way, he had. Rhian imagined it was Rory MacLeod's ambition that had led them all into this terrible conflict.

She sank to the floor on Leith's other side. "He canna see ye," she reminded Farlan. "He took a tremendous blow to the head before they brought him in."

"Aye, so ye said. And now, by God—ye say someone tried to murder him?"

"Tried to smother him with yon bolster, where he lay."

Anger kindled in Farlan's eyes. "Cowards."

"Aye, but it puzzles me. He lay here both senseless and helpless. Why no' just employ a dirk and be done?"

"Farlan?" Leith said, his voice rough and desperate. "Can ye get me home?"

"Leith, my man, I can but try."

Chapter Eleven

L EAVING THE TWO friends together, Rhian stepped outside for a word with Alasdair. The events just past had shaken her deeply. She still did not know what to make of her reaction to the man who lay inside.

Her enemy. A MacLeod.

Certainly, her compassion might be stirred by anyone, though out of self-protection, she ordinarily kept a tight hold on it. Nothing like this.

Alasdair stood with his brawny arms crossed over his chest and a glower on his face. "Mistress? Wha' happened here?"

"That is what I would like to know. When I came by, there was no one on guard and all lay dark inside. Someone had tried to smother the prisoner."

His eyebrows soared. "Smother? 'Tis a craven deed, that. Surely ye be mistaken?"

"I wish so. Whoever it was used a heavy bolster and left it behind."

Alasdair swore low and bitterly. "I left twa men I trusted here. I ken fine 'tis a duty nobody relishes, guarding a man ye wish dead. But I did trust them."

"Who were they?"

"Drachan and Marc."

"Aye." Rhian reflected swiftly on it. She too would have

trusted those particular men, who were steady and reliable. "Might someone planning to attack the MacLeod have lured them away wi' some false message?"

"If so, they would no both ha' abandoned their post. One o' them would ha' gone. Or come for me."

"I see. Who will we get to guard him, then?"

"I do no' ken." Alasdair lowered his voice. "I do no' like it, mistress. The council, as ye heard, is in an uproar. Folk do no' appreciate that one"—he jerked his head toward Farlan, inside— "having a place beside Mistress Moira. Now wi' the coming o' this prisoner, they see it all happening again."

"Aye." Rhian could only agree, if unhappily.

"I say to ye, mistress, it would ha' been better had his attacker succeeded and he lay dead."

With that, Rhian's heart, given whatever had bloomed so unexpectedly between her and Leith, would not let her agree.

She studied Alasdair. Had he been the one to dismiss the guards? For they surely would have answered his bidding. But nay, for Alasdair would have used the sharp dirk he kept in his boot.

"Best, perhaps, to send him back to MacLeod," she suggested.

Alasdair snorted. "So he might recover and return to attack us again? We have had all that before also."

"I do not know if he will ever fight again. He is blinded. And the wound to his arm has done untold damage."

"Well then." Did Alasdair look pleased?

"Only time will tell whether or not he regains his sight."

"'Tis in the hands o' fate, I suppose. There are worse places it might be."

Rhian regarded him steadily. Fate had not always been kind to Alasdair. He'd worshipped her da and served him long and valiantly, only to lose him. He'd harbored feelings for Moira, a truth Rhian had long suspected and which Saerla had confirmed, only to have her reject his suit to accept another. His enemy.

Alasdair, though, lived his life directed by a strong inner sense of right and wrong.

"Can ye try to find out who attempted to kill Leith Mac-Leod?"

"I will speak to Marc and Drachan, but if they abandoned their posts before that person came, they may no' ken. I will be having words wi' them, either way."

Rhian almost pitied Marc and Drachan.

"Let me know, please, wha' ye discover."

"Aye, mistress."

"D'ye think ye'll be able to find reliable guards?"

Alasdair grunted again. "If I canna, I will stand here mysel'."

"Ye can scarce do that both day and night."

"Here, lad!" Alasdair called to a member of the small crowd who had gathered. "Come and tak' a message for me."

Rhian slipped back inside while Alasdair set about taking care of his business.

The scene inside struck her forcibly. Farlan sat cross-legged on the floor at Leith's side and spoke to him, low and steady, his hand resting on the man's arm.

Kindness lay in the gesture, and a great measure of caring. Rhian did not want to feel any particular liking for Farlan. *She did not.* Yet when she saw him thus, she began to understand what had attracted Moira to him.

He looked up at her. "Leith, here, has been having troubling dreams."

Rhian nodded in response. Walking to Leith's side, she asked, "What sort o' dreams are these?"

Leith turned his face toward her, though his pale eyes did not focus on her. "Merciful lady, is it ye?"

His voice came rough. As she'd predicted, he was in a very great amount of pain. Such a load of pain in addition to the other injuries he'd suffered could well kill a man. Even one so strong as this.

She crouched back down beside him. "Aye, 'tis I, Rhian Mac-Beith."

"Rhian MacBeith. I canna see ye."

"Ye've suffered a tremendous blow to the head. Whether or no' ye may regain your sight, I canna say."

He nodded. "My head hurts something fierce. And my arm—" He groped there, and his features twisted in distress. "But I remember ye. From the battlefield."

Farlan questioned Rhian with a glance.

"I went out looking for our wounded," she told him. "And found…" She nodded at Leith.

"Ah. 'Tis a credit to ye, you did no' call the party and let them finish him."

"I could no' tell, wi' the dark and all the blood, wha' side he was on."

Farlan gave her a level look. "And 'tis perhaps how it should be."

Mayhap so. But Rhian was MacBeith to her bones. And both these men, whatever Farlan claimed, were MacLeods.

She turned her gaze on Leith. "Ye will be in a fierce amount o' pain. My basket has run out o' supplies. Master Farlan, will ye stay here with him while I go and mix a draught?"

"I will."

Leith reached out and groped for Rhian's wrist. "This draught, will it send me to sleep? I would rather the pain than return to that dream I was having."

"Sleep will do ye good. It allows for healing."

He looked unhappy, but did not object.

AS SOON AS the woman called Rhian left the room, Leith turned to Farlan. He wished he could see his friend. By God, he wished he could see the woman. But her face danced in his memory, as he'd seen her out in the dark. A blur of a white oval and a pair of beautiful eyes.

For all that he could not see her, he felt her compassion. Whenever she touched him, it came flooding in upon him. He wanted her to touch him and never stop.

He groped across the blanket that covered him, and Farlan clasped his hand.

"Farlan, I'm afeared. Wha' if I ne'er regain my sight?"

"Mistress Rhian is a fine healer. Do no' despair."

"Aye, but what use am I if I canna see? As a warrior, what use? As a man—"

"Gi' it some time, Leith. Rest, as she says."

"I do no' want to return to that dream. I was but a wee bairn, lost in a forest—"

"We dream many troubling things," Farlan told him. "Especially when we are ill or hurting."

"Aye." Leith thought on it. As a man, he tended to shrug off worry and troubles, preferring to keep a light spirit. He chose laughter over more serious emotions. Now he lay trapped in this foreign place, in the dark.

He did not like feeling afraid or admitting to it. But fear, like the pain, held him in its grip.

"Leith?" Farlan's voice, warm and steady, came to him like a lifeline. "Can ye tell me—us—who attacked ye? Someone tried to smother the life from ye."

"*Us*? Ye speak o' your woman, then? The MacBeith chief?"

"Moira, aye."

Leith thought about how Farlan had returned home to MacLeod before defecting and told Leith of his feelings for this woman. "Is she worth it?" he asked in a low voice. "Is bein' with this Moira MacBeith worth giving up your birthright?"

"She is. I am no' saying 'tis easy. Her choosing to be wi' me has created no end o' troubles. And I—I am like a man adrift, belonging nowhere. Save in her arms."

It must be a love, Leith marveled, such as he himself had never yet known. Och, what man would want to be so enslaved?

"But tell me," Farlan urged, "wha' d'ye remember o' the

attack?"

"Verra little. I was asleep, I think. I came awake wi' a great weight pressing down upon me. I struggled against it, to breathe. Then I fell senseless, fell into that dream. D'ye think, Farlan, I lay near death then? That the forest where I wandered was death's borderland?"

"I think whoever attacked ye thought ye well dead. Beyond that, Leith, I canna say."

Chapter Twelve

THE DRAUGHT RHIAN mixed sent Leith into a deep sleep, despite his wishes. She could not tell if he once more slipped away into troubling dreams, but he lay quiet and apparently relieved of his pain.

Rhian remained there with him in the cowshed that smelled of its past occupants and admitted the chill, which could not be good for the patient. She stayed and watched him closely. She could not say why she stayed. God knew, she had scores of other tasks to perform and other wounded to visit. This man, this one man, did not warrant her exclusive attention. She provided care for those of MacBeith blood, who should come before one not her own.

Alasdair had stationed a new pair of guards outside before going off to run down Marc and Drachan and question them about having abandoned their duty. Ask what they'd seen and who might have attacked Leith MacLeod.

She should have left also, yet each time she approached the door to go, her newfound compassion for this man pulled her back. It felt precisely like a hook embedded beneath her heart, one that tugged hard. She'd never felt the like, and her mind spun over it.

Attachment. But why should she be attached to this particular man? Because she'd stumbled over him on a battlefield? But nay, for there'd been others lying out there in the dark. Plenty of others.

True, anyone with an ounce of pity in her soul might feel for one who lay in such perilous straits. Blinded, badly wounded, and far from home. Despite that, she should be able to walk away. It distressed her that she, a sound and practical woman, could not make herself go.

But she sorted through the contents of her basket at least twice, then thought of ways the miserable prison might be improved. It was the same place Farlan had been held when first he came to them, bleak and filthy. No wonder Moira had done all she could to relocate him.

Right into her bed.

Aye well, and that would not be happening again. For one thing, Rhian never fell victim to any man's charms. For another, he was a MacLeod.

Nevertheless, when she'd done all she could to make the prison more comfortable, she sat down with her hands in her lap and watched him sleep.

A big man and a powerful one he must be, when in good fettle. She had never seen him so. At his best, he would tower over her, and she was not a particularly dainty woman like Saerla.

She could not allow herself to fall into any traps. Could not think about the body beneath the blanket that she and Moira had seen when they washed the blood from him, fine as that body might be.

Moira, as levelheaded a woman as Rhian knew, had fallen into that trap, and look where it had got her—at odds with her own people and at risk of losing leadership of the clan.

Yet, even after telling herself all that, Rhian sat on, her gaze resting on Leith MacLeod. He slept quietly for a time. When he stirred, when his eyelids twitched and his lips moved, denoting a dream, she touched his hand, which lay across his chest.

He quieted again.

Not until she heard voices outside the door was she able to

break the spell that held her and step outside.

When Alasdair saw her, he motioned, and they stepped away from the two men who stood on duty.

"Did ye chase down the errant guards?" Rhian asked him.

"Aye." His expression looked sour. "They say one o' our own brought them a message supposedly fro' me, saying the prisoner was dyin' and was no' worth guarding any longer. Since they did no' want the duty anyway, they left."

Rhian searched his dark eyes. "Who brought the message?"

"As soon as they grasped it had been false, they did no' want to say. I persuaded them, so to speak."

"And?"

"'Twas young Tearlach."

Rhian searched her mind. "Kebran's son?" Kebran had been killed by the MacLeods some time ago in a battle. Tearlach was not quite old enough yet to take up a sword, being a stripling. But he spent his time in the warriors' hall, and they all knew him.

Rhian's eyes narrowed. "Tearlach's sister, Elreadh, is married to Dannochat, is she no'?"

"Aye," Alasdair said heavily. "And Dannochat fell to a Mac-Leod sword during the battle just past. He lies even now awaiting burial."

Rhian drew a breath. "Where is she, Elreadh?"

"No one seems to know. Mistress Rhian—" Alasdair seized her elbow and pulled her still farther away from the guards, who watched them curiously. He lowered his voice. "If 'twas she who sought her revenge upon yon MacLeod, well, there be none who will blame her. 'Twill be hard indeed to get any sort o' judgment upon her from the council."

"But 'twas an act o' cowardice. Ye said so yoursel', Alasdair. We canna just let her get away wi' it."

"'Twas cowardly, aye. But who would condemn a woman who has just lost her husband for acting fro' her grief and rage?"

"The bolster that was left behind—can it be proven to be hers?"

"Wi'out a doubt. And I suspect she thought she'd killed him. From the way young Tearlach reacted when I told him the prisoner was no' dead, they both did. No doubt that is why she ran off so swiftly that she neglected to take the bolster."

In a panic over what she'd done, Rhian thought. Elreadh was a tiny thing. Even blinded and severely wounded, Leith MacLeod had withstood her attempt at murder.

"What's to do?" she asked Alasdair.

"I will go now and inform Mistress Moira o' what we've found. Ye can trust these two guards, Mistress Rhian. They ken fine they are no' to be tricked into leaving their post till their relief arrives."

"Aye." Rhian gazed at the door of the pen. She could leave now. She *should* leave now. She had no cause to worry about the man who lay inside.

Yet that accursed hook buried in the center of her belly argued differently, tugging hard every time she thought about walking away.

He is naught to me. Just a man. Our enemy.

"Go and get some rest," Alasdair bade her, not unkindly. "No' to speak out o' turn, but ye look ready to drop."

Rhian snorted. "Ye be a fine one to talk."

He shrugged. "I'll rest when I need to. Soon."

She'd have to take him at his word on that.

She watched him walk away and forced herself to follow him, even though she'd left her basket inside with her patient. She had other baskets, and other patients, for all that.

She could return for it later.

But as she made her way back to her own quarters, to the blessed silence there and the peace of it, she continued to think about Leith MacLeod.

What would it be like to awaken, as he eventually would, to pain and darkness? To blindness and the knowledge that he lay surrounded by enemies?

She'd had scarcely a chance to return to her chamber all day.

The fire had long gone out, and the room felt chilly.

She washed and changed out of her bloodstained clothing, then once more sat beside the hearth and kindled a fire. The very act brought her a measure of peace, and the terrible tension inside her eased as she watched the flames strengthen and grow.

Here was her center, the place where she belonged. She never had and never would need anything more.

She must keep a close eye on the woman she was. No lass any longer, but a woman grown, one who planned to remain a spinster. A levelheaded, practical soul with no time or room for fancies. One with a tight grip on her emotions.

Though she did feel for poor Elreadh, no matter how cowardly her actions. And she felt for the man who lay in darkness so far from home.

Chapter Thirteen

B Y MORNING IT was all over the settlement, what Elreadh had done. It had perhaps spread via the guards who'd overheard some of what Alasdair said to Rhian. No way to tell.

Rhian herself first heard the gossip when Fiona came to her door early the next morning.

Fiona, a woman of middle years and a widow, had been… Well, in truth, she'd been Da's lover. Following the death of Rhian's mother some years ago, Da had been distraught. Aye well, they all had.

Fiona had stepped in after a handful of years to comfort him. Rhian still remembered how shocked she and her sisters had been when they discovered Fiona had been spending her nights in Da's chamber. In Da's bed. The same he had shared with Ma.

Iain MacBeith had been a big, bluff, kindly man with a loud laugh. Fiona's company had brought some of that back to him, though he'd never been the man he was when Ma was alive.

Eventually, his daughters had come to terms with the relationship. It had been Saerla who made the observation. *Everybody needs someone, and I believe men do even more than women. We canna claim to love Da and yet wish him aught but happiness.*

Fiona could not be more different from Ma, who'd possessed a quiet, serene spirit. Fiona's emotions showed almost too readily, and she had a tendency to chatter. But she'd been devastated by Da's death, and Rhian could not doubt the sincerity of what she'd felt for him.

That did not necessarily mean Rhian welcomed a visit first thing in the morning following a restless night.

"Have ye heard?" Fiona demanded even as she came pushing into the chamber. "'Tis Elreadh. She tried to murder yon MacLeod prisoner last night."

Rhian said nothing. The fire in her hearth that had lent her such comfort last night had burned to nothing, and with the morning light, all her worries flooded back in. She felt scattered and found she'd gained scant rest after all.

When Fiona received no answer, her fine hazel eyes narrowed. "But here's me telling ye something ye already knew. Ye've been tending the man, aye?"

"Aye. Has Elreadh been found?"

"No' yet, though Alasdair has men looking. 'Tis believed she's left the settlement. She and her young brother have an aunt outlying. She's likely gone there, though Tearlach will no' say."

Rhian bit her lip.

"Did ye see the prisoner after the attack?" Fiona demanded, no doubt deciding that if she could not shock Rhian with her news, she might at least mine her for further details. "How did Elreadh attempt to kill him? No one will say."

Then Rhian should not say either. "It was a cowardly act, Fiona. Let us leave it at that."

Fiona's expression grew hard. Rhian knew this woman for a warm one, a generous one, qualities that had no doubt drawn Da to her. Now she pronounced almost viciously, "The MacLeod would be better dead."

Aye, so, and that was the accepted belief. Every MacLeod was better dead, including Moira's Farlan. Acknowledging that, Rhian had a glimpse of what her sister faced. Loving Farlan as she might, how would she ever convince anyone else to accept him?

"'Twas a cowardly act all the same, when the man lay helpless. He is blinded, Fiona." Though Rhian hoped the condition would not prove permanent.

Fiona hissed, "I ken fine, Rhian. Ye ha' a sympathetic heart. Your da loved ye for it. But were it no' for the MacLeods, your da would still be here wi' us now." She fought back ready tears.

"Aye," Rhian said softly. No one could argue that.

"The council has been in session since early this morning."

"Over Elreadh?"

"Nay, nay, and if Alasdair finds her, I doubt much they'll be willing to hear a word against her."

"Her punishment will be up to Moira, surely."

"Will it? I am no' so certain." Fiona's gaze met Rhian's. "For 'tis Moira's own fate they've met to discuss."

His head hurt, an unrelenting pain that spread from the back of his skull in a band across his eyes. It felt like he'd had his brains rattled all over again. That was naught, though, to the pain in his arm. That had teeth and gnawed at him, deep.

Both those things paled in the face of the fact that he could not see.

He'd never been afeared of much. Indeed, his ma routinely condemned him for it in that chiding, loving way she had.

Leith, will ye never stop wi' landing yoursel' in trouble? And laughing about it.

Aye, he'd always possessed more daring than sense, and the three of them—himself, Rory, and Farlan—had landed themselves in no end of trouble and mischief.

He'd retained an almost magical belief that if he could get into trouble, he'd be able to work—or charm—his way out of it again.

He'd never, though, been in such difficulty as this. Captive. Sorely injured. Blind.

Panic stirred in his breast. Take now, for instance. He'd awakened alone and cold, lying in what was undoubtedly his prison. Hurting. Whatever draught the merciful angel had mixed for him had long worn off.

Rhian. It was a beautiful name that fairly sang in his mind.

He could not see her, nay, but he could feel the kindness that flowed from her. He felt it whenever she touched him and even when she did not, so long as she remained nearby.

He wished with all his being she was here now.

He lay motionless, trying to breathe against the pain in his arm, enduring breath after breath. The vast and vital strength that helped him escape whatever scrapes befell him had now near deserted him.

Perhaps that meant he would die.

But nay, he was not so weak as all that. He'd fought off the attacker who'd come intending to finish him. The need to breathe had brought him up from the depths of his darkness, fighting. That meant he must still possess the will to live.

At least he had a friend nearby. Farlan was here in this place of enemies, and had come to see him. Or had that been but another mad dream? Nay, for Farlan had come here, to MacBeith. Sacrificed his name and birthright to be with the woman he loved.

And Rory was still livid over it.

Aye, but what could Farlan do to help him? Farlan would not be accepted here, would he?

Leith thought about it, figured the odds and chances, none of them good, while he breathed in and out against the pain.

If it was morning, might Rhian return? He did not know it was morning for certain because he could not see the light. But he could hear increased activity beyond the door. Foot traffic and folk calling questions to the guards who stood out there, where it had been quiet before.

He prayed Rhian would come. Then again, what reason did she have to continue tending him? He was an enemy, and perhaps she had finished with him.

That thought struck deep and opened up a new wound.

If Farlan returned, Leith could ask about Rhian. Request that she might come. If she truly were a merciful angel, she would not refuse him.

He lay so, fist clenched against his pain, concentrating on breathing in and breathing out, until he heard another voice speaking to the guards outside. A sweet, steady voice he recognized.

Thank you, God.

She came in quietly, but he could not mistake her identity. He knew her step, knew the way she moved, and he at once caught her scent. Herbs. And woman.

"Ah, so ye ha' come awake." She crossed to his side. He had his eyes clenched shut against the pain. He wished… He wished if he opened them, he could see her.

"Leith MacLeod, how d'ye fare this morning?" Answering her own question, she said, "In a great deal o' pain, as I can see."

She came down beside his pallet. He felt her bend near.

Touch me, he beseeched silently, even while trying to form a smile on his lips, to find some quip to say. That would have been his way of old, to make light of the very worst situation.

He failed now. Instead he gasped against the pain. "I think I am dyin'."

Touch me. Help me. Please.

She laid her hand on his head, across his eyes. It felt warm in the chilly air, felt soothing beyond measure. She whispered some words, just a few under her breath, words he could not catch despite how close to him she bent. The pain in his head eased. He wanted to stay like this forever, with her touching him. Instead he caught her wrist in his fingers and drew her palm away.

Slowly, slowly, he opened his eyes.

And her face swam into view, half hazy from the light that streamed in from all sides. A white oval just as he remembered, perfect in form. Wreathed by concern and filled with a beautiful mercy that rivaled the light. A pair of long-lashed, deep blue eyes. Lips pressed tight together. A cloud of dark red hair, half caught back, a glorious nimbus.

By God, her hair was red. And by God, he could see her. *He could see.*

"Rhian MacBeith," he whispered.

She nodded, and her lips parted. "Ye can see me?"

"I can now." Now that she'd touched him. "Wha' magic is this?"

He still had hold of her wrist. He slid his fingers beneath hers, which were warm and slender, and held them tight.

They remained that way for a score of heartbeats, two score, gazing deep into one another's eyes.

She was all he saw, and, from that moment, all he ever wanted to see.

Chapter Fourteen

"THIS WOUND IN my arm, it could kill me, aye?" Leith MacLeod asked.

"We shall try to make certain that does not happen."

He had let go of Rhian at last, released her fingers from his. She'd risen from his side and moved around the inside of the pen, rooting in her basket for herbs and clean bandages.

She always held hard to her calm demeanor when treating a patient. But she felt shaken to the heart by what had passed between her and Leith at the return of his sight.

The charm she'd muttered had been that—a simple charm, and spoken more by rote than aught else. One frequently whispered such charms over hurts. That had not restored his sight.

Or mayhap it had, because she'd wanted it for him. She'd wanted it so.

She did not understand why this man affected her the way he did, what there was about him that tapped into the deep well of her compassion. But when that happened—and she could not deny it happened—she felt for the first time in her life just how bottomless that well was.

He watched her now as she moved around the space. How could she deny him that? He'd been recently blind, and she was all he had now to gaze upon.

Yet it was the way he looked at her, in part, that shook her so.

No doubt, no doubt at all that his sight had come back on its own, even as she'd hoped it might. The effects of the blow he'd taken had merely worn off. It had naught to do with aught she'd said or done. A mere coincidence.

"Come, Rhian, sit beside me once more."

He should not address her so. It should be *Mistress Rhian* at the very least. Yet the roughness in his voice betrayed the great weight of pain under which he labored. And anyway—

Could she stand on ceremony with him now?

"I maun change those bandages first." Then, *then*, aye she might sit with him.

He grunted.

"And," she continued, "I might mix for ye another draught against the pain."

"Another that will make me sleep? I've nae wish to sleep any longer."

She turned and looked at him. Some emotion inside her, some hint of longing perhaps, twanged. A fine figure of a man he was. Not the sort she'd ever expected to favor. In fact, the very last sort. And yet…

"I ha' told ye, there be healing in sleep."

"And the possibility of evil dreams. By any road, sleep renders me defenseless. I ha' few enough defenses left to me as it is."

"Aye," she agreed. She brought her bandages and knelt down beside him.

He went suddenly still. *He wants for me to touch him,* she thought, and could not tell how she knew.

"This will hurt."

His only answer came in the form of another grunt. It did hurt. They both sweated through it, but throughout, he never took his eyes from her.

Handsome eyes they were, changeable like the sky—at one moment gray and the next blue, and set beneath well-marked sandy brows. The brows matched the beard on his jaw and, aye, the hair that patterned his broad chest. For she'd seen all of him. He was without question one of the most masculine men she'd ever beheld.

"There." At last she smoothed the bandages. "Does that feel better?"

"It does, while your hands be upon it."

Her gaze flew to his again. Was he trifling with her? Flirting with her? Surely not. He spoke as if he stated a plain truth. Besides, men rarely flirted with MacBeith's steady, practical, and utterly dull middle daughter.

"I will get that draught."

"Stay where ye be. Please. Just keep your hand where it is a moment longer."

Touching him. She should not. Out of simple pity, surely she might.

Only—this was more than simple pity that she felt. More even than simple attraction, if she'd admit to that. If she had to define it, she would call it *connection*. That hook in her gut that only ceased to pull so hard when she got close to him.

Could it be he felt that too? By no means could she ask him. It would sound like madness.

So she asked instead, spreading her fingers on his chest, "Like so?"

"Aye." He inspected her face again, taking minute notice of every feature. She knew it for a plain enough face, so he surprised her when he said, "Ye be a bonny thing, merciful angel."

"Me? Nay." Saerla was the bonny one. Moira the most striking. Rhian had always accepted that.

"Nay," he echoed softly. "Bonny does no' cover it. Too weak a word entirely. 'Tis beauty that describes ye. Rhian MacBeith. A beautiful woman, full grown."

She smiled wryly despite herself. Aye, and was he not a charmer? "Ye say that only because I am the first face ye've looked upon here at MacBeith."

"I say it because 'tis the truth. Nay. Do no' leave me yet."

Once more he caught her hand and wove his fingers through hers. "Iain MacBeith's daughter, are ye?"

"Aye. His middle daughter."

"Your sister, the one playin' at being chief, 'twas she who seduced my friend, Farlan? Aye, he told me all about her when he returned home. Before he left us for good, that was. For her sake."

"There are three o' us. Moira, myself, and Saerla."

"MacBeith's three daughters. I will confess, though I did sympathize wi' Farlan when he told me all, I did no' quite understand it. Aye, love is love. But fealty is fealty, ye ken."

"Aye."

"Now, beholding ye, I begin to understand."

That made her draw away, pull her fingers from his, and get to her feet. "I will prepare that draught."

"I do no' want it."

"Master Leith, 'tis far from proper for us to ha' any sort o' relationship beyond that o' nurse and patient."

"Surely, though, 'tis already more. Ye saved my life out there on the battlefield. Ye canna deny I would ha' bled to death had ye no' aided me."

"Perhaps."

"And now ye ha' restored my sight. Ye be keeping me alive." His lips worked for an instant before he added, "Ye be keeping me alive in ways I canna understand."

That made her turn back and stare at him, feeling once more that pull to the gut, the tug to her heart.

Nay. She could not let this—whatever it may be—happen. She'd seen the misery such nonsense brought to Moira.

"I ha' other patients to tend."

"Aye, no doubt ye do." He bowed his head in apparent defeat.

"If I mix the draught, will ye drink it?"

He shook his head.

"But ye will be in pain wi'out it."

"I will endure."

She did not like that. It went against her every instinct, as did picking up her basket and leaving him here.

"Are ye warm enough?"

"Aye, Mistress Rhian."

Sweet heaven, she loved the way he said her name, like music on his lips.

"The guards are just outside the door. Take what rest ye can."

She went out and walked away past the guards without stopping, even though with every step, the hook in her gut tightened.

She lectured herself firmly as she might one of her sisters. She could not, *would* not, be so foolish as to succumb to this nonsense. Leith MacLeod was but a man.

Only he was not.

At least his sight had returned, as her instincts had told her it would. A good thing that, for the life of a blinded warrior offered little. Just as she could offer him little. She must concentrate on healing that vicious wound and getting him traded back to MacLeod.

Rory MacLeod's first cousin, so Farlan had said he was. The son of old Camraith's sister. So the man should want him back right enough.

But it bothered her. It bothered her because it echoed so closely all that business with Farlan, wherein Moira had held him as a hostage and tried to bargain with Rory MacLeod over him.

Just see how that had ended.

Before anyone could bargain over Leith MacLeod, though, he had to be sound. And they, Clan MacBeith, would have to settle the leadership of the clan. At the moment, even Saerla, with her foresight, could not say how that would work out.

She entered her quarters and set down her basket, perched on the edge of her bed, and put her head in her hands. Steady and composed, that was MacBeith's middle daughter. Only, at this moment, she wanted to rage and scream and cry.

Removing her hands from her head, she pressed them against her stomach. Here, it hurt. Just beneath her heart. She had to put all thoughts of Leith away from her. Return to the sensible woman she had been.

Because living like this was bound to drive her mad. She would not know herself. And a woman who did not know herself was of use to no one.

Chapter Fifteen

"THE COUNCIL HA' come to a decision about whether Moira should continue wi' leading the clan," Saerla announced the next morning. "Ye need to come."

Rhian blinked at her sister unhappily. She'd appeared at the door of Rhian's chamber early, clad in a manner that suggested she'd been bound for the training field.

"What, did they stay in session all night long?"

"I believe they did. Alasdair was wi' them. 'Twas he who came out and caught me, said I should bring ye."

Alasdair. In session with the council while Moira, the acting chief, was not. Och, what would Da say?

Rhian searched Saerla's face, seeking clues. "Ha' ye Seen the outcome o' all this?"

"I ha' no', though I was up at the stones before dawn speaking my prayers."

The stones—an ancient circle on the rise above the stronghold, a place of magic. Da lay up there beside it along with others of their ancestors.

"Very well, I will come. I need time to pull mysel' together. I just crawled from my bed."

"Best no' take long, sister."

Saerla slipped away on silent feet, calling softly over her shoulder, "The great hall."

Rhian went back inside to try to get hold of herself. She did not often lose control of her emotions. Och aye, events did slip away from her. Da's death, and her brother Arran's before that, had caused no end of grief. The war with MacLeod, and Moira losing her heart to Farlan. But she'd always kept a grip on her reactions to such events.

Now she felt scattered and as if she held on to her composure by a thread.

And that accursed hook in her belly had kept her awake most the night. Aye, she was merely weary. Fraught. An understandable reaction to events.

She dressed as quickly as she could and bound her hair. She washed in cold water from the basin, telling herself all the while she did not have time to stop by the cattle pen and see her patient.

The air outside held a chill, and clouds poured over the western mountains from the direction of the sea, heralding rain. Indeed, before she reached the doors of the hall, big drops began to pelt the ground, her shoulders, and her hair.

Others occupied the hall ahead of her. The members of the council, of course, including the irascible Ewan. Saerla was there, and Moira had been called in. Alasdair closed the door firmly behind Rhian. No one appeared to be in a good mood.

But a fire burned in the long, rectangular hearth, and Rhian gravitated toward it, holding out her hands. Doing so, she looked into Moira's face. Her sister appeared wary—worried.

Rhian looked next at Alasdair. Had he got any sleep last night? She doubted it. He'd been here with the council and doubtless up on the walls before that, searching for marauding parties of MacLeods. Perhaps checking on Leith's guards still earlier.

Leith.

She could not let her thoughts stray to him. *She could not.*

She sat close to the hearth, and the others joined her, most of them standing, though Saerla perched at Rhian's side. Rhian could feel emotions coming off both her sisters, and strong tension dominated the chamber. From Saerla she also sensed a measure of sorrow.

Ewan began speaking. "We, the members o' the council, remained in session all last night trying to decide wha' should be done to secure the leadership o' this clan. We live in dire times."

He looked around at them all, his gaze touching each face. "Since the death o' his father Camraith the chief, Rory MacLeod has been determined to run roughshod over us and defeat us if he can. Claim all Glen Bronach for MacLeod. That means our lands, held here for long before any MacLeod ever darkened the horizon. 'Tis no time, this, for weak leadership."

Moira took a step forward. "Are ye calling me weak?"

Ewan's expression became difficult to read. He'd been a contemporary of Da's, and a trusted advisor. He'd known Iain MacBeith's daughters all their lives.

Now he seemed to choose his words carefully. "I would no' call ye weak. But I believe, as do the other members o' this council, that your judgment has been compromised."

That made Moira blink. "Because I am a woman?"

"No' just that. Though it be a factor."

Another of the council members, an older man called Rab, spoke up. "We are no' men used to following the leadership o' a woman, though not one o' us here would be foolish enough to ignore advice from our wives. Ye, Mistress Moira, ha' proved yoursel' in battle, as has Mistress Saerla. Your father was, and would be, proud o' all his daughters."

"'Tis the MacLeod," said another, younger man. "The one ye ha' taken to yer bed."

Moira flushed even though she must have been expecting this. She took it like a blow. "Farlan does no' affect my decisions as befits this clan."

"How can he no'?" the same man demanded. "He is always whispering in yer ear."

"He is no longer a MacLeod. He has renounced the name."

"He may well ha' done. And he might ha' stripped off the tartan. That does no' make him any less what he is, and for certain sure does no' make him a MacBeith."

"We trust ye, Mistress Moira," said Rab. "We canna trust him."

"So what? Ye want to cast me off as Rory did Farlan?"

"Nay, nay," Rab soothed. "But ye could gi' him up."

Anger now poured into Moira's dark blue eyes, hardening them to flint. "That is your decision, is it? The choice ye give to me. Gi' up Farlan or step down as chief? We ha' been here before."

"Aye, so we have," Ewan agreed. "But we never settled the matter. We canna ha' a MacLeod in whatever guise holding a place o' leadership in this clan. Not while Rory MacLeod beleaguers us. Both yer sisters have refused the place o' chief. We've offered it to Alasdair."

Moira looked at Alasdair, who gazed back at her. Bitterly, she asked, "And what has Alasdair said?"

Ah, Rian thought on a quick surge of sympathy. *This cannot be easy for Alasdair.* He had, aye, for some time harbored feelings toward Moira, only to see her fall for another man. The most unsuitable man possible.

"I told them," Alasdair said, his gaze still on Moira's face, "I still believe a member o' Iain MacBeith's house should stand at the head o' the clan. Wi' yer brother dead and neither o' yer sisters willing to accept the place, Moira, that leaves ye."

Moira shook her head. "I do no' understand. Ye ha' also refused the position?"

Ewan did not sound happy when he said, "After speaking half the night, we came to a compromise. We are willing to leave ye at the head o' the clan, Mistress Moira, so long as Master Alasdair leads beside ye."

Moira's lips parted. It took Rhian a moment to grasp what Ewan had just said. Moira took an instant also.

"Joint leadership? Is that wha' ye mean?"

"Aye."

"Mysel' and Alasdair?" She closed her lips into a hard line before she said, "He is to approve my decisions, is that it?"

"Nay, not so," Rab insisted. "Merely make them alongside ye so we may be easy in our minds that there is no undue influence upon ye."

Moira's nostrils flared. She said nothing.

"And one more condition," Ewan added.

"Wha' is it?"

"Ye will no' wed wi' Farlan MacLeod while ye hold the place o' chief. If ye do so, ye maun step down."

"Unacceptable! Would ye force me to live in sin?" As she already did.

"We merely ask ye," Rab said, almost gently, "to step awa' from him."

Moira cast one angry look at Alasdair as if she thought it all his fault and stormed out of the chamber. Alasdair gazed after her. Rhian thought she saw despair in his eyes.

Saerla scrambled up and swiftly followed her sister out.

"Did she refuse?" Ewan asked the other members of the council. And then he muttered, "Women are incapable o' making a measured decision."

Rhian went out in her sisters' wake, but not before laying a reassuring hand on Alasdair's arm. "She will come round. She does no' blame ye."

Out in the pouring rain, she could not see either of her sisters. Where would Moira go, and Saerla after her?

Of one thing alone was she certain—it was fatal to pin one's affections on a MacLeod, in whatever guise. She must keep away from Leith at all costs.

Chapter Sixteen

RHIAN MacBEITH HAD been right. The pain in Leith's arm soon grew teeth and gnawed at him, becoming unbearable. Many times after her departure did he reconsider having refused her offer of a draught.

But he'd had his fill of being rendered senseless, and thus defenseless. He'd been attacked once already. Who knew what threat might next enter that door?

Should Rhian return—what would he do then? Lying with his teeth clenched and his gaze on the door, he considered it. He would, nay, still not take the draught.

He would ask her to touch him again.

Her touch contained magic. Well, if not that—if, as a grown man, he'd put belief in such things behind him—it at least contained comfort. Healing.

He had difficulty not believing her palm on his brow had been fundamental in restoring his sight.

That thought allowed him to draw a breath. At least he had that, had escaped the darkness that had indeed rendered him twice as helpless as now.

He lay feeling grateful for it, and taking stock of himself. The pain in his head had gone, though the wound there still felt tender to his probing fingers. The tear to his arm, though, worried him. It had affected the whole limb so that though he could clench his left fist, he could not close the fingers of the right.

He would not be able to hold a weapon, even if he had one.

A dire position, indeed, in which a warrior should find himself. He lay struggling beneath the weight of it, trying to decide what his ma must be thinking. She most likely assumed he'd been left for dead after that last battle—which, in truth, he had. The retreating MacLeod forces had not had time to retrieve all their dead.

Would Ma weep for him? And his bonny sister, Aisleen? He hated to imagine it, to think they might shed tears on his account. He'd sought always to bring them laughter rather than heartache.

And Rory—och, Rory would be in a fury over this. Having lost Farlan already, as he saw it, he'd be livid thinking Leith either captured or dead.

Indeed, after what happened with Farlan, Rory would likely rather Leith dead than captured.

Farlan renouncing his birthright and his clan, for a woman, no less, had wounded Rory deep. Close as the three of them had been, they had harbored an unthinking kind of friendship that Leith believed nothing could destroy. He had considered them all brothers, or as good as.

Now Rory was like a bear with a wounded paw—difficult and irascible toward everyone. More determined than ever to seize Glen Bronach and become sole ruler over it.

Yet they'd lost the last two battles. He would be livid over that.

Aye, they likely all thought Leith dead. It was an odd feeling, that, knowing everyone who held him in affection believed him gone from the world. Almost as if he'd fallen off the face of the earth and ceased to exist.

Folk held those they loved in their hearts and minds. 'Twas what kept them close.

He wondered suddenly if Rhian MacBeith held him in her mind. If she thought about him even now, when she was away from him.

But nay, it was a foolish notion. Rhian MacBeith did not love him.

Gritting his teeth still more fiercely, he struggled to sit up on the pallet. His own weakness appalled him. The simple movement took three attempts, and by the time he succeeded, Rhian's clean white bandages had turned red.

But he would not lie here, by God, like a puling infant.

Having made it upright, he sat sweating and trying not to groan aloud. He had no clothing, not a stitch, which meant Rhian had seen all there was of him. Ah well, she would not be the first woman.

His clothing would have been ruined with blood. But the cool air pricked at him, and his nakedness made him feel all the more vulnerable.

Another defense, gone. All the things that made him who he was had been stripped away. It allowed him to think anew on the ordeal that had befallen Farlan. Aye, he'd sympathized with the man when he brought his tale back to MacLeod and told of his love for MacBeith's daughter. He'd felt for the man, but until now, he hadn't truly understood. Being trapped, cut off from all he knew, and all that knew him. Surrounded by ill will.

He closed his eyes, clenching them hard against a sudden wave of weakness and despair. To combat it, he reimagined the moment when Rhian had laid her hand on his brow and he'd opened his eyes. To see her.

The sweet, serene oval of her face, full of womanly wisdom. The perfect sweep of her brows and the cloud of wild auburn hair. The full lower lip that betrayed just a hint of the passion that might lie within.

He could not say that the passion lying within her might extend to him. She was a woman who disciplined her emotions. Not some pretty lass primed for seduction.

Just as he'd tried to tell her, she was not merely bonny. She was *beautiful*.

Using the conviction of it for strength, he heaved himself to his feet. When he got there, he stood swaying, nearly falling back down. His head spun in slow, sickening circles, and he half feared he'd lose his sight again.

Yet he stood on his feet, by God, and felt more the man for it.

The pallet had been provided with two blankets. He took up the smaller of them and wound it around his hips, making a rough covering. Then he stood shaking in every limb, wondering if he dared take a step.

Rhian had left a flask on the wooden table that stood against the wall. Water, no doubt. Only a few steps away, yet he doubted he could reach it. Should he fall, he would never pick himself up again.

Shuffling like an old man, he took one step. Two. When he reached the table, he caught up the flask and wondered how to open it one-handed. His throat burned with thirst, so he used his teeth on the stopper and spat it out.

Ale. God bless the woman. God bless Rhian MacBeith.

OUT IN THE rainy morning, Rhian paused and cocked an ear, wondering if someone had called her name. The rain fell so hard it looked like a silver curtain, and in the distance, thunder rumbled. She could not see her sisters anywhere.

This was madness.

She'd already tried Moira's chamber, that which used to be Da's—alarming Farlan, who waited there, and sending him out on a search of his own. Saerla's quarters also lay empty, as did the armory and any other place Rhian could call to mind.

They must have gone up on the rise. To the ring of standing stones. And Da's grave.

More madness, in such weather. But Moira had not been completely in her sane mind when she'd left the hall. And the rise—well, it was Saerla's second home.

Rhian set her shoulders, picked up her skirts, and ran. She wished she'd stopped by her own quarters for her cloak, for the hard rain soaked her to the skin. Ah well, she could become only so wet and no wetter.

The wind caught her as she climbed the rise, slipping on the wet turf as the storm blew in from the west. It covered her, crashing and tearing, making the rain of a moment ago seem like nothing. Water filled her eyes so she could not see. Yet she knew the way. She'd been coming here since a wee lass. She need only keep on.

The next time she stumbled, hands caught at her and helped her up again. Her sister's hands. She'd found Saerla, at least.

Neither of them attempted to speak as they gained the top of the rise, passed Da's grave, and reached the circle of stones. There, Moira came out to meet them.

Rhian had found both her sisters.

They huddled down, the three of them, with their heads together and the rain pelting their bent backs, in the limited shelter of a standing stone. In the onslaught, Rhian could not tell Saerla's hands from Moira's, gripping her own. But she felt the strength of the embrace.

The storm passed, pounding the ground with percussive steps and grumbling like an ill-tempered giant.

Soaked to the bone and chilled with it, Rhian raised her head.

Moira did also, her face streaked with rain like tears. Saerla's brighter head—now darkened by wet—lifted in turn. They regarded one another.

"Be we all well?" Saerla asked.

Moira shook her head. "Half deafened by that thunder. How did the both o' ye find me?"

"Where else would ye go?" Rhian asked. Aye, as she should have known from the outset.

Saerla had one arm wrapped around Moira's neck and the other around Rhian's. She tightened them. "Stay but a moment. There is strength in us being together like this. The three sisters

MacBeith."

There was magic in it. And aye, such magic remained Saerla's domain. Rhian stayed where she was.

"We are stronger all together," she said. "And we will need that strength, no doubt."

"Aye," Saerla agreed, "we will need it for what is to come."

Chapter Seventeen

"H A' YE RECEIVED a Vision, Saerla?" Moira asked. They'd climbed down from the rise in the wake of the storm, encountering both Farlan and Alasdair in passing before moving on to Rhian's chamber, where they felt they might best be alone.

There they dried off, Rhian lending her sisters fresh clothing. She tended the fire in her own hearth while they found words to exchange with one another.

They needed this time together.

"Nay, I ha' no' received a Vision." Saerla shook her head. Already her hair began to dry in the warmth from the fire, forming a halo of bright curls around her head. "I ha' no need o' one. Anyone might feel what is to come."

Moira nodded soberly. "I ha' made a right mess o' things. I wonder what Da would say."

That made Saerla lift her gaze to Moira's face. "Ye have no cause to wonder. I ha' told ye, Da believes Farlan to be your destiny."

"Aye. To be truthful"—Moira hesitated—"so do I. Yet look at the trouble it has caused. Continues to cause."

"Aye." Rhian could only agree.

Moira hurried on, "Just because I trust Farlan—and I do, I would trust him wi' my very life—does no' mean the council ever will. Or the clansfolk. Or Alasdair."

"Alasdair stood for Farlan," Saerla reminded her, "when he crossed the loch to your side."

Miserably, Moira said, "Alasdair did that for my sake. No one is fooled into thinking differently. Add to that the fact that, despite our latest victory, Rory MacLeod is no' done wi' hounding us. He will attack again and again. If we lose a man here, a man there, if we grow depleted, what will happen then?"

"He will also lose men," Rhian said. "He has already lost Leith."

"Aye, a sore blow, if Farlan can be believed. Leith is Rory's cousin and close to him as can be. But will that no' merely serve to enrage him all the more?"

"Perhaps best to send Leith MacLeod back," Saerla suggested.

Rhian felt an immediate tug just beneath her heart, as if the connection to Leith buried there tightened. She wanted to protest it. But aye, mayhap it would be the best thing.

"He has regained his sight," she announced. "Only a short time ago."

Both her sisters stared at her.

"'Tis the hand of the gods, that," Saerla breathed.

"Or Rhian's. Either way, it makes him more of a threat," Moira declared. "If we send him home, he may recover to fight against us again in the future."

Rhian shook her head. "Not soon, and perhaps not ever. That wound in his arm has his life still hanging in the balance."

"All I know," Moira said unhappily, "is I do not want a repeat o' what happened when we tried to bargain wi' Rory MacLeod over Farlan. Best to send Leith back now, I think."

So it would end that swiftly between them, would it? Whatever *it* was—this connection. This latent desire. Aye, no doubt for the best. Cut those bonds, and cut them clean.

Moira made a face. "Of course, now I will have to consult wi' Alasdair before I make any decisions. If I try to act on my own, the council will no doubt replace me entirely and make him chief."

"Likely they merely do no' want ye making such decisions wi' Farlan," Saerla offered gently. "Ye can see that, surely."

"I can see it." Moira sighed. "We maun be ready for more battles. When I go up on the rise—" She paused, and her blue eyes became almost as dreamy as Saerla's. "I can feel that we are part o' this land, all o' us. The three o' us especially." She curled an arm around each of her sisters' necks, uniting them once again. "Our roots here run deep. I will no' surrender this land to Rory MacLeod or anyone."

"Aye," Saerla agreed softly. "I will pray on it, that we might be strong enough and determined enough. That through all the strife, we may find a lasting solution."

Rhian smiled. "I will never, Saerla, doubt the power o' your prayers."

"Nor I," Moira vowed.

"And," Saerla went on, "we maun gather together this way more often. For there is, aye, strength in it."

"Aye," both Moira and Rhian agreed.

"Just think on it," Saerla added. "Rory MacLeod has lost that strength. He and Farlan and Leith were all close, aye?"

"So Farlan says."

"Well, he is now without the two o' them. Mayhap"—Saerla's gaze sharpened—"'twill be better to keep Leith here after all."

Rhian's heart leaped. Perhaps it would.

SHE WANTED TO go and see the prisoner after that, longed to make an excuse for it and check that terrible wound of his. Discover whether he wanted that draught after all. Be in his company. But the longing frightened her, because there was no sense in it. She might well be attracted to him, aye. He was a man and she a woman. Nature had made them with the purpose of being so attracted to one another.

The curious thing was she'd never been so attracted to any other man. Oh, in her youth she'd followed a few lads with her eyes—MacBeith had a surfeit of handsome men. She'd even kissed a few on feast days, after dark. It had meant nothing. And following first Arran's death and then Ma's, she'd devoted herself to running the household and taking care of others. She'd put such nonsense behind her.

Now the nonsense had caught up with her, and she a spinster.

And he an accursed MacLeod.

She would not go and see him, nay. She had plenty of other wounded to treat, folk of her own blood.

She set off about those visits, this time well-sheltered in her cloak against the rain, all the while thinking—it wasn't mere physical attraction that drew her to Leith MacLeod. There was something more. The look in his eyes. The strength and vulnerability together that lay inside him. The sense of rightness that bloomed within her every time she touched him, even if just to provide care.

There could be no rightness in being with a MacLeod, she told herself savagely while she treated wound after terrible wound, reminding herself all this came of conflict with Clan MacLeod. A clan full of greedy, ruthless, and ambitious men.

Like Rory himself. Leith MacLeod's cousin.

She must cut any ties she fancied had formed between her and the man. Was she not a levelheaded woman? One who dealt with the basics of survival? She had no business imagining anything more.

She had her place here in Clan MacBeith. A good and necessary place. She need only be content with it. And that required dismissing any thoughts of earnest blue-gray eyes and a face made for laughter.

There could be no laughter shared between them.

Mayhap it would be best to assign Leith one of the other healers. Just because she'd stumbled over him out on the battlefield, and because she'd been there when the effects of the blow he'd taken to the head wore off, did not mean anything existed between them. Did she not have the example of Moira before her?

The rain ceased late in the afternoon, flying away down Glen Bronach to pelt the MacLeods' stronghold before departing.

Rhian, with her basket now filled with soiled linens, stepped outside for a breath of air before retiring to her own quarters. How sweet the air smelled after a rain. Clean and fresh, and carrying the tang of wild thyme from high on the braes. She stood breathing deeply and felt her heart calm within her.

This place, this blessed, beautiful glen, was enough. A reason for her to work and care, to strive. If she dedicated her life to its preservation, it would be a worthy and satisfying cause.

Upon the thought, the clouds overhead, which still ran hard before a fast wind, parted and the late afternoon sun broke through. It shone down in bars of gold and lit the green turf, and the loch beyond.

Rhian caught her breath as her heart swelled. *Be content, my lass,* she told herself, and it sounded like her mother's voice. Only the greediest of women could ask for more.

Chapter Eighteen

"I CONFESS, MAN, I did no' expect to see ye up and on your feet."

"I did no' entirely expect to be here." Leith stared at Farlan with rising gladness. After a day trapped here in the malodorous cell, forsaken and alone, he could not think of anyone he'd rather see. Well, mayhap one person.

She had not come, all the long day she had not. Though he'd prayed—prayed for her to return.

Farlan studied him carefully. At home, back at MacLeod while growing up, Farlan had always been the steady one, the calm voice of reason. The member of their trio whom they could count on to talk Rory down when he'd become too carried away with himself.

Leith had been the jester, the one to make the other two laugh. He'd given Rory a dose of nonsense, once Farlan gentled him.

He could not feel farther from nonsense than now.

"I am that glad to see ye," he confessed to his friend.

"I am that glad for ye to see me. As soon as I heard your sight had come back to ye, I had to come and find out for mysel'."

"Who told ye that?" Leith asked, thinking of Rhian.

"Moira did. Her sister did mention it. How d'ye feel? Here, sit down, man. Ye look a bit wobbly to be stomping about. And I brought a flask."

Thank God. Though he would not give in and take one of Rhian's draughts, Leith would not refuse strong drink at this point.

They sat on the pallet, since there was no place else, one of them on either end. Farlan passed Leith the flask, and he drank deep.

"How's the wound?"

Leith swiped his lips with the back of the same hand that held the flask. "I tell ye, Farlan, I ha' ne'er suffered the like. 'Tis hurting something fierce and has teeth that will no' relent. And only look—I canna use my right hand at all."

Farlan appeared fittingly horrified. "'Tis your sword hand, that."

"Aye. I canna so much as make a fist. The arm's as limp as a dead fish."

Farlan frowned deeply. "Wha' does Mistress Rhian say about it? She's been treating ye, has she no'?"

And there it was. Already, her name brought her alive in the room.

"She's a fine healer, and I daresay saved my life," Farlan added.

Leith hesitated over how much to share with his friend. It sounded like madness. On the other hand, no one alive would understand his predicament better than this man.

He fixed Farlan with a hard stare and lowered his voice. "I swear, Farlan, she brought back my sight."

"Eh?"

"She laid her hand upon my brow, and 'twas as if the darkness lifted. The first thing I saw was her face." *Her beautiful face.*

Farlan swore softly.

"Aye—'twas like some miracle out o' the old stories we heard as lads. I do no' think she's an ordinary woman."

"None o' the three o' them is," Farlan declared. "Old Iain's daughters."

"I've never known her like."

"Christ Jesus, Leith! Do no' go there." Farlan looked uncomfortable.

"Where?"

"Do no' go losin' yer heart to her. 'Tis a terrible, hard road. Take it from one who knows."

"I ha no' lost my heart to her." But that was not completely true. A part of his heart, at least, felt anchored to Rhian in a way he could not explain.

"I ken fine she be a lovely woman," Farlan went on. "And possesses a good heart. But by God, man. Only see what's happened to me."

"Aye, so," Leith murmured. Cast adrift here without friends. Among enemies. Cut off by his own chief. It was a hard fate.

But then, Farlan lay every night with the woman he loved. He got to hold her in his arms and hear he was loved in return. What was that worth?

"By any road," Farlan went on before Leith could speak, "'tis what I came to tell ye. They are talking o' sending ye back."

"To MacLeod?"

"Aye, to Rory. *Home,*" Farlan added.

"Who says this?"

"Moira. She does no' want a repetition o' what happened when she held me prisoner. Holding a hostage against Rory—it did not work out too well."

Send him back. Ah, God! Emotions tore through Leith, stirring raw conflict. 'Twas the best possible outcome. And the worst.

"When?"

Farlan shrugged. "It will take some time. 'Tis no' like at home, where Rory makes all the decisions, nor even when Camraith was alive and he did. Here no one agrees, and all maun be discussed. They want Moira to confer wi' their war chief, Alasdair, before acting."

Farlan fixed Leith with a stern eye. "And ye will no' go telling

Rory any o' that when ye get home."

He would not. Learning that the leadership of Clan MacBeith was not absolute could provide Rory with an advantage. One that could come back to harm Rhian.

And yet—did not all Leith's loyalty belong to Rory, his cousin and chief?

"Ah, hell," he swore.

"Gi' them a while to hash it over," Farlan advised.

"Aye. To tell ye true, Farlan, I do no' think I am fit yet for the journey home. Though it shames me to admit it, I do no' think I could walk so far."

"They will take ye on a litter, if need be. If they decide 'tis best to be rid o' ye."

Aye, and what would Rory say if Leith turned up in his present condition?

For years, even behind the back of his father the chief, Rory had talked of taking over the glen. He'd trained for it, planned for it, lived for it. His father's death—for Camraith had kept a level head where his MacBeith opponents were concerned—had provided him the chance he'd awaited so long.

So far, however, the campaign had not been going well. Even without their patriarch, Iain, Clan MacBeith had proved far stronger than Rory expected. He'd lost battles, and men.

He'd lost Farlan, his dearest friend.

Leith said, "'Twill no' take Rory long to launch another attack. He maun be livid, thinking me either captured or dead."

Farlan nodded grimly. "'Tis too much an echo o' what happened wi' me."

"Aye, when ye were held prisoner, and when ye turned on him."

"I did no' turn on him!"

Leith eyed Farlan. "The way he sees it, ye did."

"No one wants that situation again. Aye, ye be valuable, being Rory's cousin, but they will send ye back as soon as they can."

Then he'd better accept it. Whatever this mad, unreasonable thing—connection, insipient attraction—between him and Rhian might be, he'd better surrender it.

Rhian MacBeith, so he assured himself sternly, was but a woman. A wondrously warm and caring lass for all that, with a wealth of charms and a spirit in which he began to suspect his could be at home. Just a woman like any other.

Only she was not like any other. That, he believed to his bones.

Chapter Nineteen

RHIAN SAT IN the great hall with Alasdair and Moira when Farlan came in. The big man moved quietly and stood for a moment listening to what Alasdair was telling them. A party had located the lass Elreadh, she who had attempted to kill Leith. Found hiding with family up in the hills and brought back by Alasdair's men, she now awaited an audience with him and Moira, wherein she would learn her fate.

Rhian's attention flew to Farlan. She knew where he'd been, that he'd just come from seeing Leith, and she ached to ask him how his friend fared. Because she'd resisted returning to Leith all day, had not allowed herself to go and tend him.

Soon they would send him back to MacLeod. Moira had just been telling Rhian so, asking how soon she thought Leith would be ready to travel, before Alasdair came in with his news.

'Twould solve her predicament anyway. If the man departed from her sight, he would also disappear from her mind. Would he not?

For the best. Without question.

Then why did she examine Farlan's face so closely, looking for signs of—what? Worry? Signs that his friend was much worse?

Farlan did send her a look, one she failed to interpret.

Alasdair spoke on. "She is reported to be distraught. Weeping and half out o' her mind with grief. Ye need to decide, Moira, whether or no' you and I can handle the matter or ye want the full council involved."

Moira raised her eyebrows. She too shot a look at Farlan. "I do no'. The prisoner has survived the attack. Surely, Alasdair, if you and I confer over Elreadh's predicament and arrive at a fitting punishment, 'twill suffice."

Alasdair gave an uneasy shrug. "The runner who came to me seemed all too sympathetic to the lass's plight and says she is offering no resistance. Wi' the way things are, the council will likely no' agree to punish her at all."

"Yet she tried to kill a man," Rhian heard herself say.

"She tried to kill a *MacLeod*," Alasdair corrected her with an unreadable glance at Farlan. "And as Moira points out, she did no' even succeed."

An unhappy silence fell.

"If we drag a weeping, grieving woman before them," Alasdair said after a moment, "the council will crumble."

"Still," Rhian huffed, "there needs to be justice."

"One justice for a MacBeith," Moira mused softly, "and another for a MacLeod." She looked at Farlan in turn.

"I ha' just come from Leith," Farlan said. "He is up on his feet."

"What?" Rhian felt herself go pale. "He should no' be. That wound o' his will tear open wi' any movement."

"He was nearly murdered in his sleep. He feels defenseless and wishes to garner his strength as he may."

Rhian must go to him. She'd need to check the condition of that ugly wound. She did not doubt it would need re-dressing.

Alasdair dismissed the prisoner from his consideration. "If ye call Elreadh here for judgment, the council may well hear o' it. If so, they will come on their own."

"So they will," Moira agreed. "Rhian, will ye stay and help me face them? I feel there must be some form o' justice handed out, even if 'tis no more than a slap. If we fail in that, there will be no hold upon what folk think they can do to MacLeod prisoners."

Moira swallowed hard. "Da would no' want it so. He would no' want us to become—well, those who attack the defenseless."

"He would no'," Rhian agreed.

"We maun be better than that," Moira declared, and looked at Farlan again.

Rhian wondered if Moira recalled questioning Farlan soon after he'd been taken prisoner, also with a grave wound. During questioning, Moira had laid a heated iron against Farlan's torn flesh.

Somehow, Farlan had subsequently forgiven her that deed. Such was love. But Moira had not liked the way that left her feeling, and would not do it to other captives.

Rhian could not deny Farlan and her sister did love one another. Farlan's love had, in some ways, changed the woman Moira was.

"Farlan," Moira said, "will ye go and find Saerla so she too may sit in on the judging? I think we all three should be here standing united."

Farlan went out without a word. Rhian wondered how it was for him, living among folk who did not want him here. Forced day after day to endure their enmity and disparagement. Would that ever change? Not while Rory MacLeod sought to overthrow them.

"Come." Moira held out a hand to Rhian. "Here, beside me."

A party of MacBeith clansmen soon came in, bringing Elreadh with them. The girl, whom they either led or assisted along, drooped in their grasp. She had long, fair hair hanging loose down her back and eyes turned red with weeping. Her parents came hurrying after her, concern etched on their faces.

Despite Rhian's outrage, pity flared in her heart. The girl had lost the man she loved—no one could gainsay that. She appeared utterly broken. Yet, as Moira said, they could not condone attempted murder of one who was, for better or worse, under their protection.

Moira got to her feet to meet the party. Rhian arose too from her place by the fire.

"Elreadh MacBeith," Moira said. It was a calling, a summoning, and spoken in a passable imitation of Da's tone of voice. One of command.

Ah, and could Rhian feel Da here with them in this place where he'd made so many wise decisions? They needed him now, needed his strength and forbearance.

Indeed, as Moira tipped her head and regarded Elreadh, Rhian saw a trace of their da in her. Rarely had the resemblance been so strong.

Elreadh looked up. She appeared terrified. All in all, with clansmen on either side holding her up, she made a pitiful sight.

Sternly, Moira demanded, "What ha' ye to say for yoursel'?"

Alasdair had backed off a few steps, perhaps indicating that he left this in Moira's hands. He watched Elreadh with no change of expression as her gaze flew from Moira's face to Rhian's, to his and back again.

"I did no' mean to do it. I was passing by the place wi' a load o' linens, just, for my dear Dannochat's bier. And I thought—why should that MacLeod monster live, when my husband lies dead?"

An honest question, one spoken without defiance. Elreadh was far too broken for defiance. And aye, if the council came, they would seek to impose no punishment.

Saerla came rushing in and stepped up to take the place between Moira and Rhian, clasping both their hands.

"How could ye attack a man, attempt to murder him, wi'out meaning it?" Moira asked.

"I did no' mean it," Elreadh insisted. "My heart bade me all at once. I was passing by, as I say. I'd just been sitting wi' my husband—my da and I had—wi' his body. What's left o' him after those MacLeods ran him through. I said I would fetch the linens to wrap him for his grave."

No one there said anything.

Elreadh stumbled on. "I ran by the pen and saw no one was there guarding the door. I thought, wha' if he's the one who killed my Dannochat? Wha' if he escapes and goes on to kill some other lass's man? It is no' right that he should live while my man lies cold."

Saerla squeezed Rhian's hand.

"So I lifted the bar and went in." Elreadh wept now. "He lay there sleeping. I thought how easy 'twould be to cover his face and stop his breath. I had a bolster wi' me, that we had meant to use for Dannochat." She paused and swallowed hard. "I smashed it down over his face, thinking only to hold it there till he slipped awa'. But he came awake. He struggled. He was still stronger than me." She sobbed. "I was no' strong enough to bring my man the justice he deserves."

"There now," said the man to Elreadh's right, who more than half supported her. "It is enough, Mistress Moira. Let the lass be."

Said another member of the party, Elreadh's father, "She did no' kill the bastard, after all."

The council had not come, no, not yet. Yet, in a way, they were here. These men who had followed the bidding of their chief and brought Elreadh in expressed a common feeling. No one would condemn this lass for what she had done.

"'Twas an attempt at murder." Moira sounded stern.

"O' a MacLeod." The first man spoke again. "Do we no' do the same during every battle?"

"Aye, but," Rhian heard herself say, "those men are no' lying defenseless. They have swords in their hands."

"And," Moira added, "they are no' under our protection."

"'Tis no' right," declared a man from the back, "to protect a MacLeod above our own, who is grieving."

Moira looked at Alasdair. "Alasdair? Your opinion?"

For the first time, emotions showed on Alasdair's craggy face. "Let the lass go. She has already suffered enough."

Rhian's heart fell.

Moira caught her breath. "I feel there should be some consequences—"

Alasdair sent her an unreadable look. One of the men muttered, only half under his breath, "Aye, mistress, so ye would."

"'Twas mostly my fault by any road," Alasdair rumbled. "I placed the guards who abandoned their posts. She would never ha' ventured in had they been where they belonged."

"Elreadh," Moira pronounced, "I wish ye to think hard on wha' ye ha' done while ye grieve your Dannochat. I want ye to seek forgiveness. Tak' her home," she added to Elreadh's parents. "There will be no further punishment."

They went out with a clatter, Elreadh weeping harder than when she came in. Not until they were gone, and the four of them were alone, did Rhian realize what had just happened.

Alasdair had made the decision. One that should have been the chief's alone. Did Moira resent that? Hard to say, because she had her face schooled and near expressionless.

Saerla covered her face with her hands. "We ha' to stop wi' this."

The rest of them stared at her.

"We ha' to find a way for MacBeith and MacLeod to stop wi' killing each other."

Moira gave an incredulous laugh. "Wi' Rory MacLeod at the gates? 'Twould be a fine thing."

Chapter Twenty

AFTER FARLAN LEFT the cattle pen, Leith took stock of himself with a brutally honest eye.

Weak as an infant he was, hurting in both his body and mind. It had perhaps been a bad decision to get up on his feet, because this accursed wound of his had started back to bleeding and needed the bandages changed.

But, by God, he'd be cursed if he'd lie on his back helpless and wait for the next MacBeith to walk in and try to finish him off.

The contents of the flask that Farlan had left with him served marginally to dull the pain that beset him. It remained fierce enough though to make him clench his teeth in the effort at endurance.

The word Farlan had brought tormented him almost as much. The MacBeiths intended to send him home. Too much trouble, he was, and too much of a risk after what had happened between Farlan and Moira.

He tried to decide how he felt about that. How he should feel. Despite the leaking wound, he heaved himself to his feet and returned to his plodding course around his prison.

He should be glad to get away from this grim place. To escape the hatred and the ill will. He should be eager to go home, return to his family. Ma and his little sister Aisleen would be frantic with worry for him.

He should be ready to return to Rory and provide what support he could, what sanity he could, though no one had excelled at that like Farlan.

A part of him, though, feared that if they sent him away, he would never see Rhian MacBeith again.

He paused with his good arm braced against the wall and thought about that. It might be for the best. Whatever these feelings were between them—and he'd be cursed if he could name them yet—they had no future. He might, aye, be attracted to the woman. He might think her the loveliest thing ever to draw breath, an angel, in truth, but it would do him no good. Because it did not mean she could ever feel anything more than a kind woman's obligation toward him.

Best to go. To cut whatever ties he felt forming with her quick and clean. Because look what had happened to Farlan.

By the holy mother, Leith would not choose that for his fate.

He stumped to the next wall and paused again. Rhian might be unrivaled in his experience, aye. He could not persuade himself to argue otherwise. There were, however, beautiful women at home, many of them widowed by the conflict. Widowed and with bairns to raise.

Him, he liked bairns and had always hoped for a passel of them. And a number of the women back home looked toward him favorably.

He did not need Rhian MacBeith.

Only he did.

He needed to get out of here by any road he could and forget about the woman.

Only he never would.

She'd saved his life, and that was enough.

A thousand days, ten thousand nights with her, would not be enough.

But she had cast him off already, kept away from him all the day long, not even caring how he fared.

The bar on the door rattled. He heard a voice outside—her

voice, low and rich, like music. The door opened and she came in.

Everything within Leith stopped—his thoughts, his breath, possibly his heartbeat.

She came with her head bent, wearing a gray cloak and with the familiar basket over her arm. She paused just inside the door, raised her head, and looked at him.

For several moments they regarded one another as if they could not get their fill. Leith's heart jerked back into motion with a painful lurch.

Ah, and she looked twice as beautiful as he'd remembered. How could that be?

He supposed he made an awful sight standing there with one blanket wrapped around his hips and the other cast over his shoulders. Like a beggar.

He'd be willing to beg for but a word from her lips.

But those lips pressed together in an almost painful line before she parted them and said, "*Dhe!* Ye should no' be up and on your feet. Wha' were ye thinking? Only look. That wound has torn open once again."

He might have said any number of things in reply. That, as he'd told Farlan, he could not endure lying helpless. That he feared he'd go mad if he did not regain even some small control of his life.

But she set aside her basket and hurried to him, raised her blessed, gentle hands, and laid them on the blanket slung over his shoulders.

So strongly did her touch affect him, he spoke words he hadn't intended. "I feared ye would no' come. I thought ye were done wi' me."

She gazed up earnestly into his face. Into his eyes, deep. Into *him*. She might have said a thousand things, that it was best if she kept away, that he'd soon be gone from MacBeith soil anyway. That she hated him, a dreaded MacLeod.

Instead she said, "Nay. I could no' keep awa'."

Which of them moved first then, leaned into the other? Leith never knew. She stretched up; he bent down. Their lips met.

In the past, Leith had kissed his share of women. He'd kissed other men's shares of women besides. Not like this. Never like this.

This felt inevitable and primal, like the flooding of the tide. Like the rising of the moon. Like the coming of spring after the death of winter. It was like no other kiss because Rhian MacLeod was like no other woman.

He knew that then, standing there with his lips on her. Knew it to the bottom of his heart and the depths of his soul. It terrified him so, when the kiss ended, he could find no words to say.

He merely gazed into the bonny oval of her face, into her eyes that had gone wide with her emotions, the same emotions he felt.

Amazement. Wonder. A sense of claiming.

She remained on her tiptoes, still pressing her hands to his shoulders. His arm, the only one under his command, had crept around her and clasped her tight.

She whispered, "I should no' ha' done that."

"Ye should. Och, lass, ye truly should."

He kissed her again. This time it was wild and hungry, a kiss to scare a woman away, if anything could. She did not frighten, but parted her lips beneath his, as hungry as he. Their tongues met and tangled. The kiss turned tender, so tender it fair pulled Leith's remaining strength from him.

When this one ended, she laid her cheek against his chest. He nuzzled her neck and the tendrils of dark red hair that spiraled there, having escaped the tight hold of the plait she wore.

Had her heart also escaped her hold?

"Och, Leith," she murmured. "Och, what are we to do?"

A fair and valid question. He wished he could give her an answer, wished it with everything in him. He longed to tell this woman all would be well, that he would make it so. That they'd find a way to be together.

He could not, so he kept silent, kept silent and ran the palm of his hand up her back, memorizing the feel of her. Threaded his fingers into her hair. Absorbed the sweet smell of her skin.

This might be all he'd ever have of her. Not enough.

To be sure, all too soon she lifted her cheek from his chest and stepped away from him. Gathered herself with stern mastery.

She drew a breath before she said, "What am I thinking? I maun dress that wound. And find ye some clothing. Ye stand here half-naked."

That made him grin despite her withdrawal from his arms. "D'ye mind?"

She shook her head wildly.

They should be naked together, the two of them. In a big bed somewhere, and with a month or so's worth of nights to learn each other.

But here he stood, a MacLeod prisoner. And there she stood, daughter of a MacBeith chief.

Hastily she turned away to her basket. "I ha' clean bandaging. Pray, sit down."

Half bemused, he obeyed. At least he'd have her hands on him. It would hurt when she drew off the sodden bandages, but it would be worth it.

Aye, it did hurt. He had to suck in his breath and clench his teeth, but her beautiful face hanging above him helped. And her gentle, merciful hands.

As she worked, she scolded him, "Ye never should ha' been up on your feet. 'Tis much too soon. Only look at the damage ye ha' done."

He could see—and feel—the damage. He also felt the relief lent by her touch and the healing when, having smoothed the new bandages, she laid a hand over them and whispered what might be a charm.

She gazed at him. "Ye maun be careful or ye will undo all the work I ha' done."

"I will be careful, Rhian. I will do aught ye ask, if ye will but stay wi' me."

"It canna be, Leith. Ye maun see, it canna be."

"I do see that, aye."

He dove in for another kiss, but she dodged away from him, moving nimbly to pick up her basket.

When she finished repacking it, she cast a look at him where he sat on the pallet.

"They are planning to send ye awa' back to MacLeod."

"Aye, I ken. Farlan told me."

"I do no' think ye be able to travel yet, and I will say so. But—'twill come. A parting between ye and me."

An ache started deep inside him. He said nothing.

"I will find ye some proper clothing and ha' it sent in."

"Rhian, do no' go."

"I must."

"Pray afford me a few more moments."

"'Tis no' wise." She would not look at him now. She gazed at her basket. At the floor.

"Tell me ye'll return."

"I will." Dark with misery, her eyes touched fleetingly with his. "To check your bandages. That is all, Leith." She turned to the door. "'Tis all can ever be."

She went out as softly as she'd come in, leaving Leith in pieces.

Chapter Twenty-One

RHIAN HAD LITTLE sleep that night. At dawn she rose and went in search of the one person from whom she could expect a measure of understanding—Moira.

Following Da's death, when Moira had taken the place of chief, she moved into his quarters, the same Ma and Da had occupied when the family members were young. It felt strange to scratch at that door now, and even stranger when Moira swung it open.

Clearly having come straight from her bed, Moira stood half-clothed in a simple chemise, her hair hanging loose in a wild red cloud. Rhian glimpsed Farlan sprawled in the bed, one brawny arm still stretched across the empty place where Moira must have been lying.

"I am sorry," Rhian said quickly, unexpectedly affected by that sight. "I should no' ha' come so early."

Moira blinked at her. "What is it? Is somewhat wrong? Is it the prisoner?"

"Aye."

"God, has he died?"

"Nay."

"Good," Moira said in a low voice, striving not to wake Farlan. "I can think o' naught calculated to make Rory MacLeod angrier, and he is angry enough already."

"I need to speak wi' ye, sister."

Moira measured Rhian with a swift glance. No doubt she would prefer to return to the warmth of her bed, but she nodded. "Let me don some clothes, just."

She dodged back inside but did not shut the door all the way. Rhian heard a deep murmur that must be Farlan coming awake, and Moira's voice in reply.

When she reappeared, she looked more like the sister Rhian knew, composed and in control.

"Where can we go to talk?" Rhian asked. "Where no one will hear?"

"Your quarters. Come."

"Nay, I ha' been tossing and turning there all night. I canna bear it."

That made Moira look at her more closely. "The council chamber, then."

The council chamber lay at the rear of the great hall, which remained cool, dark, and deserted at this hour. They went in, and Moira struck a light.

"Now, Rhian, what is all this?"

Where to begin? Now that Rhian had roused her sister from her comfortable bed, she scarcely knew. In the habit of caring for others, she did not often express her own feelings. When she did, she often regretted it.

Feelings were for others. And admitting to them rendered one vulnerable. She dealt in practical realities.

Not unlike Moira herself. And look what had become of her cool, disciplined sister—at the hands of a man.

Unable to face Moira after all, Rhian turned away and began laying a fire in the cold hearth. That, she knew how to do.

"Rhian?" Easing back on her heels, Rhian looked at her sister. With concern on her face, Moira hunkered down beside her. "Tell me what has frightened ye."

Frightened? She wanted to deny it, but aye, it was fear that held her in its grip. Fear that she could not evade her feelings for

Leith, and the effects of his kiss.

"I hardly know—" she began, stopped, and tried again. "I ha' feelings for him, Moira."

"Him?" Moira's baffled expression showed she did not understand. "Sister, ye will ha' to explain better than that. 'Tis too early in the day for me to guess."

Then she seemed to tumble to it. Her face filled with dismay. "Och! No—"

"I came to ye," Rhian said in a rush, "because ye ken what it is, so I imagine, to feel this way. To run up against emotions ye canna deny. To feel you're falling down a slope, helpless, wi' no way to stop the tumble."

"Aye." Moira barely breathed it. "I ken. But sister, how? When? Ye barely know the man."

"Only to treat that wound o' his. Only to watch him regain his sight. Only to help him hold on to his life."

Moira swore bitterly. Thoughts raced in her eyes. She must have been through this struggle, must have weighed the reasons for denying such feelings.

"I came to ye," Rhian whispered, "because ye canna tell me I do not feel what I am feeling. That I am mistaken."

Moira waggled her head unhappily. "Much as ye might wish ye are."

"Aye." Rhian looked away from her sister's misery, held out her hands to the fire that gathered strength in the hearth. She felt chilled right through.

"This is no' like ye, Rhian. Save for Angus when ye were but a girl, I ha' never known ye to fancy anyone."

"True." Angus had been one of Arran's friends, whom Rhian had admired from afar. He'd been killed in a skirmish even before Arran perished.

"Why, no end o' men have sought your hand," Moira went on. "Ye never gave any o' them a glance. I do believe Da despaired o' ye ever marrying."

"I made up my mind to be a spinster." Rhian spread her

hands. "My place is here. I ha' no time for such nonsense."

"And now?"

"Everything has changed."

"But why? Why him?"

"D'ye think I can tell ye? D'ye think I know?" Rhian challenged her sister. "Why Farlan?"

"Och!" Moira said in despair. "He just reached right inside me and grabbed hold o' my heart."

"Aye, so."

"But Rhian—"

"Moira, I did no' come here to discuss the ways and means o' falling in love. I need ye to talk me out o' it."

"Me?"

"Give me all the reasons why it canna be. The price to be paid for such a love."

"I think ye ken that already."

"Talk me out o' it now, before it is too late."

Instead, Moira reached out and pulled Rhian into her arms. They clutched one another desperately.

"'Tis a hard road," Moira murmured. "I kept telling Farlan, even as it happened, that 'twas impossible. But the feelings—the feelings would no' heed me. 'Tis when the impossible becomes so, becomes manifest and undeniable, ye ken ye be lost."

She, Rhian decided, was not lost yet. She might claw her way back from the brink if she used all her will and all her strength.

But if she kissed the man again—

She could not. She would not.

"Tell me what to do, how best to deny him."

"Ye came to me for advice? One who has failed at the task?" Moira drew away far enough to gaze into Rhian's face. "How does he feel for ye? Can ye tell? Because his feelings figure into it as much as your own." Slowly she shook her head. "Farlan has given up so much for me. He lives here surrounded every day by hatred. Ye canna imagine the guilt I suffer over it."

Rhian could.

"Sister." Moira caught Rhian's face between her hands. "There are but two ways ye and Leith MacLeod might be together. He would ha' to give up his life at MacLeod, as Farlan has done, or ye would ha' to give up your life here, leave home, and go with him."

Give up her life here? But how could she? Was she not the fire at the heart of this place?

Nay, rather than that, she would have to abandon the small flame that began to burn between her and Leith. Deny whatever this was she felt for him. Tell herself it was just a passing fancy.

If she could.

Looking into her sister's face, she said, "I could no' do that. I could no' leave MacBeith."

"Well then." Moira mopped tears from Rhian's face, tears she hadn't realized she shed. "'Tis the heart of it, Rhian, much as I hate to say. He is a MacLeod and ye a MacBeith."

"Aye." Rhian made herself nod. "Ye ha' the right o' it. I do no' need a man. I do no' even want one. I do no' want him."

Only she did.

Moira's expression showed she heard the lie. "Perhaps 'twould be best, Rhian, if we send him back to Rory MacLeod soon, as soon as possible."

"It would." Rhian mopped at her own face now. "He is no' fit to travel yet, though. He was on his feet when I saw him earlier and had opened up the wound something terrible."

"How long before he can make the journey?"

"I canna say."

"We can have him littered, rowed across the loch in a boat."

"Aye. Even so, I believe the journey could kill him." Resolutely, Rhian got to her feet. "I will send one o' the regular healers to tend him. I will no' see him again before he recovers enough to leave."

Moira rose also. Heartbreak looked at Rhian from her eyes. "Sister, I am that sorry."

"Do no' be. I asked ye to talk me out o' my feelings, and so ye ha' done."

"It scarcely seems fair," Moira whispered.

"Nor would it be fair to begin somewhat that could only serve to try the man, as Farlan has been tried. Sister, ye will tell no one? Not even him, Farlan."

"Your secret is safe wi' me, Rhian." Moira's lips tightened. "Though Saerla, being Saerla, may guess."

"I hope not." If she might hide her feelings away in her heart, Rhian hoped she might more easily deny them.

Chapter Twenty-Two

Though Leith waited for what felt like an interminable amount of time, Rhian did not come. He slept when he could, a refuge against the pain that ravaged him. He spoke to himself when he could not sleep. He relived a thousand times the kiss they had shared.

He lived off the feelings Rhian aroused in him. Not lust—well, not all lust, by any road. He was far too ill for that. But off the tenderness, the sense of rightness, the sure and steady bonds that seemed to have formed between them.

Those bonds tugged at him relentlessly. He'd never felt the like. A constant pull it was, and no relief to be found until he was with her again.

But she did not come.

He kept up hope, somehow, through that night and part of the following morning. When the healer arrived—a man, and a stranger—it felt as if his world came crashing down.

"Where is Mistress Rhian?" he asked when the fellow, of middle years and careworn, came bustling in.

"Busy elsewhere."

"Aye, so." Leith's thoughts raced. "But 'tis she has been treating me."

"I will be treating ye now."

The man was brisk and hurried, and employed very little of

what Leith would term mercy in his treatment. He changed the bandaging without care, offered Leith a draught, and shoved a bundle into his hands.

"Clothing."

Had Rhian sent it? She'd said she would. Despite the gift, despair settled upon him.

"I advise ye do no' move about more than ye can help." The healer cast a disdainful look around the pen. "'Tis a grave wound, that. Ye maun let it heal."

Aye, so, but how to heal his heart?

The healer went out, and Leith donned his clothing. Soon after, another rattle of the door announced the arrival of rations, brought by a scowling guard instead of Rhian.

He lay back upon the pallet, having no appetite to eat, and thought of her. *In the afternoon, she will come.*

Only she did not, and the time dragged unbearably. Having long finished the contents of the flask Farlan had left with him, he struggled under the weight of his pain.

Perhaps he should have accepted the draught the brusque healer offered.

When what he guessed must be late afternoon arrived with no sign of Rhian, he told himself he must accept the truth. She had made up her mind. She wanted naught more to do with him. That kiss—that kiss must have frightened her.

Och, and he never should have kissed her. Though, to be truthful, they had kissed each other.

Ah, but his Rhian—and he had no doubt to the bottom of his soul she was meant to be his—was a woman of wisdom. She'd witnessed all that had passed between her sister the chief, and Farlan. She did not want that for herself.

Only a madwoman would.

He could not blame her, nay. But he needed a chance to talk to her, to convince her—

Of what? That he, and what he sensed existed between them, was worth her tearing up her life by the roots?

What was he, by any road? No great prize. He was the kind of man with whom women liked to flirt. They sought his smiles and, aye, sometimes his kisses. They liked for him to make them laugh. None of them took him seriously. He'd never even been near the prospect of a serious relationship.

How could he persuade this beautiful, great-hearted woman to take him seriously? He did not know, but if he did not have a chance to see her soon, he would go out of his blessed mind.

When the light began to fade, indicating evening fell in the world beyond his pen, he went and pounded on the inside of his door. Guards stood out there on duty. He could hear them, but they did not respond. He pounded again. He shouted. He kicked the door.

Eventually it opened a crack. A guard with a face like a thundercloud peered in. "Wha' do ye want, MacLeod?"

"I need the healer, Mistress Rhian."

The man's hard gaze flicked over him. "Are ye dyin'?"

Likely not, but his wound had started bleeding again with his movements. "Aye. I think I'm dyin'. I need for her to come." He needed her to touch him again, lay her cool hand on his chest. Gaze into his eyes. His merciful angel.

The door of the pen slammed shut. Leith did not know whether or not the guard took a message.

He waited. He paced, and bled.

Rhian did not come. An unbearable despair settled on his heart.

The pain—both that of his heart and the agony in his arm—drove him to his pallet, where he lay trying to think. His right arm still hung useless. He wondered if he'd ever hold a sword again.

Was it worth it, this campaign of Rory's? Not for the first time, he contemplated that question. Farlan, before he defected, had tried to reason Rory out of his determination to conquer the glen.

Aye, Farlan had a reason. Yet he was right that the cost in

lives, in suffering, in heartache, had become very high. Could it be justified by a vow made by Rory's ancestors long ago?

The old chief, Camraith—Rory's father and Leith's uncle—had led with wisdom and forbearance. Though there had been running skirmishes and cattle raids all Leith's life, Camraith had held his hand from wreaking destruction. He'd harbored a respect for Iain MacBeith, now also a man dead.

All those years, so Leith thought, Rory had held a belief that Clan MacBeith would be easy to overthrow. The smaller and hence weaker clan just awaited conquest.

Only they had not proved weaker during this campaign.

Rory had not counted on the three sisters MacBeith.

Leith folded his left arm over his forehead and sought refuge in sleep. He felt heavy in his limbs, weak and cold to the bones, despite his clothing and the two blankets. When the fog came into his mind, he welcomed it. He came to himself only once and again, sensing dimly that the whole top of his left arm lay saturated with blood.

Perhaps I am dying. If he did die here alone in this wretched pen, would his spirit then travel home after? He'd heard from other men, some who'd recovered from dire wounds not unlike his own, that their departed loved ones came to fetch them at the end. Who would he see? His uncle Camraith, with his steady gaze and benevolent smile? His own da? His grandmother, whose busy hands had always seemed to shed love over him?

Leith, he thought he heard her whisper, *'tis a long journey. Are ye strong enough?*

He'd always been strong, aye. He'd taken it for granted. Unlike Rory, who'd sprouted first like a sapling and filled out after, Leith had grown steady into a broad, solid frame. He'd competed with the others at feats of strength.

He was not used to lying weak as a newborn lamb while he contemplated his death.

"Grandma, I am no' sure I can make it home."

Then wait, lad. It may no' yet be your time.

A voice closer to him, one that fit well into his dream or whatever else this was, spoke aloud. "Is he dyin'?"

He opened his eyes, or tried to. A flare of light blinded him, and he closed them again.

"He's bled a terrible lot. Better get the healer."

Mistress Rhian. But he did not seem able to say her name aloud.

The light faded. He wondered if night had come again so swiftly. He wondered, still more vaguely if this was his permanent night.

Time passed as he floated. He imagined he flew, flew over the glen.

He recognized it at once, though he'd never seen it from this perspective. How beautiful it all looked, the green turf cradled between the upturned mountains. There, the loch glittering the way it always did in the first light of dawn.

Morning must have come. He was flying home. He had only to cross the loch and he would be there.

And yet—did he want to go, when he left Rhian MacBeith behind? Torn by the question, he hovered, no more than a spirit in the air. He must go back, despite the sickness and pain.

Wherever she was, there he must also be.

$$\sim\!\!\sim$$

Chapter Twenty-Three

R HIAN LAY FAST asleep when someone came pounding on her door. It had taken her a long while to reach the oblivion of sleep. Prey to her thoughts, and worse, her emotions, she'd thought the refuge would never come. When it did, it came deeply and seamlessly, without dreams.

Now some idiot arrived, waking her up again. There had better be a good reason.

She sat up in the bed, her hair tangled around her, and listened. No sounds of attack from beyond the small, silent chamber. No cries of alarm. That meant Rory MacLeod had not returned.

"Mistress Rhian! Mistress Rhian—"

Curses, it was a cry of alarm after all. The pounding at her door resumed. She got to her feet and went to answer it.

Adair, a member of the guard, stood there scowling. One of Leith's guards. She snapped awake instantly. "What is it?"

"The MacLeod prisoner. We think he's dead or dyin'."

She'd known what Adair was going to say before he said it, just as if she'd already heard the words inside her head.

"What happened to him?" Had he been attacked again? Och, by heaven!

But Adair shook his head. "We do no' ken. He did no' want his supper. Was after asking for ye. Tam said we should check on him. When we went in, he lay there covered wi' blood."

The wound had reopened. That awful wound would kill him after all.

Apologetic, Adair went on, "We ken ye said ye'd no' treat him any longer, and we should send for Master Preslan, but Tam said ye were the best one to save him."

God bless Tam. "I'll come. Give me a moment."

She did not bother to dress, merely tossed on her cloak over her night rail. She threw items into her basket with frantic hands. She and Adair went out into the dark.

It must be the middle of the night. No one stirred except, presumably, those on watch up on the battlements.

What had made Leith's guards check on him? If they'd left him to lie till morning…

A torch flared outside the cowshed. Tam sprang to life when he saw Rhian. "Mistress, if ye'd rather we call Master Preslan—"

"Nay. Ye did right calling me. Bring a torch inside. I will need a good light."

She smelled the blood as soon as she went in. Leith lay on his pallet with the blanket drawn up to his chest. She hurried up and set her basket down with trembling hands.

Och, and he looked dead. Eyes closed and face pale in the flaring light, he lay with one arm folded across his breast, keeping the blanket close as if against the cold. Both blanket and pallet were soaked with blood.

They had brought her too late. But nay, nay, he breathed yet.

"How long has he been like this?"

"We do no' ken, mistress. Master Preslan saw him earlier, and we brought him his supper. Ye can see he did no' touch it." Adair repeated apologetically, "He did ask for ye earlier, but we ken ye said ye would no longer treat him."

Rhian cursed under her breath.

Tam, who held the torch, took up the tale. "I was about to go off shift, mistress, when I got a feeling—it was too quiet. He was too quiet. I thought I would take a wee look just to see, even though it made sense he would be sleeping."

"'Tis well ye did."

"Why is he bleeding so much?"

"'Tis a deep wound that refuses to close."

"Will he die?"

Did this man of middle years, one of Alasdair's most dependable men, care? Rhian glanced into Tam's face and thought maybe he did. "I canna tell."

"Aye well," Adair said, "'twill solve a few problems if he does."

That it would. But Rhian meant to fight for Leith. Fight like a lioness if she had to.

Tam asked, "D'ye need any help lifting him, maybe? D'ye want us to call another healer?"

"Nay. You help me, Tam. We maun strip this sodden clothing off him. I will change the bandages, see if I can stop the bleeding."

Leith had moved around far too much. Had she not told him to keep still? Stubborn man.

Adair went out. Rhian and Tam worked in silence. She welcomed the guard's brawn in shifting Leith's big form, and appreciated that he kept mum. Let her think. Concentrate on what needed to be done.

All the while she worked over Leith, he never roused. Never stirred nor gave any sign he knew they were there. His broad chest barely rose and fell with his breaths.

Beneath Rhian's fingers, his skin burned.

Fever. It was the last thing, the very last thing he needed. Apart from the ugly wound, which she packed with herbs and bandages, it could be enough to steal his life.

As she worked, she became angry. The emotion built in her, slow and inevitable as a kindled fire. How many more men would have to suffer like this, to die for Rory MacLeod's ambition? How much more unfairness and pain?

As she smoothed the bandages over Leith's arm, she wondered how a chief who claimed he cared for his people could put them to this.

She did not give way to anger often. A reasoned woman, she usually put away her rage and, like her other emotions, kept it under strict lock and key. She must do to get on with the tasks in front of her.

But now—now she wished she could have even a few short moments to tell Rory MacLeod what she thought of him.

Upon the thought, her ears caught the sound of hollering from beyond the pen. She turned her head, and her gaze met that of Tam in the torchlight.

"What is that?"

"I will go see, mistress."

No need to worry for guarding the prisoner from escape. He would not be on his feet again soon.

Possibly not ever.

Rhian laid her hand on Leith's brow as she had once before and spoke a charm. A prayer. For the fever to break. For his eyes to open.

See me. See me!

The shouting outside grew louder and more frantic.

"Attack. Attack!"

Rhian stiffened where she knelt. *Nay. Nay, not now. Not so soon.*

And yet this, the dead-silent hour before sunrise while shadows still cloaked the glen, made a favorable time to launch an attack. Such shadows played tricks on the men who stood watch. Allowed a force to get close before being seen.

She shuddered to the depths of her being. More vicious wounds. More pain. More death. She gazed down at the man beside whom she still knelt. It needed to stop, all of it.

She must get to her feet and leave Leith. She would be needed, all hands would. She might not fight with the sword like her sisters. But och aye, she fought.

She bent and placed a kiss on Leith's brow. His skin fair

scorched her lips.

"I will return," she whispered. "Ye hold on. Hold on for me."

<hr>

SHE STILL CARRIED her anger when she went out into the murky light of predawn. People rushed everywhere, several nearly crashing into her. Both guards had gone. They would be needed on the walls, as would her sisters.

Upon the thought, she saw Moira hurry by, clad for battle and with Farlan at her side. Aye, so, he fought with her now, and alongside MacBeith clansmen who would as soon put their swords in his back as otherwise. Madness personified.

He fought against his own folk. How? How could he, even for love?

She put out a hand, and by a miracle, Moira paused. Rhian stared into her sister's face, which looked hard, her gaze like flint.

"Where is Alasdair?"

"At the gate ahead of me. I maun go."

"How many MacLeods?"

"Enough to bring us down. Ye will be needed, sister."

Rhian nodded. "I will refill my supplies and go."

But not out onto the battlefield this time. She might condone that risk to her flesh. Her heart could bear no more.

Chapter Twenty-Four

SOMEONE HAD KISSED him. Nay, not just someone. It was Rhian who had laid her lips upon his brow. He would know her touch anywhere, and the feel of her when she bent near.

He wanted to open his eyes and see her. He tried and failed.

She whispered something, a charm that flickered over his skin and cooled the heat that consumed him. Odd that, for he burned and yet he felt cold, and racked by shivering.

She was magic, this woman of his. She spoke magic, shed it over all she tended, all she cared for. Over him. He wanted that magic as he'd never desired anything, not even laughter. Wanted to take it deep inside him and make for it a place to dwell. Within him for eternity.

Rhian. He tried to speak her name, but could not do that either. Nor could he feel her as intensely as before. She had left him. He was alone.

Steady, he lectured himself. *She will return.* If she had tried to stay away from him before, sent another healer in her place and yet returned, she would once again.

He need only hold on till then. Surely she had told him so. *Hold on for me.*

He could do that. He could do anything to be with her.

He sucked in a breath even though it hurt to do so. He had to keep breathing if he wanted to see her face again. See those eyes of deep blue gazing into him, into him as if she could see his soul. He had to keep breathing against the weakness and the pain, if he wanted her to touch him.

And he did. Och, he did.

He floated and fought the pain and breathed and dreamed, even though he did not sleep. He dreamed he was in a battle with warriors shouting all around him, the clashing of weapons, the loud rattling of shields. In the dream, his right arm once more served him. He held a sword in his hand, strong and sure. He could hear Rory's voice shouting—shouting for them to advance. *Attack. Take no prisoners. MacLeod. MacLeod!*

Leith turned swiftly toward the nearest opponent, a MacBeith warrior. They fought outdoors in the dark, the combat heavy and hand-to-hand. Kill or be killed.

But the MacBeith warrior toward whom he swung bore no sword, held no shield, and wore no leather armor. Shock poured through Leith like a douse of cold water as he stared and stared.

The warrior was a woman, and she had Rhian MacBeith's face.

FEARING SHE HAD not sufficient supplies in her own chamber, Rhian ran instead to the infirmary where the healers kept their stores. The door of the hut stood wide open, and it looked like the place had been ransacked. No one remained there, all gone out already to search for the injured.

She found a basket and loaded it with supplies, her hands shaking. The commotion outside had grown louder, and she had to pause, take a few deep breaths, before she gathered the courage to go back out.

Her anger, though, still accompanied her, lying like a hot stone just beneath her heart.

The worst of the injuries, as she knew, would be up on the ramparts at this point in the battle. Wounds from flying arrows, hacked fingers dealt by those climbing up to breach the walls. Later, if the MacBeith clansmen marched out to meet their attackers, it would become worse, much worse. Men would lie broken and bleeding on the ground.

Just like before, when she'd found Leith.

Leith. The very thought of him tangled up the thoughts in her mind. So many conflicting feelings—

Climbing up the worn stone steps that led to the ramparts, she met someone tumbling down who crashed into her. They both fell, with Rhian on the bottom. Her basket flew out of her hands, and she scraped both palms on the rough stone. Her chin made hard contact with one of the steps and all hope of breath left her body in a grunt.

"Mistress!" someone nearby hollered. "Be ye hurt?"

She did not know, but gasped, "Nay."

Feet ran to her. Hurried hands helped her up. The man who had crashed into her, a MacBeith warrior, was no longer a man but a corpse. He lay with his eyes wide open and an arrow through his throat.

Suddenly Rhian had a flashback to Da, to how he had looked when Moira, Alasdair, and the others had brought him home the night he died. So much blood, and the gaping wound at the side of his neck from where that blood had come flowing.

Anger bit at her again even as the second man steadied her. "Are ye certain ye be no' hurt?"

Hurt, aye—to the very soul. "Nay. Let me climb up."

He moved aside. She gathered the contents of her basket and navigated the narrow walkway. A dangerous place to be, up on the battlements. And as she reached the top walkway, amazement made her freeze.

A black tide of screaming, bloodthirsty men lapped about the skirts of the keep. Torchlight from the walls shone down upon them, illuminating an angry face here, a flap of tartan there, the glint of a sword. The sheer noise and insipient violence of it stole Rhian's strength. So many men. They turned her beautiful glen into a place of ugliness and horror.

Someone bumped into her again, from the side this time. An arrow arced over the battlement, nearly striking her.

"Mistress, for the love o' God, get down."

"Aye. Aye. There are wounded?"

There were, lying against the bottom of the wall, suffering. She crawled to the nearest of them and treated him while the screaming, the clashing, and the strife continued above her. She moved on, trying to avoid getting stepped on even as she dressed wounds.

"Mistress," said the second man she treated, "ye be bleeding." Agonized, he stared into her face and motioned to her chin.

"'Tis naught. I took a fall."

"Ye should no' be here. 'Tis too dangerous."

"None o' us should be here." They were people all, just people. What call had they to try to kill one another?

After that, she tried to shut away her thoughts and ignore her fear while she worked on. Her anger continued to simmer inside, and flared to life when she heard a call.

"Rory MacLeod! 'Tis Rory MacLeod!"

She stumbled to her feet. In the performance of her duties, she had worked her way down the walkway above the main gate. Here was the battle concentrated.

Here would be the man who led the MacLeods on this bloody campaign.

Rhian went to the wall and looked over, only realizing as she did that she stood beside Moira, who remained on her feet but was smeared with blood. And Alasdair—it had been Alasdair who cried out.

She gazed out, and down.

Far to the east, the sun clawed its way into the sky, and that made it easy to see their attackers.

They had a battering ram. Rhian had no idea how they'd transported it across the loch or if they'd sent men on the longer and far more arduous route around and over the burn. It was an enormous thing, the trunk of a tree shaped to a butt end and now suspended on leather straps. An engine of destruction.

Two score of men manned it. The MacBeith archers targeted them, but it was difficult to aim straight down. And to Rhian's horror, it appeared the attackers had enough men to take the places of any who fell.

The man at the head of the thing—he was Rory MacLeod.

Rhian gazed at him, this man at the heart of all her grief. A big man, he fought bare-headed and had flying black hair and a wicked, sculpted face. He stood with his sword already drawn as if waiting to burst in upon them once the gate fell.

The gate could not go down.

"The gate canna' go down!" shouted Moira beside her, stealing the very words from her mind. "No' at any cost."

Rhian stared at her sister, startled, and Moira gave her a swift, fierce stare in return. "Ye should no' be here. Go!"

Rhian could not move to save her life. She plundered Rory MacLeod with her gaze, wondering what would happen if he did break in, bringing blood and death with him.

She would lay aside her basket then, lay aside her healing. Take up a sword.

Someone pushed in beside her, hands fierce on the stone. It was Saerla, tense as a bowstring. She leaned over the stone battlement and, like the rest of them, stared down at Rory MacLeod.

For a moment he gazed back up at them, his face sharp and angular in the torchlight. Saerla said something—the words rolled off her tongue. A curse?

A prayer.

Their archers all fired. Rhian was nudged out of the way by one of them and fell back. She did not see what happened next, but a cry went up. A cry of victory.

What did it mean? Had Rory MacLeod been struck? Had her anger, like an arrow, struck him down?

It was not right to wish for anyone's death. Except, perhaps, his.

Chapter Twenty-Five

"WAS HE STRUCK?"
"Aye!"
"Is he dead?"

The questions flew when they met, the four of them, in the great hall during the aftermath of the battle. Moira, Saerla, Rhian, and Alasdair, whose wounds Rhian treated even as they spoke together.

Farlan was not there. Rhian did not know why and half feared to ask after him.

Those standing at the battlements—from whence Rhian had been pushed back—had seen an arrow take Rory MacLeod in the back. They'd seen him crumple slowly, and his men mobbing around him, shielding him from further missiles and eventually bearing him up. His second-in-command had given the order to withdraw.

No one knew whether Rory lived or died.

Rhian tied off the bandage around Alasdair's brawny arm and shot a look at Saerla. Her sister had muttered something there at the end. A curse after all?

But Saerla did not believe in issuing curses. She'd reminded them all many a time that what a person put out into the world— good or ill—came back upon her threefold.

None of them wanted more ill fortune.

Saerla, though, was not saying a lot, not now. She seemed almost stunned by the battle just behind them. Rhian had tended her wounds, which proved minor. She'd tended all of them in turn, Alasdair, as always, being the last to accept care.

"If Rory MacLeod be dead," Moira declared, "'twill change everything. 'Tis he, so Farlan says, who has been carrying the banner against us."

As if the speaking of his name summoned him, Farlan entered the hall. His gaze flew immediately to Moira, and hers to him. When he reached her, they touched hands as if they just had to make certain of one another.

Such a love, Rhian thought. *Despite everything.*

Farlan bore a big, bloody gash on the side of his face that started next to his eyebrow and descended into his brown beard.

Rhian motioned him to her. He sat before her stoically, his gaze steady, while she began to clean the wound.

"We are striving to determine whether or not Rory has been killed," Moira informed him. "Could ye tell?"

"Nay. Rory will, though, be a hard man to kill. His ambition sustains him."

"Aye, so," Alasdair said. "But I say we may ha' succeeded this morn. That arrow went straight into his back. Deep."

"'Tis no' a matter of if it went into his back," Rhian said, "but what it struck there. A rib? He will likely survive, unless poisoning sets in." Her thoughts flicked to Leith, lying seared by fever. "A lung? He has even chances o' surviving. His heart—"

"I do no' think it struck his heart," Saerla said. They all stared at her. Did she think, or did she know?

"Sister—" Moira began.

Saerla shook her head. "I ha' no' been given that knowledge."

"Well, Mistress Saerla," Alasdair said, "ye might well seek it. Rory MacLeod's death could save us."

He looked at Farlan, who still sat quiet beneath Rhian's hands.

"The next Chief MacLeod may no' be so hellbent upon conquest. Who will tak' his place, Farlan, should he die?"

Farlan pressed his lips together as he contemplated it. "A goodly question. He has no issue and nary yet a wife. I suppose in the regular way o' things, Leith would ha' taken the place, being the eldest o' his surviving cousins. But Leith lies here, in your prison."

"Near to death," Rhian put in.

Now they all stared at her. Sorrow flooded Farlan's fine brown eyes. "Truly?"

"I fear so. I was with him when the alarm sounded."

"Holy mother," Farlan whispered. "I maun go to him. He is like a brother to me." He looked at Moira. "He should nae die alone."

"Then go to him ye shall," Moira assured him. She went on, relentless, "If Rory MacLeod dies, and if his cousin, here in our hands, does also—"

"We could assure it," Alasdair growled.

"—who will take the place o' chief at MacLeod?"

Farlan pondered further. "There are other, more distant cousins, o' course. Leith has a sister, younger than him, but she is no' wed either yet, and has no bairns." He made a rueful face. "She be a strong lass, but the prospect o' a female chieftain has no' yet caught on over there."

"These distant cousins," Alasdair suggested, looking more cheerful, "may well fight it out among themselves. 'Twould gi' us some relief."

"Aye, but do no' count Rory out so swiftly," Farlan cautioned. "He is tougher than old boots."

"Well," Moira said, "here was me thinking 'twould be a good idea to send yon Leith back to MacLeod and be rid o' him." She looked at Rhian. "Now I am no' so certain. Even if he survives, why allow him back to step into the place o' chief?"

"It may no' come into question," Saerla murmured, and Rhian wondered again what she had Seen.

"Leith," Farlan told them, "would mak' a very different sort o' chief to Rory. There is nary an ambitious bone in him. Wi' him in charge there, and me here, I think we would ha' a very clear shot at a peaceful existence."

Alasdair spat at him, "Ye be no' in charge here, Farlan."

"I did no' say I was."

"Whisht, Alasdair," Moira said. "'Tis a fair point Farlan makes. And maybe a way forward for the future."

Was it? And did that make a chance, however slight, for Rhian and Leith to be something more than enemies?

All Rory MacLeod had to do was die.

Rhian did not like the thought, even though her anger, still a hard knot inside her, was mostly focused on that man.

"I must go to Leith at once," Farlan said, moving away from Rhian and back to Moira's side. "Perhaps before he is sent home, a tentative agreement might be made."

"One resting on the death of his cousin?" Moira's lips tightened. She sighed. "He will no' like that. I maun go visit the wounded and add up the damages. Alasdair?"

"I will come wi' ye, aye."

They went out, and without a word to anyone, Saerla followed, leaving Rhian alone with Farlan, who yet lingered.

Rhian did not at all dislike the man who would one day become her sister's husband, at least if Moira got her way. And she usually did. In differing circumstances, Rhian thought that she and Farlan might have been friends. They had much in common. A certain steadiness of spirit. A quiet strength. The ability to put their own needs aside for the benefit of others.

But circumstances were not different.

He approached her and gave her a level stare. "Is it true? Is Leith dying?"

"I canna say either way. His life hangs in the balance."

Hold on until I return.

"He is one o' the people in the world closest to me. Ever since we were lads, it was so." Farlan did not add that now the other person closest to him—Rory—might also be dead or dying, but she saw it in his face.

She touched his arm. "I am sorry. Ye had best come soon, if ye wish to say aught to him. In fact"—Rhian made her mind up swiftly—"I am bound there now, if ye want to come along wi' me."

"I will."

It felt strange walking through the settlement in Farlan's company. The sun had now risen on what looked to be a beautiful day. Clansfolk were everywhere, discussing what had occurred. They glared at Farlan with—not quite open hatred, but a wealth of enmity.

Imagine living so. Imagine living so for the sake of love.

Chapter Twenty-Six

"H E HAS TAKEN a fever," Rhian told Farlan as they went, "on top of that stubborn wound that refuses to close." Refused in defiance of her best attempts to heal him.

Farlan slanted a look at her. "Why does it refuse to close, d'ye ken?"

She shook her head. "'Tis a dire wound, much torn when the sword went in and even more so when it came out again. And he will no' stay still, so it opens again and again."

They reached the cattle pen, and Farlan eyed it with disfavor. "I canna blame him for failing to keep still, trapped in this vile place. I was held here mysel'. I felt I would lose my mind wi' the confinement."

And now he slept in the chief's bed.

Rhian scowled at the door that once more stood unguarded. "The men Alasdair assigned here abandoned their posts when the attack came. I hope—"

Fear had her moving through the door without finishing the thought. Farlan came behind her.

The interior of the pen lay dim, the light having guttered out. Rhian struck another with unsteady hands and looked at the man on the pallet.

He lay unmoving beneath the blankets. So still was he, his profile appeared carved from stone.

Farlan breathed, "By God! Is he gone?"

Rhian hurried to Leith and hunkered down, her heart pounding. It could all end here, whatever troublesome and inappropriate feelings she had for this man. Fate could take it from her hands.

But nay, for he still breathed. "Alive." But terribly still, and burning with fever yet. The draught she'd tipped into him had done nothing. "At least no one attacked him."

Farlan grunted. He stood watching compassionately while Rhian checked the wound, found it had once more bled through the bandages, and changed them with hands far clumsier than usual.

Not until she finished did he ask, "What can I do? What to help?"

"He is one o' your closest friends, ye say."

"Aye." Farlan's throat worked before he said, "I wish ye could ha' known him." He gestured at the prone form. "No'—no' like this. Laughing all the time. He has a big, great laugh."

Like Da, Rhian thought.

"Forever teasing and telling stories. He is the only man I know who can jest wi' Rory, and get awa' wi' it."

Rhian could see it, could imagine this man laughing, his eyes crinkling in a smile even before his lips did. The contrast with what lay before her pained her heart. She wanted to heal him. She did not know how.

"Your chief will be missing him," she murmured.

"He will." Farlan did not bother reminding Rhian that, in truth, Rory was no longer his chief. "Especially wi'—wi' me being gone as well."

"Aye." If she had a lump of anger lodged beneath her heart, Rory must also. If he lived, that was.

"Speak to him," she urged Farlan. "Perhaps if he hears your voice, it may encourage him." She herself had bidden the man to hold on. Yet any fool could see he lay far distant.

Farlan lowered himself to the floor. He began speaking to

Leith in a calm, steady voice.

"'Tis me, Farlan here, Leith. I will sit wi' ye a time and speak o' the old days. Remember when we were lads, the three o' us— you, me, and Rory? The trouble we would get into wi' Chief Camraith, and your da also. Remember the time we stole those swords fr' the armory in order to spar wi' them and Rory took that dire cut to his thigh? Nearly unmanned him. We refused to tell whose idea it had been, though o' course 'twas Rory's own. Most the mischief was. Or remember the great challenge to swim across the loch—"

Rhian let Farlan talk on, spinning his memories while she bustled about. She went out and fetched a basin of water, returned, and set about bathing Leith's brow, battling against the fever, for she knew very well—

She knew such a fever could steal the life of a man, even one so strong as this.

As she worked, she too listened to Farlan's tales, and she willed healing into her hands.

⇥⟫⟪⇤

SOMEONE SPOKE TO him in a low, persistent voice, the words filling his ears. He knew the voice, felt certain he did. Familiar and comforting, brimming with good connotations. If he thought hard enough, he might put a name to it.

Someone touched him also, though not the same someone. He knew the feel of those hands upon his skin and the very scent of her as she bent low over him.

Hold on for me.

He did so—he held even against the current that wanted to sweep him away.

Each time she touched him—his arm, his hand, his chest, blessing the agony that gripped him—he felt a little frisson of magic. Of healing. It allowed his mind to surface and the breath to fill his lungs more deeply.

"D'ye remember the time we stole that ale from Chief Camraith's stores? We could no' ha' been more than ten. If I recall, that was no' Rory's scheme but yer own."

Leith's lips moved. "I remember."

The hands that comforted him froze. Those who kept him company—two persons, surely—became still.

"He spoke," Rhian said.

Ah, Rhian! His Rhian with the deep blue gaze and the cool hands, and the lips he wanted to kiss for an eternity.

He whispered, "Beautiful lady."

She laid her hand upon his brow. And suddenly he had the strength to open his eyes.

He saw her just as he'd been imagining her all this while. The perfect oval of her face, the brow now furrowed, as if she worried for somewhat. Those lips, parted slightly. And eyes brimming with beautiful compassion.

He said slowly and clearly so she'd understand, "I held on. For ye."

A sound drew his gaze to his other side. His friend Farlan hunkered there, wearing a look of wonder.

At the sight of him, Leith smiled so wide it hurt his cheeks. "Och, so 'tis yourself blathering at me."

"Aye." Farlan smiled back.

"Tellin' stories."

Farlan waggled his head slowly. "Just trying to remind ye of who ye be. No' a prisoner. No' a dying man."

Leith told Farlan with great sincerity, "I am no' ready to die."

"Ye keep thinking that way."

"I canna die, ye see, before I kiss Mistress Rhian."

A small gasp drew his gaze back to her face. Hope and anguish warred in the depths of her eyes.

"Ye great fool," Farlan said. "Ye've given her a grand excuse to keep from kissing ye, ye ken. She's a healer and wants to keep ye alive."

"Some things," Leith said directly to Rhian's lovely face, "are probably worth the dyin'."

Her fingers tightened on his brow before she lifted them clear away. "A typical man." He could tell she strove to speak lightly, even though he thought he glimpsed tears before she lowered her lashes. "Thinking o' such things even at death's door."

"Such thoughts," Farlan assured her dryly, "are calculated to keep a man alive."

"Is it so?" Lightly still, she appeared to contemplate it. "Then here is something to be going on with." A soft kiss landed on Leith's brow just where her palm had been. "And this." A second, still more fleeting, touched his lips.

His soul—his very soul—rose and rejoiced. For an instant, all pain fled his body before crashing in upon him once more.

Farlan laughed softly and with sympathy. "If that does no' cause ye to stay wi' us, Leith, naught ever will."

Chapter Twenty-Seven

"THE PRISONER MUST be moved from that filthy pen," Rhian declared forcefully, "if ye want him to survive. It is cold and malodorous. No place for a man barely clinging to life."

She spoke before Moira and Alasdair, who she supposed now made a pair of sorts, representing Clan MacBeith. They'd met at her request in the great hall that otherwise stood cold and empty.

Moira and Alasdair exchanged speaking glances.

"The council will no' like it," Alasdair said. The big man sported a number of his own bandages, some of which Rhian had placed. His face bore new lines, yet he appeared indefatigable. Did he never tire?

Rhian told him, "I do no' care about the council. Tell them that Leith MacLeod is an important prisoner, one who must be kept alive."

Alasdair made a face. "They ha' heard all that before." He rolled his eyes at Moira. "Wi' the last one."

"Aye, so." Rhian had to admit it. Men like Ewan did not like where that had gone. "We almost lost him this day." It took her a moment to gather her emotions and go on. "If he remains where he is, I canna promise we will not lose him yet."

Moira looked at her with concern. Rhian could not quite decide from whence that concern stemmed. From the possibility of losing a valued prisoner, or something more? Moira knew what

Rhian felt for Leith MacLeod. The worry might well be for the state of her heart.

Moira took a turn around the room. "I say move him."

"Ye would," Alasdair muttered unhappily.

Moira swung to face him. "Ye disagree?"

"The council, as I say, will disagree. Moira, they ha' seen all this before."

"So ye ha' said. That does no' change the fact that Rory Mac-Leod may be dead or dying. We may ha' the future chief MacLeod in our hands."

"So," Alasdair sneered, "treat him well now and he may spare our lives later?"

Anger flashed in Moira's eyes. It must be galling for her to be deprived of the full place of chief and forced to make her decisions jointly.

"Farlan says this Leith would make a far different sort o' chief to Rory."

"Farlan." Alasdair's lip curled.

Moira's chin jerked up. "Much as ye might dislike it, much as the accursed council might, I will be wedding wi' him. Soon. He will stand at the head o' Clan MacBeith."

Alasdair growled.

"If he has an understanding wi' the man who will likewise lead Clan MacLeod—d'ye no' see, Alasdair? We could ha' a future before us that holds peace."

The very thought made Rhian draw a breath. It was like one of Saerla's Visions.

"For that to happen," she put in, "Leith MacLeod must survive."

"'Twill no' be accepted." Alasdair tossed his hands into the air in frustration. "They did no' like it, Moira, when ye moved yon Farlan out o' that selfsame pen and into luxury."

She snorted. "It was no' luxury."

"Close enough! They beat him near to death. D'ye think they will no' do the same wi' this one?"

"Then send him home!" Moira blared. "He and Farlan can form an alliance first."

"Aye. You can be certain," Alasdair said with great scorn, "the only one who does no' disdain Farlan for renouncing his birthright is Leith MacLeod."

Obviously infuriated, Moira reminded him, "Ye it was who stood to defend Farlan when he came across the loch to us."

"I did that for ye, Moira. For *ye!*"

Rhian had to look away from Alasdair's agony. In the past, he had asked Moira to wed with him. For the benefit of the clan, supposedly, though Rhian did not believe it the only reason.

"We canna send him home," she put in. "No' yet. The journey would kill him."

"I see no choice, then," Moira cried. "'Tis leave him where he is to die, or let him do so on the way to MacLeod."

Alasdair heaved a great sigh. "I wish we had never taken the bastard prisoner."

So did Rhian. Only, she didn't. She thought of brushing her lips across his earlier, the pure need and longing that had seemed to flow out of him and into her. To never have known that seemed an abomination.

"Ye do realize"—Alasdair looked at Moira—"if the council does no' approve of our joint decisions, they may well strike ye off as chief?"

Moira toed up to him. "I am still Iain MacBeith's daughter and still ha' a right to head this clan. Let them gainsay that."

"They *will* gainsay it," Alasdair retorted, "if ye marry yon MacLeod."

"Farlan is a MacLeod no longer."

"Wha' is he, then? A free man? Wi'out any clan at all? Do no' be a fool, lass. MacLeod blood flows in his veins. And any offspring he gets on ye will carry that blood."

"So be it." Moira narrowed her eyes to slits. Without looking at Rhian, she said, "Mak' arrangements to move the prisoner, sister."

For the first time, Rhian faltered. "Aye, but where? No' where ye held Farlan before."

"Nay. Farlan was attacked there. We maun keep Leith closer by." Moira spun to face Rhian. "I think he should be moved to your chamber. Ye can share wi' Saerla, for the time."

Alasdair grated out, "Family quarters?"

"Let us see if attackers dare intrude there. Ask Farlan to help ye move him." Moira hesitated. "Where is Farlan?"

"With the prisoner."

"Aye, so he will help ye, then. Keep Leith in your care, Rhian. If ye share with Saerla, ye will be close by."

Or she could merely keep to her own chamber. Stay there with Leith.

Shocking, should it get out. Tempting beyond measure.

"Once his condition improves," Moira pronounced, "we shall meet and speak again. Perhaps by then we shall know whether Rory MacLeod is fatally wounded. And perhaps by then Farlan will ha' an agreement wi' Leith."

Rhian nodded and went out before Alasdair could argue it further, or perhaps change his mind.

She stood for a moment outside the doors of the hall, drawing air into her lungs. Leith MacLeod in her quarters. In her bed. The thought fair stunned her senses.

She wanted, aye, to take care of him. Wanted to take care of the man in ways that had naught to do with healing.

In the past, she'd heard women talk. While she'd provided them care, she had. Both matrons and maidens alike speculated on and recalled acts they'd performed with their menfolk. Some quite intriguing acts.

If Rhian had been intrigued, it was in a distant way. She'd never considered indulging in those pleasures herself.

Until now. The prospect of having Leith in her bed had opened a door in her mind, letting certain images flow through. Prompting particular questions.

How would the man taste—everywhere? Salty? Spicy? Arousing?

How would his skin feel beneath her tongue? Coarse? Rough? And if she plowed her tongue through the hair on his chest? Followed the trail of hair that led ever lower?

By heaven, what was wrong with her? The man was far too ill for such indulgences. He was dying.

Still. Still and all. Once she had him tucked up in her bed, once they were alone in her chamber, she would have the chance to find out.

If she chose.

Chapter Twenty-Eight

T HE VOICES CAME to Leith from a distance and roused him from the welter of pain in which he lay. Easier by far to ignore them, give himself up to the burning oblivion that held him.

And yet—he recognized both, and one of them called his name.

"Leith, man! Can ye no' open yer eyes and look at me?"

He could not. He lay there breathing, just breathing against the agony.

The second voice said, "Mayhap 'twould be best to move him while he remains senseless. It might hurt him less."

Aye, that voice he knew. The power of it flooded him with awareness and strength enough so he could open his eyes after all.

They hung above him, the both of them, in the stone hut. He remained here then, a prisoner, even though it felt as if he'd flown far. Farlan looked direly worried and somehow grief-stricken. Who had died? And Rhian MacBeith's lovely, calm face also showed unhappy emotions.

She looked at Farlan. "I do no' want to hurt him anymore."

Farlan shook his head. He spoke to Leith as to a child. "Leith, we need to move ye. We will do it as carefully as we can."

To Rhian he said, "The wound has been bleeding."

"I ha' never seen a wound to match it. It refuses to close over, whate'er I do."

"Where—" Leith tried to speak and could not tell if he succeeded. "Taking me?"

"Hush now." Rhian laid her hand on his chest. Comfort and healing flowed into him in equal measures.

She touched him. But not for long enough. All too soon she stepped away, and he heard her speaking to someone else. A commotion ensured.

Suddenly the hut became crowded with people. They swarmed him, jostled him, lifted him, which gave the pain sharper teeth. He could no longer see Rhian, but he got a glimpse of Farlan. Steady, reassuring.

He floated, tilted, felt as if he would fall. Before he could, the darkness came crashing down.

⸙

"LEITH, CAN YE hear me?"

He had stopped moving, and it had gone quiet apart from Rhian's voice. Dim light flickered against his closed eyelids. The pain blotted out everything else.

"Rhian?"

"Aye, 'tis I. Drink this."

A vessel was tipped against his lips and a small amount of liquid flowed into his mouth. He choked on it.

Arms came out around him and lifted him up. The vessel tapped his lips again.

"Drink. 'Twill help wi' the fever."

If she told him it would, it would. He trusted her implicitly. With his life and aught else he had.

"Where?"

She eased him back down. Her fingers flitted over his head, brushing the hair back from his brow.

"Whisht, Leith. We ha' moved ye out o' the cell for your safekeeping."

"Farlan?"

"Aye, he was here. Gone now. 'Tis but the two o' us."

The desire to see her allowed him to open his eyes. Astonishment widened them.

He lay on a bed in a chamber where he'd never been before. The softness of a mattress cradled him, and a bolster snuggled behind his head. Firelight danced behind Rhian, so he could not see her face as clearly as he might wish.

He did not need to see her, though. He could feel her with every part of him.

"Am I dyin'?" He felt like it. If he was, he wanted it to be here, with her. Perhaps he merely dreamed all this. He'd had a wealth of strange dreams since the fever came on him, including that in which Rhian had kissed him.

A funny thing—of all he'd dreamed, he wanted most for that to be true. Another funny thing—he'd never imagined he could come so low as this. In the past he'd taken a great deal for granted. His strength, which he hadn't expected could fail him. His confidence. His immunity to love.

He could not tell what he felt for this woman now. Mayhap not love. Something equally huge and powerful.

She did not immediately answer his question. Her calm face did not register distress, but her eyes did. Deep blue, they held his gaze for an instant before filling with tears.

She placed her hand on his chest in that way she had, as if—as if claiming him. "I will no' let ye die."

"Good." Because he was not ready to leave this world. Not without more of her kisses. Not without a lifetime to spend with her. That, and only that, mattered.

"Though"—her voice came choked by tears—"if ye could gi' me some help in keeping ye alive, 'twould be welcome."

"Verra well. Do no' weep." He reached with his left hand, since the right still did not serve him, and brushed a tear from her cheek. "I will do all I can."

"Ye maun gather up your strength. Rest when I tell ye to. Drink your draughts."

"Aye, Rhian. Aught ye say." His eyelids weighed heavily. He did not want to close his eyes because then he would not be able to see her face. "Will ye bless me?"

"Bless ye?" Her expression turned confused.

"Wi' another kiss."

"Leith MacLeod." She sounded almost chiding. "Even lyin' at the door o' death, you're a rogue." But she bent to him. Her fingers brushed his forehead. The scent of her came upon him, herbs and warm woman. "There is your blessing."

"I did no' mean—"

She silenced him by placing her lips on his, a fleeting kiss only, and far less than he craved. He wanted to drink of her. Consume her. Make her his own.

Was he too sorely hurt for that? Only one answer for it: he needed to grow well.

He could do that. He could do anything for her kiss.

"Rhian," he said, just to speak her name again.

"Leith."

And aye, it was as if they claimed one another there in the silence, with the flames flickering behind her, and the scent of her surrounding him.

He reached up again, with wonder this time, to touch her hair, a nimbus of fire around her head.

"Beautiful, merciful angel."

"Rest. 'Tis that will heal ye, if anything can."

"Ye will heal me." *If anything can.* "Do no' leave me," he begged even as his eyes dropped shut.

"I will no'."

He slept and dreamed he was once more on the battlefield, lying beneath his fellow clansmen—all dead. He saw her face appear before him and awoke with a start.

To discover he lay in her arms.

But nay. Nay, he had to be still dreaming. For none of this could be true. Him, lying in a clean, soft bed with the warmth of her pressed against him and her arms flung around him as if—as if she would hold him from all harm.

Such bliss could come to a man only in dreams.

He shifted carefully, both because he did not want to rouse the tortuous beast in his arm, nor to wake her. He eyed her, testing the reality. Her red head lay on the bolster beside his, so close he could feel the tickle of wild curls against his cheek. She lay on her side, curved toward him, sound asleep.

Och, bliss! Could a man ask any more than this?

But where was he? Where were they? The fire had died while they slept, but light came in through a narrow window. The chamber, small but comfortable, seemed to cradle him just like the mattress. Just like her arms.

Not a cell, then.

Unmoving and still unwilling to disturb her rest, he took stock of himself. He no longer shivered with cold. That might be because Rhian gave off a steady heat. And the pain in his arm—not gone, nay, but not so fierce as it had been either. He could move his left arm, both legs. The right arm still lay useless. Another part of him, though, was on the rise, reacting to Rhian's nearness.

Nay, but he could not allow that. He wanted Rhian, aye, but not in a carnal way. He softly corrected himself—not *just* in that way. Her kisses were welcome. But he desired her, needed her on a much deeper level.

So he disciplined his body, all of it, to quiet, and just lay waiting for her to wake.

She did so slowly, first stirring against his shoulder; the arm flung across him twitched. He knew the moment her wits came alive because her breathing changed. She released her hold on him and shifted away in the bed.

"Och, I must have fallen asleep."

She sat up and eyed him. He looked back at her, heart swelling.

The dark red hair spilled in a mass down her back. Her cheeks had flushed with sleep. She looked impossibly beautiful.

"Forgive me. Ye would no' stop shivering last night. I lay down to keep ye warm."

"I do no' mind."

She narrowed her gaze at him. Leaning forward, she placed her palm on his brow. "Your fever has broken." Gladness filled her face. "It must ha' been that draught."

He did not argue it, even though he knew very well it had been the night spent in her arms.

Chapter Twenty-Nine

Farlan arrived not long after Leith and Rhian finished sharing breakfast. Rhian kept eyeing Leith all the while they ate, assessing his condition and looking happier than he'd seen her before.

"How d'ye feel?" she asked as he fed himself, using his left hand.

"Weak as a lamb," he answered ruefully. But better, as he had to admit.

"And the pain in your arm?"

In truth, it had spread to his whole shoulder. "Less. Much less."

"Good. I will bandage it again once we are finished here."

Before she could, Farlan knocked at the door and peered in. He too eyed Leith, sitting up in the bed balanced against the bolsters. "I hoped for a wee word wi' Leith."

"Come in. I ha' some others to see," Rhian said, gathering up her basket. "I will leave him wi' you."

She went out. Leith stared after her while Farlan watched him closely. Then Farlan glanced around the chamber.

"I see ye ha' landed yoursel' in some comfort."

"Only because they feared I was dyin'."

"As did I. Ye look better."

"My fever has broken, so it seems. I will tell ye, Farlan, I ha' never felt so sapped o' strength. I doubt much I could get up on my feet wi'out assistance."

"And that is saying somewhat. Your strength has always been a matter o' renown."

"I may regain some strength, especially wi' Mistress Rhian's help. I do no' ken whether I will e'er regain the use o' this arm."

"Aye, so." That made Farlan look concerned.

"And wha' good is a one-armed warrior, eh? Especially one lacking his right hand. Even Rory will no' want me back again."

"'Tis about Rory I wanted to speak." Farlan came and sat on the edge of the bed. "D'ye ken he was wounded during the last attack, when he and the men tried to breach the gates?"

"Was he?"

"Aye. Took an arrow straight through the back. Everyone on the wall saw it."

A feeling of sick dread crawled up from Leith's belly to his chest. "Did he go down, then?"

"Nay. He was helped awa'. And they broke off the attack immediately after."

Leith's eyes met Farlan's brown ones, and he saw there a reflection of his own fear. "D'ye ken what happened to him?"

"Nay. How could we? But 'tis a subject o' considerable speculation."

So Leith would imagine.

"Och," he declared, denying his own dread, "Rory is much too tough to be brought down by a mere arrow in the back."

"Unless it touched his heart."

Leith's own heart began to pound. It could not be. Rory, at only a score and seven years of age, was in his prime, a force in his own right. He'd waited his whole life to take the place of chief—not that he'd desired the loss of his father, whom he'd adored. But the three of them, Rory, Farlan, and Leith, had sat together for countless hours while Rory aired his plans for the day he would claim all of Glen Bronach for MacLeod.

Such a fire, burning so bright, could not be gone from the

world.

"Nay," Leith said, half whisper and half groan.

Farlan shrugged. "I ha' to say, even though he has broken wi' me," he added more deliberately, "cast me off, I hate to think it."

"'Tis difficult to imagine."

"Aye. Yet naught has been heard of him since our men, the MacLeod men, took him awa'. He has no' launched another attack to win ye back."

"Perhaps he has but given up on me. Maybe he thinks me dead."

Farlan shook his head. "Ye be his cousin, his own blood. Can ye see him giving up?"

Rory, like a hound with a bone, rarely gave up on anything. He might worry at that bone, but he did not know the meaning of surrender.

"Listen." Farlan leaned forward and laid a hand on Leith's dead arm. "Those here, Mistress Moira and Alasdair in particular, were ready to send ye home to MacLeod before that happened. They waited only for Mistress Rhian to declare ye fit to travel."

"Aye?"

Farlan nodded.

"But do I no' make a canny hostage?"

"They have had their fill o' hostages, after wha' happened wi' me. They are no' happy having a cuckoo in their nest and wanted well rid o' ye. I maun say I encouraged it, to get ye home. Both for your sake and Rory's, thinking o' him half mad wi'out ye."

"Ye do still care about him, then."

"Of course I care about him. We are like brothers, or were. Now, though, they do no' want to send ye home before I negotiate wi' ye for a truce. A peace."

"Negotiate wi' me?"

"Aye." Farlan met Leith's gaze steadily. "If Rory be dead, ye will be the next Chief MacLeod."

It hit Leith so hard, he gasped as with a physical pain. His mind had been through so many loops and over so many hurdles, in and out of consciousness and dreams, that he could barely grasp this. That he must be his cousin's heir.

Rory had always been there, the man to lead MacLeod after his father. Young and vigorous, there had never been any doubt he would take a wife and sire any number of sons—just as soon as he could take his mind from his ambitions long enough to choose a woman.

If he'd been taken from this earth betimes by an arrow—

Leith swore softly, and Farlan nodded. "They will no' send ye back now, even if ye recover. Not until they are certain o' ye, that is."

"Certain o' me?"

"That, as I say, ye might be swayed toward striking a peace."

"So they sent ye to persuade me, did they? One o' my closest friends."

"Aye," Farlan admitted.

"That woman o' yours, the chief, she came up wi' the idea?"

Farlan's chin jerked upward. "That woman is fighting for the survival o' her clan. She will do as she must."

Leith's wits moved sluggishly still, though he pushed them to motion. "Does that include killing me? For a Clan MacLeod wi'out any chief at all would be far easier to defeat."

"Would she allow her sister to nurse ye, only to cut yer throat?"

"I do no' ken. She began wi' nursing me before there was a possibility o' Rory dyin'."

"And d'ye think Rhian would allow any harm to come to ye?"

Leith did not know what Rhian would do. She seemed determined to care for him. She treated him with such kind compassion and tenderness that he wanted to trust her. He'd slept the night secure in her arms. But if it came down to it, would she choose protecting him over her loyalty to her clan? He could not tell. Would he be willing to bet his life on her?

He might mean little more to her than any other patient. And she might, just as Farlan said of her sister the chief, be fighting for survival.

What a fool he'd been! Half seduced when he was the one used to doing the seducing.

His lips pressed into a tight line. He had come close, perilously close, to losing his heart. Only he knew how near.

He asked Farlan in a hard voice, "Wha' happened to the lass who tried to kill me?"

Farlan withdrew his hand and sat up a bit. "She's been apprehended. Naught has been done wi' her. Her emotional state—"

"Her wha'?"

Grimly, Farlan said, "She'd lost her man in the fighting and acted out o' grief."

"Aye well, no harm in it, then. Mayhap they'll use her again when they decide I'm better dead and out o' their way. But nay, they'll want to make sure o' the job and send a warrior the next time." Leith glared at his friend. "Mayhap they'll send ye." Or Rhian. They could bid Rhian to slit his throat while he lay beside her, all trusting.

"How could ye think, man, I'd raise a blade against ye? You are my friend."

Leith sneered. "Ye raise a blade against me each time ye accompany your new chief into battle, d'ye no'?"

"That is different."

"It is no'. Tell yer chief, yer woman," Leith said scathingly, "I will no' turn on Rory or on my clan, as ye ha' done."

Farlan's gaze narrowed on Leith's face. "I thought ye understood. My feelings for Moira—"

"Love, aye? Or lust? A wee bit o' both?"

"Leith, man, think carefully. We, the MacBeiths and the MacLeods, do no' need to go on killing one another. There's room for all o' us in Glen Bronach."

"Aye, but a man's heart can hold only one loyalty. I suppose," Leith said, "that is why you are here, on this side o' the loch."

"I suppose it is. That does no' mean I wish to see MacLeod brought low or Rory dead."

"I would like to believe that. I stood up for ye back at Mac-Leod, before ye defected."

"Aye, so ye did."

"But now I wonder."

"That ye could doubt me, Leith—'tis a wound I take. D'ye truly wish to see MacBeith destroyed? For ye ken if Rory lives, he will no' stop until it is so. I see the way ye look at Mistress Rhian—"

"What way?"

"Wi' a softness. I thought—"

"She is a beautiful woman."

"Aye, inside and out."

"I like to admire beautiful women."

"That is all, is it?"

"Wha' more should there be? D'ye think I'm likely to fall under some—some spell she might weave?"

"Aye," Farlan said softly.

"As ye did?"

Farlan drew a breath that expanded his chest. "I would no' wish what has befallen me on anyone, least o' all one o' my dearest friends."

"Leave her, then. Come back to MacLeod wi' me."

"I canna."

"I know Rory would tak' ye back." *If* Rory yet lived. "He will be angry for a bit, but ye ken his anger never lasts."

"I will no' leave Moira. Not till I die."

Leith tried to tell himself over again that Farlan was a fool. Yet he sensed something fine and brave in the statement.

"Look," Farlan said, "the old chief here, Iain, and our Camraith had an unspoken truce for years and years. Aye, we raided one another's cattle. There were skirmishes. Men died, men who shouldn't. All I ask, Leith, is for ye to consider a return to that. Should ye tak' up the place o' chief—"

"I will no'. Rory is no' dead. I refuse to consider it." Just as once he would have refused to consider this man before him could turn his coat.

Or that Rhian MacBeith might lie to him with her beautiful, merciful eyes.

Chapter Thirty

A GOODLY AMOUNT of time passed before Rhian returned. When she did, she gave Leith a blithe smile, making a swift assessment.

"Ye look so much better this morn. Does your wound still pain ye? Shall I mix another draught?"

Leith strove to mask any response he might have to the kindness in her gaze, and that soft smile. Yet the very air of the chamber changed when she came in. And that place deep in his gut, where his awareness of her seemed to be anchored, tugged hard at him.

"I do no' need a draught." He did not need his senses dulled. If they decided to move against him—

Rhian approached where he lay propped up against the bolsters on the bed, and laid her palm on his forehead.

He found himself gazing at close range into the depths of her eyes. And aye, despite himself, her touch soothed him; her nearness eased the wanting. The warmth of her gaze embraced him.

Mayhap she had cast some spell on him after all.

"Are ye hungry?" she asked softly, not at once moving away after she withdrew her hand.

He shook his head.

"Aye well, once your appetite returns, we will ken for certain ye are on the mend."

She sat on the bed facing him, her legs tucked up beneath her, and her hands folded loosely in her lap. "Ye should take somewhat to eat whether ye be hungry or no. 'Twill help ye to regain your strength."

He said, trying hard to discipline his tangle of suspicions and emotions, "And ye want for me to grow strong, d'ye?"

"I want for all my patients to grow strong."

"Farlan sat and spoke wi' me while ye were awa'."

She nodded. "I ken."

So they'd cleared it with her, had they? All that happened in this room. They spoke of him, made plans for him. Did they all know he'd slept in her arms?

"He told me there's a chance Rory was fatally wounded during the last attack at the gate."

That made her gaze quicken. She seemed to study him still more intently. "He took an arrow in the back. No one could tell how grave was the wound, but his men helped him away and they broke off the attack."

"His death would change everything in Glen Bronach."

"It would."

"Since ye ha' Farlan here speaking in your sister's ear, there will be no doubt how 'twould alter things."

She tipped her head as if sensing the antagonism that simmered within him. "Farlan talks to us, aye. 'Tis a good thing. It allows us a hope o' achieving peace."

"That is your goal, is it?"

"It is Moira's goal." Rhian made a rueful face. "Alasdair has other ideas."

"He wants to kill me off."

"He has wanted to kill ye from the first. Send your bones back to Rory MacLeod as a grisly message. But ye can see"—she spread her hands in a graceful gesture—"ye are being kept safe here instead."

"Wi' ye." He held her gaze steadily.

"Aye."

"Because Farlan has told them, should Rory prove dead and him having no direct issue, wi' me being the eldest son o' the old chief's sister, I am earmarked for chief after him."

"Aye."

"They ha' me in their hands and think they may influence me into some sort o' truce."

She drew a breath. "Would that no' be a fine thing? To cease wi' the killing and all the heartache?"

"I do no' ken if it would or it would no'. Generations ago my ancestors came to this glen and claimed it for their own."

"Only," she said softly, "my ancestors were here first."

"A small number o' them, to my understanding, and easily chased off."

"Only," she repeated, and leaned forward slightly, "they would no' leave. They had sacred places here, and the graves of their dead."

"They were dug in. I will give ye that."

"Your ancestors could not defeat mine."

"They say the MacBeiths had magic on their side." It might well be true. Rhian might have used that magic on him right along with her herbs. She might have employed it to influence him, to soften him, to make him turn his coat just as Farlan had.

"We fight still the battles o' our ancestors," she told him. "Is that no' foolish?"

Leith no longer knew. He had been languishing here in a weakened state, half killed and at times barely conscious. He'd begun falling in love with this woman, with her graceful hands, luscious lips, and generous nature.

He needed to think clearly. Come out of the spell, if she'd woven one. He'd never wanted to be chief of Clan MacLeod. He liked to keep a light heart, to laugh and enjoy his life. He wanted no part of the weight that rested on Rory's shoulders. He'd not been cut out for it.

And he'd never believed he stood within reach of it. Rory,

aye, a bull of a man, young and vigorous, could fight through any battle. He had only to choose a wife and grow a crop of sons. Who would think a stray arrow could bring him down?

He looked at the woman before him, she who had somehow anchored herself to his heart. "Ha' they asked ye to influence me? To—to sweeten me? Is that why ye lay here wi' me last night?"

For the first time, she looked disconcerted. A mild flush warmed her cheek, and her fingers, still in her lap, tensed.

"No one has bidden me sweeten ye, Leith MacLeod. I am my own woman."

"Ye be a MacBeith. Rooted here like—like those stones up on the rise."

"Aye."

"Your twa sisters fight wi' swords. Mayhap ye fight another way."

"O' what are ye accusing me?"

He was not sure and could not say. He wanted this feeling between them, this deep connection, to be real. He ached for it even though there could scarcely be a worse woman upon whom he might center his affections.

He wanted to love Rhian MacBeith. Because he'd never seen another woman to match her, and he'd never felt this way. Now, though, doubt and suspicion had entered the wild mix inside him.

He shook his head. His gaze dropped from hers for the first time. "Wha' will they do wi' me, your sister and yon Alasdair?"

"'Tis no' a simple decision. They ha' the council wi' whom they must deal, and their sympathies are spread wide. I believe Moira would as soon send ye home."

"So she sent Farlan to talk me round." Or, failing his oldest friend, her, Rhian.

"I do no' think the council will agree to send ye back. And as I said before, ye are no' fit to travel yet."

So she would continue to nurse him. Shed her smiles on him. And perhaps the blessings of her kisses. So that by the time he did return home, should he find himself in the place of chief, he would not be able to imagine raising his hand against her, and hers.

By God! Already he could not imagine it. He might be angry and let it be admitted, hurt by the possibility that she had been leading him by the nose all this while. That did not mean he could bear seeing harm come to one wild red hair on her head.

Lost—he was lost to this woman. Sitting there facing her in the quiet of her chamber, he admitted that to be true. But he could not let her see she had such a hold on him. Just in case—

In case she was not what he'd sell his soul for her to be. In case he, the charmer, had been charmed.

And she in truth cared naught for him.

✦ ═══════ ❧ ═══════ ✦

Chapter Thirty-One

RHIAN SHIFTED UNEASILY, and her gaze once more strayed to the doors of the hall. How long had she been here, shut in a meeting between her sisters, Alasdair, and the members of the council? It felt an eternity.

She did not understand quite why Moira wanted her here. She had little to contribute to discussions of warfare or, for all that, clan politics. She held no real authority. And she had other, more important things to do, like make a round of the wounded under her care. Make sure there were sufficient bandages and other supplies, should Rory MacLeod prove still alive—that being a question much argued during this meeting—and eager to bring another attack.

She had other things to do, like gazing into Leith MacLeod's gray-blue eyes.

She pushed that thought away from her with some difficulty. Inappropriate, to say the least, while the others sat debating whether he was likely to be the next Chief MacLeod and whether, in such case, they would be better off taking this opportunity to slaughter him.

She did not think Moira would let that happen. Not with Farlan speaking in her ear. Yet the council seemed to want just that, and Ewan, their undisputed leader, was, as usual, in a stroppy mood. And Alasdair. Alasdair's bent was to take the hard line. To show no mercy.

If it were up to Alasdair, she thought Leith would already have been executed.

After all her work to heal him. After the time she'd spent getting to know the man, while looking into those fine eyes of his.

But did she truly know him? She had impulses, aye, ones foreign to her that had driven her to touch his lips with her own. To sleep in his arms last night.

Yet when she'd spoken with him earlier, after he'd seen Farlan, something had changed. A coolness had entered those eyes made for smiling. Or perhaps 'twas wariness.

Perhaps it was just that he grew stronger, returned to better health, and began to comprehend his situation. Enough to make any man wary.

It made her uncomfortable, though. Caused her to fidget on the bench where she sat. To worry about what Leith might be doing even now.

If he got up on his feet too soon, if a renewed energy caused him to do so, he could reopen his wound still. She did not know that he would ever again be able to use the injured arm properly. At least he'd have his life.

"Rhian?" Moira's voice had an edge, as if she'd sought her sister's attention more than once. "What d'ye think?"

Rhian lifted her gaze. Everyone in the chamber stared at her, awaiting a reply. She had none.

"Forgive me. My mind wandered."

Some of the council members exchanged glances. With deliberate patience, Moira said, "When do ye say the prisoner will be fit for travel?"

The prisoner. The MacLeod. The man who seemed to have taken root inside her.

"No' soon," she blurted a bit too abruptly. "His condition improves, aye, but an attempt to move him any distance could prove disastrous."

"Yet"—Ewan stretched his lips in a ghastly smile—"ye ha' moved him. Into your own chamber, so I understand."

"Aye. And I am bunking wi' my sister, Saerla, for the duration o' his stay."

Saerla sent her a swift look. She alone knew Rhian had not bunked with her last night.

Another of the council members waved his hand. "Aye, why no' situate the MacLeod bastard in luxury?" He shot an antagonistic glance at Moira. "'Twas good enough for his fellow clansman before him, aye?"

Moira stiffened. Farlan was conspicuously absent from the meeting, and, in fact, Rhian figured he guarded the door of her bedchamber.

She hoped he did. If somewhat happened to Leith MacLeod, she—

"The prisoner was moved to Mistress Rhian's chamber for safekeeping," Moira said, breaking into Rhian's thoughts, "and so she might better care for him. Given his possible importance, we will tak' no chances on another murder attempt."

"I say," Ewan grated out, "his possible importance is reason to slaughter him. End the problem before it begins. 'Tis the opportunity o' a lifetime."

"We do no' ken," Moira argued, "but he may represent an opportunity for peace."

"Peace!" Ewan spat. "Here in Glen Bronach, where there has been naught but strife for time out o' mind?"

Saerla spoke up in her soft voice. "Things can change, Ewan. Sometimes they need to change."

They had argued all this already, up one side and down the other while Rhian fretted, wishing for escape. While the now-familiar tug beneath her breastbone became more acute.

She needed to see him. Needed to be with him.

Now everyone looked at Saerla.

"Mistress," the eldest member of the council half whispered, "have ye Seen?"

"Nay."

"D'ye ken," Ewan said, far more harshly, "can ye tell if Rory MacLeod be alive or dead?"

Aye, for that was the question. Like everyone else, Rhian stared at her sister, barely breathing.

Again, Saerla shook her head.

Alasdair spoke up unexpectedly. "Can ye, Mistress Saerla, perhaps seek that knowledge? We all ken fine ye ha' the magic upon ye."

Saerla raised her gaze and regarded them one by one. "It comes when it comes. I ha' asked. I ha' prayed on it—"

"Mayhap," Moira said gently, "ye might do so again, sister, and we will hope the spirit moves wi' ye."

"But," Ewan began, "this is information o' vital importance. Should no' Mistress Saerla devote hersel' to it and try harder?"

Rhian startled herself by surging to her feet. "I will no' ha' ye badgering my sister."

This was unprecedented for Rhian, who usually held her tongue during such meetings, and they all stared at her now. She rarely lost her temper, but aye, it did happen.

"It is all right, Rhian," Saerla said softly.

"It is not!" Bad enough Rhian had to spend her own talents to heal a man they might then take out and slaughter. She would make them leave Saerla alone.

Ewan, too, stumbled to his feet. "'Tis no' my intention, Mistress Rhian, to badger Mistress Saerla. I prize her abilities. We all do."

"Ye might try respecting them instead. Respect the magic that lies in this glen rather than seeking more ways to drown it in *blood*." Rhian could feel the heat flame in her face. She fair trembled with indignation. "Flesh and blood can bear only so much. I suggest ye look to your souls."

She stalked out, breaking through the doors and into the cool, open air. She went at the behest of the pull anchored inside her. She needed to answer that pull.

To see Leith MacLeod.

She felt like she was losing her mind.

Did a woman lose her mind when she fell in love? From what little Rhian had observed, aye. She'd watched it happen to Moira, and to countless others before her.

It felt very different when it happened to her. A preposterous observation, because she could not be falling in love with Leith MacLeod. Some other ailment beset her. Some sickness, aye, of the mind.

She half expected one of her sisters to come out of the hall after her. Saerla, most likely. No one did. Clansmen and women, passing by, cast her curious glances as she stood there letting her fury die.

She had a hundred things to do besides returning to her chamber. She needed to keep well away from Leith MacLeod. She folded her hands together and pressed them against her body just beneath her breasts, trying to quell the almost painful pull there.

Head high and cheeks still flaming, she moved on.

Chapter Thirty-Two

INTENTIONS WERE FINE things, Leith thought as he tried to shift himself against the bolsters of the bed. He intended, now that the fever had lifted from him and his head felt clearer, to look after himself. Having spoken with Farlan, he'd meant to move cautiously. Guard his tongue.

Stop longing for Rhian MacBeith.

He could do so, surely. He could perform that one small, simple task. Was he not a grown man, after all? One who had entertained many women. Not a green lad caught in the rush of infatuation.

Yet lying here—in the woman's bed—he could smell her. He could almost feel her lying next to him as she had last night. He wanted to see her so much it hurt.

Och, but he must stop playing the fool. He found himself in a dangerous position here, among enemies. They thought they might well hold the next Chief MacLeod in their hands.

They would either seek to influence him, or slaughter him.

He needed to protect himself, and that included keeping away from Rhian. For she—not that great lump Alasdair's dirk— was his greatest danger.

Leith knew that right well, aye.

He lectured and sought to steel himself, yet when he heard someone at the door, his whole body leaped.

It was not Rhian, but an older woman who delivered a basket of food. She eyed him closely and looked as if she wanted to say something to him, but she ducked back out without doing so.

After she left, Leith heaved himself off the bed and onto his feet. It hurt to move, and Rhian would likely tear him up one side and down the other if she saw him.

But she was not here. And his emotions would not allow him to lie still.

He paced as best he was able, winding a track on the floor, noticing the contents of the chamber. This was her chamber, the core of her, with all her possessions in place.

A clothespress that he did not open. Women's things—women's things were private. A chest beneath the single slit window. Not much else besides the supplies she kept here, the tools for healing. Herbs that scented the air and piles of bandaging. Small pots containing what must be unguents. Powders he had seen her use for mixing draughts.

A single, small mirror, no bigger than the palm of his hand, lying beside a comb.

That he did touch, feeling intrusive. The comb contained a few twined red hairs. He raised it to his nose, and aye, it smelled like her pillow.

Sudden longing hit him so hard that he nearly staggered. He wanted to be lying with her again as he had last night, his face almost buried in her hair. He wanted—

The door rattled once more. Rhian slipped into the chamber.

She looked upset, her cheeks flushed and her lips twisted with anguish. Leith should not be able to feel what was inside her. Only he could.

"Rhian? Wha' is it?" he asked. "Wha' has happened?"

She ran her gaze over him. "Ye should no' be on your feet," she said almost absently.

"I ken. Wha' has happened to upset ye?"

She moved farther into the chamber, shutting the door behind her carefully. "I ha' just come from a meeting o' the council.

One where they are busy discussing what should be done wi' ye."

"Has a decision been made?" Would he be dragged out of here? Slaughtered like a stirk out front of the stronghold?

"Nay. They speak in circles." She turned her gaze on him, deep blue and brilliant. "I suspect ye do no' trust me, Leith MacLeod. Were I in your place, I doubt I would trust me either. But I mean ye no harm. I do no' want—" She had to pause and draw a breath. "I do no' want ye dead."

Something inside him let go its fierce hold and allowed him to ease.

In a rush, she went on, "I would no' spend my time healing ye, only to see ye taken to the slaughter."

He believed her. Despite all his doubt and the fact that she had no real reason to defend him, he did.

"Yet," he said regretfully, "ye canna protect me."

"I canna. And that is why, should the opportunity present itself, ye maun return to MacLeod."

And they would see one another no more.

She went on, "I can do my best to argue for that, as will Moira, so I believe. But it may do no good. Such decisions are no longer up to Moira alone."

"I understand."

"Ye balance on a knife's edge. But I want ye to ken, I am no' the one to push ye off."

"I do know that, aye."

She moved a step closer, and another, her gaze still fastened on him. "Ye should no' be on your feet," she whispered again.

And then she was in his arms. Just like that, as if it happened by magic, she pressed right up against him and laid her hand in that claiming manner on his chest.

Her hand on his heart. Her compelling eyes gazing into his. Her lips just beneath his own.

Once again, he never knew which of them closed that distance, whether he bent his head to claim her lips or she reached for him. Maybe both.

When their lips met this time, a momentous thing happened. All doubt flew. All remnants of suspicion. Certainty took their place, lodging just like the ache that lay beneath Leith's heart.

This could not be. Only it was. He should not trust her. Only he did, with his very life.

"Rhian." He breathed her beautiful name into her, and she parted her lips to accept it, and let him in. Tasting of her was like nothing he'd ever experienced or dreamed of experiencing. Arousing, aye, and exciting. She had the blood pounding in his ears. But more than that, it felt almost sacred and holy, as if he'd found an answer for which he'd searched all his life.

A controlled woman, Rhian MacBeith, and a careful one. He felt that control shatter as she leaned to him. As she ran her hand up from his chest across his cheek and into his hair. As she tangled her tongue with his and invited him deeper in.

He wanted to weep. He wanted to holler. He did neither, but caught her close with his one good arm. He kissed and kissed her.

Naught in his world, after this, would ever be the same. That thought burst across his mind, along with the glorious warmth she seemed to shed upon him. No going back from this moment. Everything had changed.

Not till he began to sway on his feet did she withdraw her mouth from his, look into his face, and smile. If her kiss stole his breath, her smile had the power to fell him.

Beautiful woman, merciful angel. The darling of my heart.

Softly, softly, she said, "I did no' mean to knock ye off your feet."

"Ye steal my strength, Rhian MacBeith. And ye give it back to me again. A curious thing."

"All o' this is curious. Beyond reason. Out o' time."

He touched her cheek. He did so tenderly, as if he'd never before touched the flesh of a woman.

"Come." She caught his hand and steered him to the bed.

"Rhian—"

"I want to kiss ye again, and I'll be cursed if I'll undo all the good work I ha' done by sending ye to the floor."

He lay already at her feet. He, a great lump of a man who could make two of her.

He fell backward onto the bed and scarcely noticed the ensuing pain. Like a man in a dream, he made room for her beside him, and she cuddled into his side as she had last night, and raised her lips to his.

Time passed. He had no way of telling how much. Nor did he care, for Rhian lay with him, warm and fragrant with the scent of herbs, and the knot that had held tight within him so long—the wound where was embedded the cord that connected him to her—became at last acquiescent.

In this life or one beyond, a man could ask no more.

Chapter Thirty-Three

R HIAN KISSED LEITH. She kissed and kissed him with no thought for stopping. She ran her hand up the broad strength of his chest to the corded column of his neck and into his hair. Only this moment existed—warmth and sensation. Naught else.

So *this* was desire. This was how it felt to lie with a man and want only him. This longing to mingle flesh with flesh, touching soul to soul and life to life.

Could this be what Moira had felt with Farlan? If so, Rhian had not been fair to her sister. Because this was grand and magnificent. This was beyond irresistible.

How could it be that Leith was what she'd wanted all her life, without knowing?

She withdrew her lips from his, leaving lingering kisses at each side of his mouth, only so she could back off and look at him. A man's face, his was, heavy with bone and broad in the forehead, with tiny lines carved by laughter at the corners of his eyes. A splash of freckles he must have carried as a lad.

He was no lad now.

He murmured so the sound rumbled up from his chest, "Beautiful, merciful angel, why d'ye look at me so?"

"I can look nowhere else."

That made him smile, crinkling his gray-blue eyes with delight even before his lips curved. Her smile caught from his, and they grinned at one another like fools.

Such an intimacy, to smile with a man while holding him in her arms.

She'd already glimpsed all of him while treating his wounds. The broad, deep chest patterned with sandy hair, the strong thighs and what lay between them. Now she ached to touch it all. To run her fingers there while kissing him.

Bonded, mouth to mouth. Unbreakably. Forever.

She needed to keep her head. But nay, all hope of that had gone the moment their lips met.

"Am I hurting ye, lying against ye this way?"

"I can feel no hurt. I feel only you."

He dove for her mouth again, took it savagely this time, hungrily. She rose to meet him, opening, opening to him in a helpless parody of what she wished might happen lower down.

She forgot to breathe. Her mind floated in a golden haze, connected to his mind by their lips. She wanted him naked. Here, in her bed.

He began to laugh. It came to her through his kiss, and when he broke away, his eyes danced.

"Ye want me naked?"

They stared at one another, both realizing at the same instant what he'd said.

Ah, but it could not be. Rhian was a practical woman. A sensible one.

"Aye, so," he whispered after a moment. "I would grant ye that, Rhian, and aught else in my power to gi' ye pleasure."

"And I, you." It shook her to admit that. But how could she do other than trust him with her heart?

"Ye please me right fine just the way ye are." His gaze still holding hers, he ran his palm across her cheek and in a caress down her throat. Still lower, he cupped a breast.

Rhian, never a woman for fine trappings, wore a plain woolen gown of undyed gray and a simple chemise beneath. She could feel him, the heat of his hand, right through both layers of cloth.

He traced his lips over hers while he caressed her. Once, twice, thrice. The heat that bloomed between them became so intense that she sat up. Drew away.

"Rhian, forgive me. I thought—"

"Hush."

Her fingers trembled as she unfastened her bodice, but they trembled with eagerness. He lay against the bolster and watched her with wonder. She untied the front of the gown and pulled it from her shoulders. The chemise followed. She sat half bared to his gaze.

"Rhian."

He lifted her somehow with but the one arm. Hoisted her so his face nestled between her breasts, just where she wanted him. His mouth made a hot trail across her skin to her nipple, which he captured. She cradled his head while he suckled her, and she wondered how a woman could endure such pleasure.

"Do no' stop, Leith. Please," she murmured as she arched to him, urging more. "Never stop."

"Never." He whispered the word against her damp flesh before taking her into his mouth again. Making her part of him.

One breast and then the other, stoking the fire within her. It rose steady and strong. It rose wild.

"I need to taste ye," she told him raggedly. When she looked into his eyes now, she saw what she felt. Hunger and flames.

She caught his face between her hands and kissed him. Good, but not enough. She kissed him deeper, and he growled. Tearing herself from his mouth, she kissed a path downward, tasting the skin at his throat, his chest, followed the trail of hair still farther. She slid her hand ahead of her till she found the bulge there.

"Rhian—"

Still not enough. She slid her hand inside his leggings and wrapped her fingers around the heat of him. Hard for her, he was.

She wanted to straddle him. To take him inside her. She caressed him instead, marveling at the smoothness, the strength.

With a gasp, he exploded, fountaining warm seed over her fingers. Her reaction—a rush of power and titillation—shocked her.

This she could do to him with a mere touch.

She wanted that to happen again, only inside her.

"Rhian," he moaned, and drew her back up to lie on his chest. They gazed, searching, into one another's eyes.

She saw there what she felt. Wonder. Victory. Naught of doubt.

"Beautiful lady, fro' this moment, I am yours. Understand that? Yours alone."

Foolish tears clogged her throat.

He said, still more devoutly, "I will no' give ye up. Never for aught. I will no'."

"Ye may have to go back to MacLeod. If Rory be dead—"

"Hush. Do no' speak o' that now. We will strike a truce. We will find a way."

"To be together."

"We are together." He threaded his fingers through hers, clenched them tight. "Just like this."

Unbreakable. A bond that twined the two of them together. Against reason, against common sense.

How strange it was that he had lived the whole of his life at MacLeod—a place she could see on a clear day. Going about his life. Practicing at arms. Paying court to other women, for she knew full well such a man had done. Laughing and drinking and enjoying.

And she here, following her more serious pursuits. Lighting fires, and putting them out. Soothing troubled waters. Taking the place of her ma, the born peacemaker. Neither of them aware of the other all those years. And now neither of them able to live without the other.

Gravely, they gazed at one another. "How can this be?" she whispered. "So strong. So complete."

He shook his head slightly. All humor had fled his face. "I

canna say. Rhian, merciful angel, promise me but one thing."

"What is it?"

"That ye will no' doubt me. Do no' doubt wha' I feel for ye. It is true."

"If ye promise no' to doubt me in turn. I ken how hard it maun be. There are so many influences upon the both o' us."

He tightened his fingers on hers. "Ye might ha' been sent to seduce me."

She gave a snort. "They would ha' sent a better seductress than I, were that true. Leith, I am a simple woman, interested in only the tasks before me. I never—I never expected this."

"Nor I." He gave a rueful grimace. "I ha' always been a man to skip fro' woman to woman. They touched me all, but never laid claim to my heart." He seemed to struggle for words. "Ye ha' done just that, Rhian. My heart lies in your keeping, whether ye will ha' it or no'."

"I will ha' it, Leith MacLeod." Softly she kissed him again. "We will trust one another, aye? No matter what else may happen around us. Whether they decide to send ye awa'. Whether or no' ye become chief o' my enemies."

"Wha'ever may happen," he vowed. "Do no' doubt me, Rhian."

"Do no' doubt me, Leith."

They sealed the promise with a kiss, a strength, Rhian thought, against whatever might come.

Chapter Thirty-Four

LEITH DOZED AND woke and dozed again, and tried to convince himself what had happened had been more than a dream. Rhian, holding him in her arms. Taking him to her bosom. Shedding kisses upon him like separate shards of brightness. Wrapping her fingers around him as if it were the most natural of things, and she could do naught else.

He had to believe it. Though she'd left him now to go about her duties, she had been here. It had all happened. He could feel her still.

That was the truly uncanny part of it. He could feel her in the lingering touch on his skin. In the ache beneath his heart. He'd even had a glimpse of what lay in her mind.

A quiet woman, Rhian MacBeith. One used to giving to others. She did not make waves, and she took little for herself.

Leith would have said she was the last sort of woman to suit a man like him. Yet from the moment she'd found him on the battlefield, they had fit. She filled up the empty places inside him. His need for her frightened him.

Big, strong warrior, he marveled, half mocking himself. With this flaming need for a gentle woman.

Ah, but he would be a strong warrior no more if he did not regain the use of his right arm. And anyway, he could not deny her.

Rhian MacBeith—what she meant to him had the power to change his world.

Bonded with her, he was. What did that make of his loyalties? Those he owed to Rory, and to MacLeod.

Nay, he'd never expected such a thing to happen to a man like him.

The door rattled, and a voice called to him from outside. "Leith? Lift the bar, man."

Farlan. Leith had placed the bar across the door after Rhian left. He got to his feet now and padded across the chamber to let Farlan in.

Anxious and unhappy, Farlan entered the chamber, which at once felt too small with the two of them in it, and replaced the bar with his own hands. He turned and surveyed Leith through narrowed eyes.

"Ye look better, man."

"I feel it. The fever is gone and the pain has lessened. If only this accursed wound would close up for good."

"Ye'd best lie back down. We need to speak together."

Leith eyed his friend. "We ha' talked and talked. 'Tis enough."

Yet he returned to the bed and eased against the bolsters, since there was no place else in the chamber to sit. Farlan perched at the foot, facing him.

Gravely, he said, "We maun discuss wha' is to be done, if Rory be dead."

Their eyes met, and they shared the impossibility of it. Surrounded as the two of them were by strangers—even those who might no longer be strangers—only they experienced the weight of that possible grief.

In the past they'd weathered other terrible losses together. That of Ainsley, who'd been Leith's little sister and Farlan's child bride. Of any number of friends lost in skirmishes. Of Camraith, with his bottomless kindness and wisdom. People went from the world, unbearably and unfairly.

But Rory? Rory was a force of nature. The leader of their tribe of three. The one who got them into trouble and out of it again. Quick to anger and equally quick in thought, he drove through life like a bull, allowing naught to get in his way.

Such a man could not be dead.

Leith replied, "I am no' sure I countenance that possibility."

"Nor I. But all men die, do they no'? Even men such as he."

Slowly Leith shook his head. Two years older than him, Rory had been there all his life. The lad grown into the man who would one day lead the clan. One tolerated his faults—that all-too-hasty temper, the stubborn, single-minded ambition, the refusal to acknowledge all but perfection in himself and others.

Because he was Rory MacLeod, a man who, like the chiefs of old, inspired men to greatness. Rory was a walking legend.

But aye, even such men fell.

"I regret," Farlan said steadily and with sorrow, "I may no' have a chance to make up my quarrel wi' him. We were like brothers once."

"And are still." If Rory lived. "Brothers fall out. The bonds between them do no' break."

"I think those bonds sundered when he banished me, stripped me o' both my birthright and my name o' MacLeod."

"He loves ye still. I saw the grief upon him after ye left. Grief." Leith's gaze met that of his friend. "And wounded pride. He did no' believe ye would go through wi' it and forsake him."

"For a woman." Farlan's lips twisted.

"For a woman," Leith concurred.

"He is all pride, is Rory. I sometimes think 'tis mostly his pride behind this campaign to take over the whole o' the glen. He wants to be the man who achieves what his ancestors could not."

"Aye, but Farlan, it has no' been going well for him, this campaign. I tell ye, he thought wi' both the old chiefs out o' his way, he would roll right over Clan MacBeith. So far he's done naught but throw himself against the stones o' this keep and be driven awa' again. It maun have him in a rage." *If he lived.* "He will no' give up."

"He is too stubborn to give up. But Leith"—Farlan leaned forward and clapped Leith's knee—"we ha' a chance to salvage things. For the good o' the clan. For all o' us."

Farlan got up from the bed to pace and swallowed hard before he went on. "If Rory be dead, ye are chief o' Clan MacLeod."

"Aye." Leith did not want the place. Nor could he dispute it.

Farlan went on steadily, his voice soft. "Rory has no idea what lies here. There's a kind o' magic. I believe that's what has kept him from succeeding in overthrowing this clan. That and the courage o' the three sisters MacBeith."

Leith eyed his friend doubtfully. A big, strapping man to be speaking of magic. And yet—there was healing in Rhian's touch. And he'd heard the words in her mind. Could he say a kind of magic did not exist in this place?

Farlan went on just as if he did not discuss wonders. "Mistress Saerla, the youngest o' them, has the Sight. She has gone up on the rise now, where the sacred stones lie ye ken, to try to See whether or no' Rory remains alive. Her two sisters ha' gone wi' her to lend their support."

Leith did not know what to say to this incredible pronouncement.

Farlan stumbled on. "If she returns wi' an answer, if Rory be dead—no' that I want him to be—'twill change everything."

"Aye." So it would.

"Wi' me here at MacBeith and ye in charge at MacLeod, Leith, we could choose peace."

Leith made a face. "But I am no' at MacLeod. I am a prisoner here, and maimed."

"No' maimed. Put your faith in Mistress Rhian. I believe she too possesses a measure o' magic. She can heal ye, man."

Och, aye. Rhian could save him, if anyone could.

"Still and all, even if I do regain the use o' my arm, for all ye ha' said, I am no' likely to be released and sent home."

"If we can come to an agreement, I believe ye will."

"An agreement. For peace."

"A treaty. For peace, aye. Ha' we no', the two o' our clans, existed here for generations? If ye as chief, and Moira along wi' me strike an agreement to divide our holdings fairly at the loch and leave off wi' killing one another… D'ye no' see?"

Leith did. It fair made him dizzy. "Would this council ye keep banging on about agree?"

"If we can offer them peace? I think so." Again, Farlan slapped Leith's knee. "You and I are as good as brothers. Joined by love o' Ainsley, we were. And the best o' friends. Ye be no' a man for war."

No, Leith was not a man for war. He preferred laughter and feasting. Games and singing. If they managed to strike a peace…

What was to say he could not then convince Rhian MacBeith to come to MacLeod and live with him?

As his wife.

Och, and only listen to him! A man such as he, thinking about marriage. Yet she lay already inside him, deep inside. What else was there but to put all his trust in that, even as he placed it in her? To forge earthly bonds to match those of spirit that already held him to her.

Farlan was a reasonable man. So was he. Two reasonable men should be able to come to some sort of agreement that might benefit everyone.

He did not want to be chief, nay. But if it meant Rhian Mac-Beith might be his for all time…

"Aye," he said softly. "Aye, Farlan. Let us, you, me, and your lady, come to an agreement."

"Ye be willing?"

"I be willing."

And so it seemed the future rested on whether or not his cousin, chief, and best friend in all the world was dead.

Chapter Thirty-Five

As it so often did, the wind on the height blew strong, making Rhian feel almost as if she might take flight.

Now it gusted the gloaming into the glen. The sky never truly grew dark at this time of year, but the hills cast shadows and the shushing of the wind made them seem alive, as if they breathed. Great, crouching, shaggy beasts, she used to think the hills were when she was young. Da had laughed about it.

Da.

His grave lay just behind her, the great cairn raised by the hands of his people. Each stone laid with honor and love. She herself had laid many of them, and with every one had relived a memory.

They should not be up here alone in the creeping dark, the three sisters MacBeith. Not without a guard, anyway. Still, Moira wore her sword, Saerla carried a dirk in her boot, and Rhian, as always, had a wee sgian-dubh hidden in her pocket.

No woman, not even a healer, should go without a weapon. She *was* a healer, though—to her bones a peacemaker and a soother of troubled waters. Could she use her sgian-dubh, if a horde of ugly MacLeod warriors came screaming up the rise?

To defend her sisters? Och, aye. Not all MacLeod warriors, though, were ugly.

She remembered Leith MacLeod lying against the bolsters of

her bed, looking at her with eyes the color of the gray-blue distances on a dreamy morning. She recalled—relived— unfastening the front of her dress for him. The warm tug of his lips at her breast. Claiming her soul.

She wanted to be with him again so much she ached. She was here with her sisters instead.

They stood in a row, hands linked, with Saerla at their center facing the glen. Saerla had requested Rhian and Moira's presence, insisted they would help strengthen her as she sought to use her Sight. Her previous attempts to See whether or not Rory MacLeod still lived had been inconclusive. So she'd brought them here, the holiest spot on MacBeith land.

Rhian had no idea how Saerla did what she did. In the past, her dreamy-eyed younger sister had tried to explain it to her.

'Tis a bit like chasing the remnants o' a dream right after ye've awakened. The harder ye try, the more it slips awa' from ye.

The Sight could not be forced. It came when it chose, often without warning, or not at all. But with courage, it might be sought.

As Saerla now aimed to do.

She stood with her eyes closed against the pull of the wind, her expression intent. Rhian held her right hand and Moira her left. Through the connection made by their fingers, Rhian could feel…

Saerla's tension, aye. Her concentration, all intermingled uncannily with her determination. Fragile, did Saerla often seem, despite the armor and weapons she so frequently donned. But now Rhian felt her strength, like the granite that lay beneath the green turf of this place they loved.

Rhian shot a glance across Saerla's back and met Moira's gaze. Moira looked as incredulous as Rhian felt, her lips pressed together in a tight line, her gaze wide with wonder.

They had both witnessed Saerla enfolded by the Sight before. Rhian did not think she'd ever seen her seek a Vision this way.

Saerla's fingers, clutching hers, suddenly tightened. "Sisters, lend me your strength. Gi' me your power."

Power? Rhian did not think she possessed any. Not at least anything akin to what she could feel now within Saerla. Rhian had kindled many a fire in her life, and nurtured them. They started with a spark, reached out for fuel and air, grew and fed and gathered heat.

So did the magic inside Saerla. Rhian, catching but the edges of it, ceased to breathe with wonder. She closed her mind to the beauty of the glen and gave herself over to the sensation.

Suddenly they were one, the three sisters MacBeith. Aye, so, they'd always been linked. Close. Now it was as if they shared one life, drew one breath. The bonds that united them stretched deep into the earth beneath their feet, to the glen below, to the ring of stones behind them and the grave beside which they stood. Da's grave. He was here with them.

Rhian could feel him just as she could feel the magic inside Saerla. Strong, but like the mist above the loch on a soft day, it swirled.

Take what ye need o' me, sister, Rhian thought at Saerla, and felt the pull as her sister did just that. The magic inside Saerla re-formed and made a picture.

Rhian could see only the edges of it, a flickering of light. Movement and dark and brightness. Not enough to tell—

But Saerla engaged. The power reared up inside her so she rose onto her toes. Fully taken by the Vision, she *Saw.*

Rhian dared not breathe, for fear of spoiling it. She could feel Moira from all the way on Saerla's other side, doing the same. They stood so, eyes closed, anchored to the rock and the magic in the stones, and to each other, until Saerla made a choking sound and went down.

She fell so suddenly, so abruptly, that Rhian felt it like a blow. Saerla crumpled, and her fingers pulled from Rhian and Moira's, breaking their connection. Rhian exclaimed and went down on her knees beside her sister.

"Saerla?"

Saerla lay half on her back with her eyes closed and absolutely no color in her face. She did not appear to be breathing.

"Saerla!" Moira cried, her voice sounding like that of a bird, echoing Rhian's own. "Rhian, by God! Do something."

Rhian laid her hands on her sister's breast. A healing gesture it was, one she had used instinctively many times with many patients. She had touched Leith just so.

Now she felt the healing flow from her own fingers into her sister, and for the first time recognized it for what it was.

Love.

Da! Da, help us. Help me save her.

Saerla did not stir beneath Rhian's hands. Rhian leaned closer, seeking, seeking…

A hint of a breath, the thud of a heartbeat.

"Saerla," Moira sobbed.

She could not be gone, this beautiful sister of theirs. Not like this. They had already lost so much.

Rhian closed her own eyes, massaged her sister's chest with imploring fingers, and called, *Come.*

She might have been calling her father still, or Saerla herself. Something else came. She felt it surge up from the green turf beneath her knees and from the stones. From Moira.

Strength. Healing.

Saerla twitched beneath her hands. Low but strong, her heart began to beat. Breath surged into her lungs.

Rhian opened her eyes and looked at her sister. The wind still buffeted the three of them here on the ground. It stirred Saerla's bright hair. It seemed to flutter her eyelashes when she opened her eyes.

"Aye," Rhian crooned. "Aye, wee love, ye are back wi' us."

Wee love had been Ma's pet name for Saerla. Rhian wondered if, in that moment, she had not become her mother. For just one instant.

Long enough.

"Is she all right?" Tears flowed down Moira's cheeks. She

wept so seldom that it made Rhian stare. "Wha' happened?"

"I do no' ken. Saerla?"

"Here, help me sit up." Saerla struggled, and they both assisted her, once more lending their strength. A bit of color returned to her face, though not as much as Rhian wanted to see.

"Sit quietly yet." She laid gentle hands on Saerla's shoulders, both supporting and holding her down.

Saerla began to draw great, deep breaths. Through the remnants of their connection and her fingers on Saerla's shoulders, Rhian felt her calm.

Moira did not wait long to ask of Saerla, "Wha' happened?"

A few moments longer Saerla took to quiet herself. "I did no' receive the Vision I sought. Or"—she gazed away, out over the glen—"mayhappen I did."

Rhian and Moira exchanged glances, Moira appearing as concerned as Rhian felt—and Rhian's concern ran deep.

She never should have allowed Saerla to make this attempt. Aye, her sister was fey and steeped in magic. But all too plainly, somewhat had gone awry.

"Wha' did ye see?" Moira asked. She licked her lips before going on, "Somewhat terrible bad, was it? Ye canna deny ye received a Vision, for I caught the edges of it."

"Aye," Rhian whispered.

Instead of giving them an answer, Saerla lowered her forehead to her upraised knees and pressed tight.

Again, Rhian and Moira exchanged horrified looks.

Moira's voice sounded dry as that of an old woman when she asked, "Are we to be destroyed, then? Is MacBeith to go down to defeat?"

"Nay. That is no' what I Saw."

"Then what?" Rhian trembled badly.

Saerla lifted her head, and Rhian got a glimpse of her face—pale, stark, and with terrible knowledge.

"I will no' say."

"Sister." Moira put her arms around Saerla's shoulders.

"There is naught so terrible ye canna share it wi' us."

"There is, and I will no'. All ye need to know now is, Rory MacLeod lives. He lives yet."

Chapter Thirty-Six

"WHAT DO YE think she Saw?"

Moira whispered the words to Rhian as they worked together over bundles of provisions to be given the sick and elderly. Fiona had been helping them with the task, but she had gone off with two younger women to make some deliveries, leaving Rhian and her sister alone.

Rhian glanced up into Moira's face, which reflected her own unease.

"I do no' ken, and she will no' say."

"That is verra unlike Saerla." Rhian would have said Moira, with the cool head, was not one to fret though she clearly fretted now. Of course, Rhian would have said Moira was not a woman to lose her head over a man, either.

"Usually," Moira went on, "she feels it her duty to speak o' what she Sees, especially if it concerns someone else."

"True." Rhian thought about it. "Mayhap it does no' concern anyone else." Her gaze met Moira's again. "Perhaps 'twas somewhat to do wi' Saerla alone."

"Aye. But what?"

"Something that frightened her." Rhian felt sure of that, if nothing else.

Moira looked stricken. "D'ye suppose," she asked in a hushed voice, "she saw her own death? She said—she said Rory MacLeod still lives. That being so, there will be further battles. As we learned wi' Da, anyone can fall."

It was true. Saerla might, or Moira. Or Farlan. Saerla would not want to say.

Rhian swallowed something bitter. "If we could persuade her to tell us, we might be better prepared. Keep whomever it is fro' battle. Try to protect him or her."

"Aye. 'Tis always my instinct, that, to protect. But sister, can one protect against destiny?"

"I do no' ken. The way Saerla explains it, there can be more than one destiny laid out, like paths to be chosen."

"She did tell me that, back when I was trying to decide wha' I must do about my feelings for Farlan."

"So aye, if she would tell us the danger, we might try to prepare for a choice, at least."

Moira gave Rhian a hard look. "Ye maun persuade her to tell us. I think she will better confide in ye than me."

"Will she?" Rhian doubted it. "If she believes she is protecting one o' us, or all o' us, by keeping the information to hersel', she will never say."

Moira squeezed Rhian's hand. "Try, sister, will ye no'?"

Rhian nodded. "I will go and search her out just as soon as we finish here."

"Fiona and I can finish. Ye go and find Saerla."

It took the better part of the afternoon. Wherever Rhian went in search of Saerla, it seemed she had just left. The armory. The kitchen. The training field. At last she ran Saerla to ground on the battlements, having been directed there by no less than Alasdair.

The wind still blew hard up here, as it had earlier on the height. It seized Rhian's hair and tore it from the loose knot she wore, scattering it around her face. When she clawed it out of the way, she saw Saerla leaning on the top of the wall.

"Sister?"

Saerla did not look pleased to see her. In fact, her expression revealed little emotion. Careful. Shut down.

So unlike Saerla.

"Wha' are ye doing awa' up here?"

"Naught." Yet when Rhian first came up, she'd caught Saerla staring away across the glen. Toward the MacLeod stronghold.

She stepped into place beside Saerla, trying to decide on the best approach. "How d'ye feel?"

"I am fine."

"Are ye certain? Ye did fall senseless, up on the rise."

Saerla turned her head and looked at Rhian, her eyes wide and filled with mist. "I am no' senseless now."

"Nay, but—"

"I ha' all my wits about me, sister."

"Verra well. I only wondered—"

"Do no' ask, Rhian." Saerla's voice throbbed with intensity.

"But 'tis plain ye Saw something troubling, something that has frightened ye. If ye share wi' us what it was, we may the better seek to defend ye or whomever ye ha' Seen."

"There is no defense fro' this, Rhian. And it concerns only me. In this"—she gave a sad smile—"my twa sisters canna protect me. I maun look after mysel'."

Rhian's heart trembled with love. "That does no' seem right."

"Trust me, it is. Can ye trust me?"

"Of course. But there are times we all need one another. And—and it seemed so terrible, what ye Saw. Why should ye try to bear it alone?"

"Because I must. I am well now, sister. No ill effects from what struck me down. Ye would better spend your time tending those who need your care."

"Aye." Rhian's mind flailed over it, but she could think of no more to say. Except… "If ye need me, Saerla, if ye need at any time to unburden yoursel', ye should come to me. Day or night, aye?"

Saerla gave her a challenging look. "Even when you lie wi' yon Leith MacLeod?"

Heat rose to Rhian's face. "I did no' lie wi' him!"

"Perhaps not, but ye did no' share my chamber either, as ye claimed. So at the very least, ye shared yours wi' him instead."

Breath gusted from Rhian. "Is that wha' ye Saw? Me and—and Leith?"

Saerla shook her head. "I told ye, it concerned only mysel'. Why, is there somewhat I might See as regards ye and him?"

"Nay. Mayhap. 'Tis no' easily explained."

Saerla stared away across the glen. "Wha' is it about these MacLeod men?"

"He is a good man, Saerla, when ye come to talk wi' him. Not like ye would suppose. And the feelings I ha' for him are strong, I will no' deny."

"Ewan and the other members o' the council will ne'er countenance it. And I canna imagine what Alasdair will say."

Rhian did not want to imagine. "There is naught at the moment to countenance. I thought—hoped—if Rory MacLeod were dead, if Leith became Chief MacLeod, he and Farlan might forge some alliance. For peace."

"A fine dream. But Rory remains very much alive. Gravely wounded, but alive."

"It was him you Saw, then?"

Saerla nodded.

"Well, if he be gravely wounded, at least that may give us some time." Time to get Leith up on his feet. Time to talk him around and attempt to argue out a treaty that he might try to persuade Rory to accept when he returned home.

When he left her. Unbearable even to imagine.

Saerla looked at her. "Does Leith say Rory MacLeod is a man disposed for peace? Because I do no' think it so. Fro' wha' I ha' Seen, he is a man of anger and violence."

Again, Rhian wondered precisely what Saerla had Seen. Naught of good, not for any of them.

Chapter Thirty-Seven

RHIAN RETURNED TO her chamber at nightfall. The soft light of the gloaming filtered in through the narrow slit window by the time she arrived, filling the chamber with soft radiance. Leith, listening hard, caught the quick patter of her footsteps and lifted the bar on the door for her.

It had been a long day without her company. He'd tried to keep off his feet as much as possible because he did not want the accursed wound to start bleeding again. He'd spent the time, much of it, thinking about Rhian and wishing she would return.

The balance of his thoughts had all revolved around Rory, and what Farlan had told him. The possibility he could become chief, and for the very worst of reasons.

His cousin was difficult at times, aye. Hotheaded and single-minded. But he remained close to Leith in blood and heart.

Were Rory MacLeod gone from the world, naught would ever be the same. No one could fill his place. Leith, in particular, could not—he had less ambition in his whole body than Rory harbored in his smallest finger.

He did not want the place of chief.

Not even if it meant he might have Rhian MacBeith in his life? Ah, well, that was a different matter.

Could he discipline himself to take up duties and responsibilities he loathed if it meant a treaty, an end to the slaughter, and the right mayhap to wed with Rhian? To live with her somewhere, either here or at MacLeod. Sleep with her in his arms every night. Feel the peace that came of being in her presence.

He could not fairly say what he would give in exchange for that. Quite possibly anything he had to.

She slipped into the chamber and swept him with one bright glance before dropping her gaze to the basket she carried. The swift look, though, betrayed much, as did the warm color in her face.

He could feel her desire. Rhian MacBeith, though, was not the woman to put herself forward or boldly express such desire.

Good thing he was bold enough for both of them. "Rhian—"

"How is that wound? Has it been bleeding?"

"Nay. The pain is less." He did not want to talk about that. "Rhian—"

"Good. Let me change the bandages and get a fair look at it."

He moved back onto the bed. It was where he wanted to be anyway, at least if she joined him.

She perched on the side of the bed and bent to him. He could smell her—the same scent that haunted this chamber and her pillow even when she was not here. Herbs and woman.

Her hands moved competently. "I will try no' to hurt ye."

He watched her work over him, the rise and fall of her lashes. The deep wisdom in her eyes. The luscious lips that betrayed the passion he'd tasted in her.

He waited till she smoothed the bandages before capturing her hand and bringing it to his chest. Och, and he could feel it, that almost magical sense of claiming and peace.

"Kiss me, Rhian."

He thought she meant to refuse, make up some excuse, say she was there only to tend him. Instead she leaned to him, face bright. She pressed her mouth to his.

The taste of her defied words. Like ripe berries in summer, perhaps. A draught of cold water when he was dry. All the good things that had ever come to him.

He let her kiss him. For the space of twenty heartbeats he did, while he held on to his passion. She did it delicately and yet with heat. The combination fair turned him inside out.

Releasing her hand, he wound his arm around her and drew her down to lie atop him. They kissed and kissed, and kissed.

He wanted to memorize her. The taste and the heat of her mouth. The way her tongue flirted with his. Shy, and then unabashedly forthright. That was Rhian.

His Rhian.

He broke the kiss only to say raggedly, "Stay wi' me tonight."

She did not gainsay it. She did not play at being coy or pretend she did not feel what he felt. "I will."

He threaded his fingers into her hair, forcing her to meet his gaze. "I do no' mean just stay wi' me. I mean, let me mak' love to ye."

"I will."

No shadows filled her eyes now, no doubt. Only desire.

He'd already barred the door after she slipped in. The fire burned low and the gloaming crept in. Leith drew a breath, aware that his heartbeat shook his whole body. That he was being given a priceless gift.

"Lass. Beautiful, merciful angel."

"Let us see," she whispered, "just how merciful I can be."

THE LIGHT OUTSIDE the window faded to muted gray as they tangled together in the bed. Leith felt half afraid that if he moved too quickly or spoke too loudly, it would break the spell. For it was a spell of magic that brought Rhian here to him.

When she undressed for him, he lost all his breath. He'd seen her with her bodice open, aye. Had buried his face between her breasts. This seemed different. She shed her garments while resting her gaze upon him, revealing skin of pale white, those rosy-tipped breasts, and long, long legs with a triangle of auburn curls between them. When she came down onto the bed and laid herself against him, he thought he would die.

He did not deserve such a woman as this. She made him humble and hard as iron. A bewildering, if delightful, condition.

"Allow me to undress ye, Leith."

He was not wearing much. No sark, since he'd not wanted to wrestle that garment on over his bandages. His kilt only, and his smalls beneath.

She divested him of both, using those soft, competent hands. She, being a woman of some knowledge, could not possibly mistake his condition.

Wrapping his good arm around her, he drew her down to lie on top of him. Slim and supple, she might make half of him in size. Likely twice of him in strength.

"Rhian MacBeith." He gazed into her eyes. "I ha' ne'er known a woman to match ye."

"Ye do no' know me, yet."

"That's readily mended."

"I ha' never been wi' any man."

"Ha' ye no'?"

She shook her head, her gaze not shying from his.

"I'll do my best no' to cause ye any pain."

Her mouth drew upward in a curious smile. She dropped a kiss at one corner of his lips and then the other. "'Tis my understanding," she said almost teasingly, "desire takes awa' the sting. If that be true, I will feel naught o' pain."

Whether she did or she did not, he heard nary a whisper of it from her, nor a complaint. Sighs, a moan or two, sobs of pleasure. A word or two of demand. When they joined…

But Leith had no words for that either, no way to express what felt to him like a holy experience. He understood the act of lying with a woman. A man brought his partner as much enjoyment as he could, and took his own pleasure in the doing. He might laugh with her along the way, and glory in the rush of it all. Naught more.

This, though, caught his emotions and drew them hard into the act. Just as if that longing Rhian had somehow placed beneath his heart was connected to what she felt, each movement and each caress. Her desire became his, and his became hers.

And when he slid into her and they became one—he wanted naught so much as to stay buried to the hilt for the rest of his life.

Aye, and that had never happened to him before either. Usually, after bedding a woman, he was off and away as soon as the pleasure peaked. He'd ascertain his partner's state of body and mind, don his clothing, and leave her with a smile.

This could not be more different. This stole all his breath and half his sense. Claimed his spirit. Unwilling still to ruin the spell, he remained there inside her after he spilled his seed, and she lay beneath him as quiet as he.

He opened his eyes and looked at her. Her face lay just beneath his own, transfixed with some emotion he could not name. He knew, because he had felt it, that he'd brought her pleasure, waves of it that had drawn him more deeply inside her. He wanted no more from life than this.

Was it the same for her?

Words appeared in his mind, those he'd never spoken to any woman he'd bedded.

I love ye. I love ye right well.

Her eyes opened, deep, deep blue the color of a night sky. Breath surged into him all at once, and he knew he would never in a lifetime plumb the depths of this woman.

She said, "And I love ye also, Leith MacLeod."

They realized at the same instant what had happened, that once again they'd shared what had been no more than a thought in his mind.

"Och, lass," he whispered. "How can this be?"

"I do no' ken. I do no' care." She dropped the softest of kisses on his bottom lip. "'Tis a wonder. But for ye to love a MacBeith and me to love a MacLeod—"

Rueful now, he told her, "It has been done before."

"Aye. But no' wi'out a heavy load o' sorrow."

"I will tak' the sorrow," he vowed to her. "I will tak' whatever may come if it means I might ha' ye also."

"Whatever comes," she returned, "I am yours, both body and spirit."

⸙ ⟞⟞⟞⟞⟞⟞⟞⟞⟞ ✦ ⟞⟞⟞⟞⟞⟞⟞⟞⟞ ⸙

Chapter Thirty-Eight

THEY SLEPT IN one another's arms, and when Rhian awoke, she felt changed. So a woman would expect to feel, she reasoned, lying there with her cheek on Leith's warm chest. Being plucked for the first time was, by anyone's accounting, a transformative occurrence. No longer a maiden, and she'd waited long enough for it.

Still and all, she'd never imagined it would feel like this. Women who had confided in her in the past, both as friend and as healer, reported far different experiences. A measure of awkwardness sometimes. Pain, aye. Not this—this sea of desire that had carried her almost without thought. Not this powerful rightness.

When he had been inside her—well, it had felt so perfect that she'd been afraid to breathe. It felt as if, for the first time in her life, she was complete.

How could that be, when she never suspected she'd been wanting?

And what about the fact that she could sometimes hear the thoughts in Leith's mind?

Right now, she heard no thoughts. He slept. The chamber had grown very dark, the embers of the fire dying to sparks of orange. She could barely see Leith.

She did not have to. The warmth of him enfolded her. His

good arm wrapped around her and cupped one breast. The bad arm, on the side away from her, hung limp. She could feel...

She could feel all of him. Hints—like brief flickers—of pain from that arm. The movement of dreams in his mind. *He dreamed of her.*

And she, she wanted the man again. The desire—also unexpected—was ferocious. She, being anything but a ferocious woman, found that surprising. But the scent of him stoked that fire. The feel of the crisp hair on his chest. The memory of him filling her.

She had only to tip up her face in order to brush a kiss on a cheek rough with beard. His body was so different from hers, yet something in him was so much the same. They fit to perfection.

She wanted that perfection again.

Ah, but she should let the man rest, sleep, and heal. Only a few days ago he'd been near death. She was a healer and needed to let him gather his strength.

Knowing that, she put out her tongue nevertheless and tasted him. The skin of his cheek and the seam between his lips. She felt it, delightfully, when he came awake. Felt his desire spike like the hearth fire when she tossed on a handful of dry kindling.

"Rhian."

Did he say her name aloud, or only in his mind?

"My love." She said that because she wanted to, needed to. These words she'd never addressed to any other man felt so good on her tongue. Just like him.

His hand stirred on her breast, the rough palm sliding over her skin till he found her nipple. She wanted his mouth there, though his fingers felt almost as good.

"How d'ye feel?" she asked him because, as a healer, she should.

"Grand." He smiled, and she felt as much as saw it in the dark. "And braw."

"Aye, so." The braw part of him grew against her thigh.

"In fact, I do no' ken when I felt better. 'Tis ye, Rhian Mac-

Beith." He dropped a kiss on her lips. "Ye mak' me—But I have no words."

She had none either, so she pressed her open mouth to his, and he dove into her. Time passed, unmeasured. She sensed it when their hearts began to beat in time.

Make love to me. She thought it so she would not have to stop kissing him in order to speak.

As ye wish, merciful angel.

His name for her, that was, though she was definitely no angel here with him. In the moments that followed, she knew not the meaning of resistance. She embraced abandon instead. Nothing was too much for her to give to him, or take.

The pleasure—och, the pleasure was enough to make a woman lose her mind. But above all that, she needed one thing.

I want ye inside me, she told him either aloud or in her head; she could not tell which. And when he was...

She wanted to sob for the rightness of it.

Stay, she begged him. *Inside me.*

She'd ended up on top of him, knees cradling his hips, joined to him with all of her. She raised her head and looked into his face. The first light came through the window. Morning. And she could see him.

This man she loved.

His fair hair lay in a tangle on the pillow. In his face remained no trace of humor. Serious, they both knew this was. A claiming. Sacred as marriage.

"Do no' move. Do ye no' dare move. I want to keep ye inside me."

"No' two persons," he agreed gravely, "but one."

"Aye. Leith—I had no idea I could feel this way."

"Nor I."

"I should let ye rest," she said, almost weeping. "Ye be an injured man."

"I do no' feel injured when I am inside ye. I feel—" He shook his head slowly, unable to say.

"Strong?" she suggested.

"Like naught can harm me. Naught could touch me. I will live forever."

"Forever wi' me."

"Always wi' ye."

"I must go out soon. I maun get up from this bed, go out and act as if—"

"As if ye ha' no just lain wi' the man who may or may no' be the next chief o' MacLeod?"

Rhian gasped. "Oh, I forgot! How could I forget? Saerla Saw that Rory is no' dead. Injured, aye, but still alive."

"Saerla *Saw?*"

"She sought and received a Vision."

All the breath left him in a rush. "That is good. I am no' the man to be chief MacLeod. Though"—he hesitated—"perhaps 'tis no' so good, for ye."

"What is good for you is good for me."

"But—"

"We will find a way, Leith MacLeod."

"But—"

"I *said*, we will find a way."

A smile lit his eyes. "Aye, m'lady. Whate'er ye say. I am ever obedient."

⇥⟫⟫⟫⟪⟪⟪⇤

SHE HURRIED OUT, intent on going about her duties and her visits, and almost at once met Moira. The two of them were up so early, she about her mother's former tasks, and Moira, if Rhian was not mistaken, about Da's former ones.

"Sister, where are ye bound?" she asked.

"The battlements, to check the guard." Doubt and unease flickered in Moira's eyes. "Now that we ken Rory MacLeod is alive—"

"Aye." Rhian drew a breath. For a short time in Leith's embrace, she'd been able to lay the fears and worries aside. How could she have thought, even with him inside her, she could defeat them entirely?

With him inside her.

"But surely," she suggested to Moira, "he will no' renew the attack so soon. Saerla did say he was sore hurt."

"Aye." Moira pressed her lips into a tight line. "And Farlan has told me again and again, that will no' stop him. Rory has met defeat on our land time after time. Each attack he has launched upon us since Da's death has left him creeping awa' again. Farlan says Rory does no' accept such defeats readily. 'Twill mak' him more determined than ever to overthrow us."

The very idea had Rhian's fears rising again. "Wha's to be done?"

Moira jerked her head at the battlements. "Keep up an eagle-eyed watch and a strong defense. Decide wha' will be in our best interest."

"Such as?" Rhian asked with considerable trepidation. She did not think Moira the woman to carry the battle forth and attack MacLeod while the injury to their chief made them vulnerable. But Alasdair was quite possibly the man for it. And Moira no longer led the clan on her own.

Moira shook her head. "There will be another meeting of the council later today to discuss just that." She hesitated but a moment. "Sister, in your opinion, how much harm will it do the prisoner to be sent back at once to MacLeod?"

Dismay washed over Rhian, so powerful her knees trembled. How much harm? To Leith, physically—and to her own heart. She flashed back to last night—him lying beneath her, his gaze locked to hers as he flexed his strong body and came to her. Came *in* her.

"Sister? What is it? Is he dying?"

"Nay. I believe he is on his way to recovery," Rhian lied to her sister, something she'd done but a few times in her life. "But no' ready—no' ready to travel that distance yet."

She needed him with her. Inside her. Needed it with unprecedented hunger.

Moira, of all women, should understand that. She was in love with Farlan, he of the even temper and steady gaze.

Aye, but this thing between Rhian and Leith was private. Pure and magical. She could not speak of it yet.

Moira laid a hand on Rhian's forearm. "I ken, sister, that ye hate losing a patient. Heal him up well, and heal him up fast. He may need to return to MacLeod as soon as possible."

Rhian nodded. When she parted from her sister, it was with a heavy heart.

✦ ━━━━━━━━ ✦ ━━━━━━━━ ✦

Chapter Thirty-Nine

RHIAN NEVER KNEW at what point during that long day she became aware—aware of the change within her. It might have been while she tended her many patients, her attention focused on them. When she peeled away stinking bandages and administered draughts.

While she treated the festering stump where young Fergus's hand had once been, as Calan, Fergus's best friend, stood by anxiously waiting for reassurance she could not give. The two young men were just barely eighteen, and had grown and trained at arms together.

Rhian did not think she could save Fergus. It was going to break Calan's heart.

Or it might have been during the later meeting of the council, which Moira had begged Rhian and Saerla to once more attend. Calan was there also, one of a few younger men joining that august body.

It was possible the knowledge just crept upon her, filtered through like the blood in her veins—the desire that simmered inside her, a steady fire in a hearth. She was the hearth, and the fire quickened.

She carried Leith MacLeod's child.

She'd always had an instinct for such things, as had her mother before her. Women could come to her early and ask whether they were carrying a child, and she could sense it. She could often also tell whether the bairn was a lad or a lass.

As soon as conviction flitted through her and became undeniable—during the meeting in the hall—she knew that also.

The child Leith had given her was a boy.

It must have happened that morning when he remained so deep inside her, leaving his seed and staying seated in place. When their hearts had beaten as one, and it seemed impossible, now that she thought about it, that she could *not* conceive his child.

His child. A MacLeod.

The prospect both thrilled and terrified her—that it should happen so quickly, so easily, whatever their feelings for one another.

As a healer, she knew it did happen, even after only one mating. Even after a rape. Whether the child was desperately wanted or not.

Did she want this child? This bairn she sensed like a sliver of flame stirring within her?

She'd never planned on having children. She took care of so many others. She did not need anyone else looking to her for care.

Yet this child, half MacBeith and half MacLeod—surely he was meant to be?

This she contemplated even as Ewan, along with other members of the council, including Alasdair, reviled the MacLeods. While they floated wild schemes for attacking their enemies before Rory MacLeod made a recovery. While they pondered the advantages of Leith's death.

Calan, who harbored a fierce anger Rhian had no doubt was enhanced by his grief over Fergus, dragged the discussion back to Moira and Farlan.

"I still say it is no' right to ha' a MacLeod here clinging to the skirts o' power. I say he should be sent back to MacLeod along wi' this Leith, who might or might no' be Rory MacLeod's heir.

Rid ourselves o' the filth once and for all."

There were mutters of agreement from a few council members.

Moira's face went white with anger, though she gave no other sign of it. She glanced at Alasdair before she said, "Farlan is going nowhere. He canna be sent back to MacLeod, at any rate. He's been cast out and is no longer welcome there."

"No' welcome here either," said one of Calan's fellow warriors.

Ewan turned to Saerla with a hint of desperation. "Mistress, be ye certain yon Rory MacLeod still lives?" She'd already told them so at the beginning of the meeting, but they were enamored of the idea he might be out of their way, and reluctant to surrender it.

"Aye."

"Then," Ewan declared, "this Leith MacLeod is no good to us, if he is no' due to become chief in his own right. I say we either slaughter him or send him back."

And what would happen, Rhian wondered madly, when she began to show? When she at last revealed she carried Leith's child?

Moira drew a breath that said she fought for patience. "We ha' been over and over this. Leith remains o' use to us because he and Farlan may be able to forge a plan for peace."

"Farlan!" Ewan fairly spat the name. "I am interested in naught that traitor says. He could no' remain true to his own clan. Why should he deal honestly wi' us?"

Moira surged to her feet beside the fire. Something sharp as a naked blade shone from her eyes. "I trust him."

"Aye." Far more slowly, Ewan rose also. "And there, I am thinking, lies the problem. Alasdair? Wha' d'ye say?"

Alasdair, seated beside Moira, did not stir. In fact, he seemed a bit *too* still, and his stony expression did not change.

"Farlan," he said, "is a man wi'out a clan and has no reason to betray us."

"If," Calan interjected, "this story about him being cast off is true and no' some ruse to get him in close to our heart."

Rhian looked at Calan with new respect. The lad had the makings of a tactician.

Alasdair ignored the outburst. "Leith MacLeod, though, is another matter. His loyalty to his chief is undisputed. He is Rory's cousin and purportedly his heir." He raised dark eyes to the room. "Leith MacLeod is a dangerous man."

"I think they are both dangerous," Calan declared. "I believe 'tis a danger to all o' us if Mistress Moira takes Farlan MacLeod to wed."

"I will wed wi' him," Moira vowed, and Rhian heard her seething anger now. "I ha' but held off at the request o' this council."

"That is no' important now," Alasdair stated. "We ha' the advantage, thanks to Mistress Saerla, o' knowing Rory MacLeod is no' dead. We ha' only to decide wha' to do about it."

"Slaughter his heir," Ewan cried.

"Attack," said another of the men, "before he has time to recover."

"Send the MacLeod back," Calan added.

And Ewan asked again, "Alasdair, wha' d'ye say?"

Alasdair got to his feet, moving like a mountain. "Ye all ken I want revenge for the death o' our chief. And I would no' mind seeing every male o' MacLeod blood dead. But Chief Iain would no' wish us to disrespect his house. And his house is represented by his daughters now. I say Mistress Moira has a place at the head o' this clan, Farlan or no Farlan.

"And I think," he went on, "we would be far better wi' Leith MacLeod dead. Toss the coin and tak' our chances that Rory may die o' his wound after all, and pass wi'out an heir."

Nay. Rhian did not say it aloud, but Saerla turned her head sharply to look at her. Rhian wondered again—what was this terrible thing Saerla had Seen? She insisted her Vision had only to do with herself. But they were all so closely connected. Had she possibly Seen that Rhian would bear Leith's son? The next heir to MacLeod, if Rory did not survive. Did that somehow affect what would happen here, and to Saerla?

Rhian gasped, and Moira also looked at her. For a moment the three of them stood again united, their wills one.

Defend, nurture, enchant.

Rhian found words in her mouth and spoke them. "I think Leith is more use to us alive. Once he recovers, he will deal with Farlan and carry an intention for peace back to MacLeod."

"I agree," said Moira.

"I agree also," Saerla added in turn.

Members of the council glared. Alasdair nodded. "Iain Mac-Beith's daughters ha' spoken. We will do naught for now. Let Farlan talk wi' his friend. See wha' comes o' it."

Ewan cried in frustration, "We will miss our opportunity."

"Then we will ha' another, anon. Rory MacLeod may die after all." Alasdair shrugged. "We will stand strong and wait."

Rhian pressed a hand to her belly. She would. She must. She had double the reason now.

She turned as the meeting broke up and caught Saerla's gaze on her. Saerla, who saw far too much.

Chapter Forty

"YE LOOK BETTER, a good deal better," Farlan told Leith as he came in through the chamber door.

"I feel it." Leith replaced the bar across the door behind Farlan. "I believe this stubborn wound may be on its way to healing at last."

What he truly thought, though he would not say, was that Rhian herself had healed him. Nay, not in the ordinary way that she'd attempted all the while. Making love with her had changed him. Made him strong. Launched healing through his very blood. He felt better when she touched him and stronger when he was inside her.

Where he wanted to be again. Immersing himself in her presence. Feeling her all around him.

Instead, she'd not come near him today, not since she'd left him here this morning. Now the day grew old. He wanted her, and not just physically.

Would she return to him tonight? Could he endure that long?

He made a face at Farlan. "I am growing restless, that is certain."

"Means for certain ye be on the mend. I near went mad when I was penned up."

"Aye, so." Leith took a turn around the chamber, and Farlan eyed him, arms crossed over his chest. "Well? Ha' ye come to tell me they've decided to cut my throat?"

"Nay. For now, Moira wants to keep ye alive, and for now, Alasdair is respecting her wishes."

"For now."

"Aye. From what Moira tells me—for a turncoat such as I is no' allowed in meetings o' council—there are others who bitterly disagree."

"I do no' doubt it."

"Moira..." Farlan drew a breath. "Moira wants peace. She believes you and I, being close as brothers, can lay the ground-work for it, and then ye can take that back to Rory. Moira believes there is meaning in the fact that the three o' us—ye, me, and Rory—are so close."

"Moira does no' ken Rory."

"Nay. I ha' tried to explain to her he is driven and that the chances o' diverting him from his chosen path—conquest—are no' great. She seems to think there's some magic in it."

"There is a great deal o' magic here, Farlan. I ha' fallen victim to it myself."

Farlan nodded gravely. "Rhian?"

"I canna think for wanting her. 'Tis as if a spell has fallen over me."

"I am victim to that spell also."

"Is it the young sister, Saerla, who weaves it? She with the Sight?"

Farlan shrugged. "Mayhap. Or it may come from those stones on the height."

"I tell ye truly, I ha' never felt for any woman wha' I feel for Rhian."

"And ye, a charmer o' many a woman."

"Aye, so." Leith turned and looked Farlan in the eye. "I ha' no objection to forging a peace wi' ye, Farlan. I would do it for her sake alone. But ye and I forging a peace means naught. Rory will ne'er respect it."

"Aye, I ken. But I believe if ye agree to carry such an offer home, it will get ye awa' out o' here with your life."

Away. Out of here, apart from Rhian, unable to touch her, catch her scent, taste her again. Unable to experience the blinding rightness of being one with her.

"Farlan, I am no' certain I can leave."

Understanding flooded Farlan's eyes. "Aye, I ken. But if 'tis ultimately for Rhian's good—if we just may achieve an end to all this heartache and strife—"

"I do no' think we can. And leaving her will tear the heart out o' me."

Farlan said nothing. Aye, Leith figured he understood. This was a man who had surrendered his birthright and swum the loch near naked for the woman he loved.

"I ken fine," Leith burst out after a moment of silence, beginning to pace again, "there is such a thing as the greater good. 'Tis part o' the reason I never wanted the place o' chief. For ye ken as well as I, man, I ha' lived my life for my good, and little else."

"That changes. All that changes when ye lose yer heart to a woman."

Magnificent, it was. Terrifying.

"Think o' it this way, Leith. If we can forge a peace, the two o' ye will be able to be together. Someday."

"*Someday*. I am no' sure I can live long wi'out her. Besides," Leith cried in frustration, "I do no' believe Rory can be convinced."

"Leith, man, ye ha' to believe. Ye maun believe in the magic ye say binds ye and Rhian together."

He did believe in that. Up to a point.

"Me," Farlan went on, a bit ruefully, "I ha' been living for the belief that Moira and I are destined to be together. Despite all."

"Aye." And that had not been an easy road. "But ye are here wi' her now. No' awa' across the glen."

"I am here. Hated by everyone. Mistrusted and wished dead. By God, the only time I am at peace is when I am in her arms."

"I hear that, Farlan."

How strong was Leith? He'd lived his life lightly up to now, with enthusiasm and laughter. What would he give up for Rhian?

He drew a breath that expanded his chest and looked Farlan in the eye. "Verra well, my friend. Let us talk about a peace."

"Is all well wi' ye?"

The query sounded in Rhian's ear and startled her. She'd been so focused within that she'd failed to realize Saerla stood at her shoulder.

Now she spun and gazed into her sister's eyes. What did Saerla know? What had she noticed there in the meeting?

"Ye seem distracted," she said gently. "'Tis no' like ye."

"I have far too much on my mind."

Saerla nodded. They'd met on the path that led to the infirmary. She laid a hand on Rhian's arm and drew her aside to the shelter of a rowan tree.

"Sister, I wanted to ask ye. Did ye stay wi' yon Leith Mac-Leod last night? Because ye were no' wi' me."

Rhian had been expecting this question. Suddenly she found she could not quite meet Saerla's searching gaze. "Aye, I stayed wi' him."

"Rhian—"

"Ye need no' tell me 'tis madness. I already ken that. 'Tis mad and reckless and utterly unlike me. I canna help mysel'."

"The two o' ye made love?"

Again, Rhian wondered what her sister knew. Had she Seen that Rhian would bear Leith's child? His son?

"I love him, Saerla. And that is somewhat I never thought I would say of any man. I ken wha' men are. And women. I understand the traps and the consequences o' desire."

"Ye be a woman grown. I canna tell ye wha' to do, or wi' whom ye should or should no' lie down. But—"

"But?" Rhian repeated when Saerla's voice died away.

"I fear it canna end well."

Rhian seized Saerla's shoulders. "Ha' ye Seen his death?"

"Nay." Saerla shook her head. "No' that."

"Then what? Tell me."

"I canna, Rhian. Do no' ask it o' me. I—" Agony flooded Saerla's face. "I do no' even want to think about what I Saw."

Rhian shuddered.

Saerla looked at her kindly. "Rest assured, it had naught to do wi' ye."

What, then? Rhian could not ask again. If Saerla had Seen some terrible loss—well, Rhian could not bear it. They had already lost far too much.

Saerla said, "Ye walk a dangerous path loving this man." Her lips worked before she said, "A MacLeod."

"Just like Moira before me, choosing to love the verra man who struck Da's deathblow."

"I am no' certain we can choose where we love."

"Nay." Rhian shook her head. "Once, I would ha' thought so. I would ha' said, in my ignorance, a woman had full control o' her future and where to place her heart."

For an instant, despair looked at Rhian from Saerla's eyes. "I fear," she whispered again, "it will end in terrible sorrow."

Rhian did not know what to do. In the past she had comforted her younger sister in times of distress. Both she and Moira had. They'd looked after the smallest of them.

Now Saerla's strength had grown, as had her ability. She'd set up certain barriers that kept Rhian from simply pulling her into an embrace.

In days past, Saerla would have blurted out all she'd Seen, no matter how terrible, if only to unburden herself. Now she kept quiet.

To protect them.

That knowledge sent uneasiness crawling up Rhian's spine, as did Saerla's expression when she leaned close and said, "Take care, sister. And if ye do love him, ha' the strength to send him awa' from ye, when ye get that chance."

Chapter Forty-One

THE GLOAMING HAD once more come down before Leith heard a soft knock at the door of the chamber. By then he had nearly become convinced Rhian intended not to return to him, that she would sleep elsewhere. In the infirmary, perhaps. Or with her sister.

Half mad with desperation, with the need to see her and touch her, he'd doubted he could endure for a whole night. As soon as he heard the rap on the door, though, he knew it was her just as if he could see through the oak and glimpse her standing there.

Clumsy in his haste, and using but his one hand, he lifted the bar. She slipped in, and all came right with his world. Just like that, it did.

He'd imagined all day long what she might say to him if she did arrive. Explanations, mayhap, of why she'd stayed so long away. A speech describing all the reasons it was mad for them to be together, for he had himself thought of them all.

Instead she merely stepped up close and wrapped her arms around him.

He had but the one sound arm, aye, but he folded that around the sweet, fragrant warmth of her and drew her in tighter. The relief of having her there staggered him and made him begin to tremble.

"Rhian," he breathed into her hair. "My beautiful lady, merciful angel."

He'd been missing her, aye, aching for her all the day long, but he did not realize how much until this moment, when the agony eased. Och, sweet agony.

They stood so while the minutes flew by, and his heartbeat calmed. Then he asked, still speaking into her hair, "Will ye stay wi' me the night?" If she did, then he could survive.

She did not reply. Instead, to his dismay, she drew away from him and stepped to the door. But ah, it was only to place the bar across it before looking at him.

"I should no' be here."

"I ken."

"I should no' stay. I would do better to share Saerla's chamber this night."

"And will ye?"

Still she did not answer him directly. "I ha' always been a prudent woman. Able to weigh my decisions. Act according to wha' is right."

"Will ye say 'tis no' right, ye being here wi' me?"

She shook her head. "I canna say that."

Again she stepped up to him, raised both hands, and twined them around his neck. Her fingers tangled in his hair, and her gaze, deep blue as a midnight sky, engaged his.

He lost all his breath, even before she kissed him, and when she pressed her mouth to his, giving and taking in equal measures, he did not know if he'd ever breathe again.

He did not care.

Nothing existed but Rhian. The taste of her, the warmth. The sense of completion that overshadowed all.

She'd thought herself a prudent woman, as he'd thought himself a contented man, neither of them suspecting what they'd been wanting.

Rhian, my beautiful angel, he thought at her, since his mouth was otherwise occupied.

Leith, my love.

Her love. Of all the things he'd ever wanted to be—accomplished with a sword, accomplished with his charm, light of heart—he'd never wanted to be anything more than hers.

When the kiss ended, when he'd swept the inside of her mouth with his tongue, chasing every hint of sweetness, when her bones had dissolved so she hung limp against him, they gazed again into one another's eyes.

"This day was an eternity wi'out ye," he told her.

"I ken. I want ye inside me."

"I ken."

He shook again before they reached the bed, with need this time. Physical need, that was, for did he not need her presence with every breath?

He barely noticed the shedding of their clothes. Her slipping beneath him on the bed, her legs spread wide. The need, pure and strong, outshone all else.

"Look at me," he begged just before he slid inside her. "I want to watch your face when I make ye mine."

Her gaze clung to his. He felt her surrender, equal to her demand.

They flew with their wings on fire. He did not know if she caught fire from him or the other way around, only that they burned up together. After, she folded her legs around him, keeping him where he was.

He wanted to weep with the beauty of it. But a man, especially a warrior, did not weep over making love to a woman.

The room had grown dark and dusky; the fire was out. A bonny night, it was, and sweet air came in through the narrow window. Leith lay knowing he wanted for nothing. There was naught more to want, besides this.

"Leith. My love." Her lips slid across his cheek to his ear. "I maun tell ye somewhat."

Whatever it was, he did not want to know. He wanted nothing to ruin this moment.

And yet she might need to tell him they'd decided to execute him, his captors. For, make no mistake, that was what they were, even though he lay here in her bed, in this fine chamber.

If they meant to slaughter him, if they intended to haul him out onto the stones before all their clan and slit his throat, at least he'd had this first.

"Wait. Let me hold ye." For this moment was intimate. Unbearably so.

She made a soft sound that denoted agreement. She trailed her lips across his before urging his face down to her breast. He sucked her and felt her pleasure spike, felt her tighten around him where he lay at the entrance to her womb.

He grew hard again inside her. Made for her, he was. And she for him. How had he lived so long without her?

He came to himself an unmeasured amount of time later to find the room pitch dark. He lay still inside Rhian. She slept.

He knew because he could feel her deep, even breaths and the slumber in her mind. She slept the sleep of exhaustion. Of trust.

She had not shared with him whatever she had to tell.

A ball of dread formed in his gut. Such perfection as this could not endure. They meant either to kill him or send him back to MacLeod.

Away from her.

Suddenly, he understood what Farlan had felt. What had made him give up everything and go to live among strangers. For Moira's sake.

Leith did not think he would have that choice. Having suffered such an insult once, Rory would never let him go. Besides, as had been pointed out, he was, for the time, at least Rory's heir.

"Leith." Rhian spoke his name in her sleep. She dreamed, and all at once he was there in the dream with her.

They walked together in a meadow, through bright sunlight. Leith knew this place, the high mead back at MacLeod. He, Farlan, and Rory had played here a thousand times as lads, secure in the knowledge that their world belonged to them.

That, if Rory could be believed, one day, the whole glen would.

Now Rhian stepped beside him, holding his hand. He barely noticed in his rush of joy that it was his right hand she gripped. That his fingers were able to clutch hers. Healed. For she had that power, to heal him.

She turned and looked at him. He could see himself in her gaze, in the joy and contentment there. For she looked carefree, confident. Full of bliss. This he brought to her.

This they brought to each other.

"Ye could no' stay wi' me," she said with a smile, "and so I came to ye."

He awoke with a start because Rhian had jerked violently within the circle of his arm. She came awake with a gasp. For an instant he thought she would push away from him, for she planted her palm on his bare chest. She curled her fingers into the hair there and drew him closer instead.

"Do no' leave me."

Leith did not know what to say to that. He could not promise. He might be sent away.

He did not want ever to lie to this woman.

In the past, aye, he'd spun lies. Pretty ones. *Ye be the bonniest lass I ha' ever seen. That was the best tumble I ha' had from anyone.* For the most part, the women knew they were lies and were charmed by them, as intended.

Rhian, though, demanded truth from him by her very being.

"My love," he murmured instead, and they clung to one another for several moments while his heartbeat accelerated once more.

She murmured at him also, saying it plainly into the dark air of the chamber: "Leith, I am carrying your child."

"Eh?" He must have heard her wrong.

She reached a gentle hand to touch his face. "I am carrying your child, and 'tis a son."

Chapter Forty-Two

"H OW D'YE KEN this?" Leith sounded thunderstruck, and who could blame him? Rhian, lying upon his chest, could feel the thundering of his heart and a wealth of emotions uprising. "How could ye ken?"

"That, I canna tell ye. I just know."

Were any of the emotions she sensed rushing through him dismay and regret? Because even if he believed her—and why should he?—he might not wish to sire a child that would be brought up here at MacBeith and become a pawn in a generational battle.

She believed he loved her, aye. That truth lay between them. She did not want him ever to regret the begetting of this child.

He raised his good hand and stroked his fingers through her tumbled hair, brushing it gently back from her cheek.

"Is it magic, Rhian, that ye can tell this thing?"

"I do no' ken. Mayhap so."

"Is it true, and no' just fancy?"

"No' just fancy." She slid her hand between their bodies and touched her belly. "I can feel him. Here."

He went silent, a rarity for this man. His next words would reveal what he thought, whether he believed her and whether he trusted her.

"I am to ha' a son."

Rhian's whole body melted at the wonder in his voice. At the pride.

"Ye are, so," she told him softly. "And he will be half MacBeith."

"Half of ye." He stroked her hair again. "Rhian, I ask again, how can ye know this?"

"I just felt him. Felt him there. He must ha' been conceived last night."

Leith nodded. "Aye. And he be hale and hearty? Can ye tell that also?"

"I believe so. Ye—ye are no' sorry, Leith?"

"Beautiful angel, how could I be sorry?" He kissed her softly and with devotion. "He is made o' the love I feel for ye."

"And that I feel for ye."

"To regret that would be—well, an abomination."

"Aye." She rested her cheek back on his chest. Contentment and trepidation warred inside her. "There will be ramifications. Once this is known, once it can no longer be hidden, there will be anger. Folk will no' like knowing a member o' Iain MacBeith's house has lain wi' a MacLeod."

"The people here ken already that Moira has done just that."

"But she does no' carry Farlan's bairn. Our child, Leith, will be heir to MacBeith and—at least for the time being—to MacLeod."

Leith swore softly. "So he will."

"Wha's to be done?"

"We ha' some time yet. 'Twill be autumn before anyone can tell, unless ye share it wi' them."

"I fear this will upend life here at MacBeith. Already, the council teeters on the edge o' casting Moira out for her love o' Farlan. In their view, this will be worse. Far worse."

"Aye. And I may no' be here to support ye in it. If they insist on sending me awa'—Lass." He wove his fingers into her hair. "I do no' think I will be able to do as Farlan has, and return to ye. Rory will kill me first."

"Och." Tears stung Rhian's eyes. "Would he, so? But ye be his cousin. His heir."

"Aye, and his friend. But he was deeply hurt by Farlan's abandonment. He will see me dead before he lets me treat him the same."

"Then—then all I can do is try to keep ye here. Here wi' me."

"Can it be done?"

"I do no' ken. Mayhap, if I lie." Aye, she had always been a truthful woman. But now—now all such considerations had flown. "If I tell them ye are unable to travel… Ye lie under my care, d'ye no'?"

"I lie under your care, beautiful angel."

"If I say your wound still refuses to heal, that ye may die if ye mak' the journey back to MacLeod—"

"Yet," he said carefully, "ye ken as I do, my stubborn wound heals at last."

"Aye. No one else knows it, though."

"And if Saerla receives knowledge that Rory has worsened and died after all? If your council decides I am better off dead?"

Rhian tightened her arms around him. "I will throw mysel' in front o' their dirks, if I ha' to."

"And risk our child?"

"They will no' harm me, surely?"

"By all that is holy, Rhian." He puffed out a breath. "If ye suppose I would take a chance ever on your safety or that o' our bairn… I would die ten times over to spare ye."

She wanted to weep. Lying there with him in the dark, she did. Because what lay between them was so beautiful, so true. And because she could not see a way forward, no matter how she tried.

"There is only *now* for us," she whispered, her lips but a breath from his.

He kissed her softly. "Aye, Rhian, but the future lies beneath your heart."

So it did. And she needed to nurture and grow that tiny fire, at all cost.

LATER, WHEN THE sun rose and Rhian went out about the stronghold to perform her duties, she could feel Leith yet. She could, in truth, feel the both of them. The lad who nestled like a spark within her, and his father, anchored to her heart.

She could not help wondering how it would be if the council or Alasdair did insist on sending Leith back to MacLeod. Would the bond that connected them stretch so far? Would she feel it clear across the loch?

Halfway through the morning, Saerla found her. Rhian had gone to the infirmary for supplies and discovered her sister waiting when she emerged.

The sight of Saerla made Rhian's heart leap alarmingly. Had she received another Vision? Did she come with some dire warning? Aye, and she appeared grave enough for it.

"Saerla? Wha' is it?" Rhian clenched the handle of her basket in a death grip.

Saerla inspected Rhian carefully. Did that gaze linger a beat too long on her belly? "I wished to see how ye are. Ye look better."

"I feel well." It was true. The child within her seemed to lend a strength.

"We maun talk, sister." Saerla glanced around. "No' here."

"Ha' ye Seen somewhat?"

"Nay, not that."

"I ha' no' the time now, Saerla. I am busy." How long before this sister who Saw so much guessed the truth? Or received the information in a Vision? But surely Rhian could trust Saerla, of all people.

"We will speak later," she said hurriedly, turning away from Saerla's searching gaze.

"But—"

"Sister, I ha' wounded to tend."

"Aye." Saerla nodded. "Come to my chamber tonight. We will speak together there." *Come to my chamber. Where ye should ha' been last night.* Rhian heard the words Saerla did not speak.

The next person she encountered was Alasdair. She nearly bumped into him when he came down the stone steps from the ramparts. He halted abruptly and glanced at her. "Mistress?"

"Master Alasdair."

"How fares the prisoner?"

And here it came, so soon. The need to lie. Aye, they had lied to the whole clan, the five of them, when Da died. That had been for the greater good.

This was not. She lied because should something happen to Leith, she did not know whether her heart could continue beating.

"No' so well." She shook her head sorrowfully. "Each time I think I ha' got that stubborn wound to close, it opens up again."

Alasdair scowled harder. "I ha' been thinking. Mayhap he could be littered back to MacLeod lands, rowed across the loch. Once he be there, I do no' care wha' happens to him."

Rhian's heart began to pound. "And should he die?"

"Eh?"

"If ye take and abandon him there on MacLeod soil and he perishes, what' do ye think Rory MacLeod will do?"

"Rory MacLeod," Alasdair pronounced with some satisfaction, "lies wounded still. No' to the death, so Mistress Saerla insists. At least, no' yet. Wha' can he do?"

"Rise up in vengeance? Come to mak' answer for the death o' his cousin and heir?"

Alasdair straightened. "I do no' ken if ye ha' noticed, Mistress Rhian, ye bein' situated as ye be on the healing side o' things. Every time yon Rory MacLeod has sought to attack us, he has failed and gone awa' whimpering." He leaned toward her and lowered his voice. "I believe there is some magic in it. I even begin to believe that Chief Iain, up there at his cairn, is giving us these victories. Let Rory MacLeod come if he is able. Let it be done."

Rhian caught her breath. "That is why ye want to kill Leith, or see him die one way or another. Ye seek to provoke Rory."

"It maun end, mistress. This feud maun end one way or another. We canna go on so forever."

"You are right."

"Mayhap Rory MacLeod will find that in the end, 'tis Mac-Beith that may be holding the whole o' this glen."

Chapter Forty-Three

A SON. HE was going to have a son. Leith contemplated the prospect again and again, and each time, his wonder grew.

In the past, given his dealings with women, he'd done his best to avoid that particular outcome. For the most part he'd held back from giving his partners his seed, whether they'd been maids or widowed matrons. He had wanted no permanent ties to them.

With Rhian, the ties had formed first and were unbreakable. He could as soon have kept from breathing as kept from giving her all of him.

How she might know already that they had created a child together, he could not say. There was some magic in it. He did not doubt her.

He tried to imagine such a child. Half of him, and half Rhian. Half MacLeod and half MacBeith, as she said. A doomed child, scorned by all? Or one full of promise?

He paced the narrow floor of the chamber and tried to lay aside his wonder in order to make plans. So much felt beyond his control right now, pent up as he was in this room, unable to make his own choices. Instead of choosing to leave here, he might be sent. Or slain out of hand.

He did not want his son to grow up without him. Before this, let it be admitted, he'd thought mostly of himself. Yes, his loyalty to Rory and his clan had been absolute. Unthinking. And he'd taken pride in his abilities as a warrior. The rest had been laughter and levity, taking pleasure where he could.

The prospect of becoming a father changed all that. Becoming the father of *Rhian's* child changed it doubly so. It seemed almost a holy prospect. She gave him a beautiful gift, this woman he adored. How might he be worthy of it?

He had grand examples before him. His own da, a bluff and hearty man from whom Leith had no doubt inherited his own strength, had always taken time to teach and train him. He'd been gentle, unexpectedly so, with his children, even as he cherished Leith's mother. He'd been especially gentle with his daughters. They'd all wept, including Da, when Ainsley died along with her and Farlan's wee son.

And then there was the old chief, Camraith, who had been father to all the clan. Wise, patient, slow to anger, and quick to choose for the benefit of all, no one could ask for a better man to follow. He'd taken Farlan in and been a true father to him after Farlan's own da was killed.

If Leith could choose, he wanted to become a father like that to his lad. Could he do that from a distance?

How best might he provide for his son and for Rhian? No matter how he paced and pondered, he did not know.

If he went home, if he tore himself away from Rhian, which would feel like yanking out his heart by the roots, could he influence Rory? Try to persuade him from this course he'd chosen to pursue, that had so far brought nothing but defeats, to some sort of truce?

He knew his cousin, and he did not think so. God himself could not sway Rory once his mind was made up.

Rory might still succumb to his wound, though Saerla insisted he had not yet. Then Leith would become chief, and then his son after him, if he could persuade Clan MacLeod to accept the boy. A peace could be forged between him and Farlan, acting through Moira.

Almost as if it were *meant*.

For all that, and given all Rory's faults, he could not bring himself to hope for his cousin's death. Aye, Rory might be stubborn. He might be hotheaded and Camraith's opposite in almost every way. But he was also Leith's lifelong friend and companion.

He loved the man.

Och, and he would lose his mind trying to figure a way out of this.

Perhaps there was no way. Possibly Alasdair and the council would win their argument with MacBeith's daughters and he'd be slain.

In such case, he would never see his son grow up. He would not even see him born. And how would such a lad be treated, growing up here at MacBeith without him? Leith hated to think.

He sank onto the edge of the bed, weary from his thoughts, and weighted by hopelessness.

The door rattled, and Rhian called softly, "Let me in."

He did so as swiftly as he could lift the bar. She came into the chamber, and everything changed.

With Rhian here—aye, even though she too looked distressed—his hopelessness lifted. Strength took its place, and healing once more flooded through him. With her here, he had all he needed.

She replaced the bar on the door and faced him, filled with anguish and uncertainty. "I canna stay."

Leith's heart, which had just buoyed, sank like a stone.

"I came only to gather some o' my things. I maun lodge wi' Saerla this night."

Dismay rendered Leith silent.

She went on precisely as if he'd asked why. "Saerla says I should no' be here wi' ye. Perhaps she is right. I am meant to be bunking wi' her. Next door. If someone were to find out I ha' been staying here instead—"

Leith's voice sounded hoarse when he forced it between his lips. "Tell them ye but stay to care for me."

"That is what I thought to do. I ha' already let Alasdair think ye fare worse than ye do. That ye are no' fit to travel across the glen."

"That is what they ha' decided, then? To send me awa'?"

She shook her head. "'Tis no' decided."

So, they might still kill him.

"Here." He drew her by the hand to the bed. "Sit before ye fall down."

"The worst thing I can do," she said miserably, "is cause further suspicion to fall on ye. If they find out I am doing more than nursing ye, and if they think I ha' fallen under your influence, they will no longer trust me."

"I see." Leith's heart indeed felt like a stone in his chest.

"'Tis wise, ye see, no' to tak' the chance. I strive always to act wisely. And"—her lips trembled—"in a practical manner."

She was coming apart, was his Rhian. Had he done that to her? And what best might he do to heal her, as she healed so many others?

She said again, "I maun gather my things. I will be right next door." She lifted her gaze to his. "If ye need me."

I need ye. He did not say that aloud, did not need to. He knew she heard.

He fell to his knees in front of her and took her hand in his good one. "Do as ye must. I ha' already caused ye enough in grief."

"Grief?" She pressed her free hand to her belly. "Ye suppose this bairn causes me grief? Nay and nay, naught but joy. 'Tis as if I was born to carry this child. Your child." She leaned forward and kissed him, the action a gift bestowed with warmth and devotion. "I was born for ye, Leith MacLeod."

"And I for ye." He added ruefully, "Though I never knew it."

"Nor I." She drew a breath. "I believe there are times when God or fate or some other power moves us beyond ourselves. Just look at Moira and Farlan. At ye and me."

At least, Leith thought, Farlan had leave to be with his woman. Though he'd traded much.

"Go if ye must," he told her. "Spend the night wi' yer sister. Only allow me to hold ye first." *Somewhat to keep me warm. Somewhat to keep me sane.*

They clutched one another. Comfort flowed into him—and another strong wave of healing.

Her lips but a breath from his, she whispered, "Let me dress your wound before I go."

He would let her cut off his arm, if it kept her longer. "It is better."

"Aye, but do no' tell anyone."

He took her place on the bed while she bustled around fetching supplies from her basket. He did not need her to tell him the hole in his arm was at last healing. He felt the difference. The healing came every time she touched him.

"There now." She smoothed clean bandages with careful fingers, then dropped a kiss on them. "For healing."

"Heal me, Rhian," he begged. "Heal me before ye go."

She dropped a second kiss on his lips before unlacing the front of her gown and drawing him to her bosom. She cradled him there, weaving her fingers through his hair while he feasted on her warmth, on her strength.

"I maun go," she whispered.

Nay. Everything within him wanted to protest—*did* protest, though he held the words from his lips.

She no doubt heard the ones in his mind. In his heart.

With trembling fingers, she refastened her gown and turned away to gather her things. A clean chemise from the clothes press. Her comb and a few pots of unguents.

"Wait," he said just before she turned to the door. He rose and went to her, laying the palm of his hand on her belly. "Bless this child. Keep him safe at all cost."

Chapter Forty-Four

R HIAN DID NOT sleep that night. Her emotions rather than her thoughts kept her awake. A curious thing, for usually she was able to force her emotions into line.

Not now.

She could feel the child within her, a flutter deep inside where his father had put him. Another curious thing, for she knew very well it took many months before a mother might feel her child move.

Leith had upended everything, overset her world. He'd torn her apart and put her back together again, a new woman.

Saerla, beside her in the bed, was also restless. When they were young, the three of them barely five years apart from oldest to youngest, they had slept in the same bed. She remembered Ma coming in each night and telling them stories—beautiful ones about heroes and mystical beasts, and their ancestors—and kissing them *one, two, three.*

Goodnight and sleep ye well, my beauties. All the powers keep ye safe.

Now neither she nor Saerla felt particularly safe. She hoped Saerla, who at least did sleep, if only restlessly, was not caught in the throes of another Vision. Rhian did not think she could bear more mystery or ill news.

She lay staring wide-eyed into the dark of the chamber, wondering again what Saerla had Seen. If it was naught to do with her or Leith, then what?

She wanted so much to be with Leith, it hurt.

If she went next door, if she did no more than slip out of one chamber and into the next, she could be with him. He would touch her, slide that broad-palmed, calloused hand over her skin. Kiss her everywhere. This terrible feeling of longing would fade, and rightness would flood in to take its place.

She could not be so weak, though, as to rise from this bed and go. Surely she had more self-discipline than that.

She must have dozed at last near morning, for she awoke abruptly to find Saerla out of the bed, at the door, and admitting Fiona to the chamber.

The older woman, a strapping example of MacBeith femininity, swept Rhian with a look where she lay in the bed.

"I came to tell the both o' ye," Fiona cried. "The guards ha' spied signs o' movement over at MacLeod. Just now, wi' the first morning light."

Rhian sat up far too quickly, and her head spun. Saerla stared at Fiona in dismay. "Moving upon us?"

"Aye, lass."

"Are they certain? Mayhap the MacLeods but train there on the green sward."

They did that, aye, frequently.

Fiona shook her head. "They think no'. The men called Alasdair, who went up and took a look. He is mobilizing the warriors. I thought ye should know."

"Aye." Saerla looked grim. Rhian wondered if this was what she had Seen. "I maun don my armor," Saerla said, almost to herself, "and strap on my weapons." She looked at Fiona. "Has Moira been told?"

"Aye. Alasdair went to her himsel'."

"This must mean Rory MacLeod is recovered enough to fight," Rhian said.

"Aye." Saerla shot her a look. "And it will change everything."

Fiona went out, doubtless to spread the dire news elsewhere.

"At least," Saerla told Rhian, "Fiona will now be able to attest that ye passed the night here wi' me. Are ye no' glad?"

Nay, not if Rhian might never have another chance to spend a night in the circle of Leith MacLeod's embrace.

⤖⤖⤖❮❮❮❮

"I SAY WE march out to meet them," Alasdair declared. He looked angry enough to spit nails. He also looked like a mountain in his heavy leather armor and helmet, bristling with weapons.

"I agree wi' ye," Moira said, surprisingly. She too stood clad for battle, and appeared grim and as sleep deprived as Rhian felt.

Alasdair looked startled. He did not often hear those words from Moira.

"Ye do?"

"Rory and his warriors ha' met defeat each time they tried to attack us. 'Tis time they learn we hold this side o' the glen in a firm grasp. Let us march out and show them our strength."

Farlan, beside Moira, did not appear happy with the statement. He too stood clad for battle. Would he fight against his own clansmen? Would he be able to cut down men he knew?

As if she wondered the same, Moira turned to him. Her blue gaze seemed to measure the man, the breadth of his shoulders. His steady stance. "Farlan, I want for ye to stay here and direct the defense o' the battlements."

He stiffened. "Nay, Moira. I stand—and fight—beside ye."

She shook her head. "We need someone we can rely upon if the fight goes badly and comes back upon our own walls."

Farlan flinched. If that happened, Moira would likely be either dead or wounded. Captured. Taken from him. Rhian understood the pain of that much better than she had only days ago.

Not a sound broke the waiting silence before Farlan spoke.

"Your men will no' tak' orders fro' me, here on the walls."

"He is right," Alasdair growled. "The men still do no' trust him. Ye stay here, Moira, the both o' ye, to defend the walls. No one does that so well as ye. I will lead the men out to battle."

Moira looked at Alasdair, who towered over her. She knew, as did everyone else in the chamber, that Alasdair had long harbored feelings for her.

"Nay," she decided. "We do this thing together, Alasdair. Ye and me."

"I do this thing for ye. For Chief Iain and MacBeith."

Tears stung Rhian's eyes.

Saerla said, briskly for her, "Are we going to stand here arguing it, or are we going to fight Rory MacLeod?"

"Aye, so." Moira tore her gaze from Alasdair's. "Farlan and I will keep the gate—at all costs."

Alasdair, looking relieved, immediately dashed out. Rhian wondered if it was the last time she would ever see him alive. And Saerla…

As her sister moved to follow Alasdair, Rhian caught her arm and asked in a low voice, "Is this what ye Saw? Will we lose this battle?"

Saerla shook her head. "Stop wi' wondering wha' I Saw." She glanced back at Moira and Farlan, who stood facing one another, hands linked.

"Saerla, will we survive?"

"There are partings, Rhian. There are always partings."

Saerla dashed off, and Rhian asked herself how someone so ethereal could engage in battle. Could it be that Saerla spoke of her own death? Of Alasdair's?

Rhian could not bear it. She loved them both. Ah, God! She loved every soul that belonged to this place.

And that meant she must be strong. She might not fight with a sword, but she did fight.

She needed to gather her weapons. She should go to the infirmary to stock a basket. She would watch the battle from the walls when the two forces met, and be ready to tend any wounded.

She went instead to her own chamber.

Leith admitted her, looking frantic. "Wha' is it, Rhian? Wha's happening? I could feel, well—" His gray-blue eyes widened. "I could feel that ye were afraid."

"Could ye?" She moved into the circle of his arm, craving that closeness. A moment's shelter only before she went out to face the unendurable.

"MacLeod musters for an attack."

"Rory?"

"He maun be at their head, aye? They would no' move wi'out him."

"They would no'."

"He maun ha' recovered from his injury. Moira and Alasdair decided we should march out to meet him, only—only Alasdair will no' allow Moira and Farlan to go. I am afraid we will lose him."

Leith said nothing.

"Saerla has Seen somewhat so dire she will no' share it wi' anyone. She speaks only of partings."

"Rhian, listen to me." He tipped her face up and gazed into her eyes. "We can ne'er truly part. Understand me? No' even though distance comes between us. There is some magic in it."

"Magic?"

"Aye. Only look at this."

He lifted his hand, which was no great feat.

Only, it was his right hand.

"Leith!" she gasped. "How long—"

"It has been coming along slowly since the wound closed over. A twitch at first. I could scarce believe it, so I did no' say. But Rhian, beautiful angel, I believe 'twas loving ye that has healed me. Touching ye. Being inside ye."

Quite possibly so. But this meant he might someday hold a sword again. And wield it against those she loved.

He'd gone from being the man she adored to being a threat.

"I maun go. We keep watch from the walls in case the fight comes back upon us. I will try to keep ye abreast o' it."

"Be careful, my love." He kissed her sweetly, and she felt the pull deep inside. "Be careful, for ye carry my heart."

Chapter Forty-Five

H ELL MIGHT WELL consist of standing helplessly and watching a battle from afar, or so Rhian decided sometime later. She had climbed to the wall above the gate as soon as she left Leith, and joined Moira and Farlan, who held a place there.

Farlan stood quietly, his big hands resting on the stone, but Moira could not keep still and paced the walkway like a lioness.

It did not help that the distance was great and they could not see all of what transpired. What happened out at the loch side did not seem real, though Rhian understood all too well that it was.

Alasdair had set up a defense on their side of the loch—a wise tactic, since it meant the MacLeod forces must launch boats and row across, and might be attacked as they came ashore. So it was, and the MacLeods came in ferociously.

"Is that Rory at the head o' them?" Moira demanded of Farlan. "The man in the foremost boat? Can ye tell?"

Farlan narrowed his gaze. "Aye. He moves like Rory."

"Curse him! He was supposed to be dead or dying."

Rhian, striving to follow the distant forms and to pick out Saerla's, could clearly feel Moira's tension. Everyone there on the walls could, and it made their men restless and edgy.

"Ha' faith," Farlan said. "The MacBeith forces ha' taken up a strong position."

"Perhaps"—Moira fairly spat the word—"this will be the

battle to convince Rory he should leave off wi' attacking us."

At first it seemed it might be so. Rhian watched the battle ebb and flow, there at the loch side, certain she was able to pick out Alasdair, their spearhead. He fought like a whirlwind, and the other MacBeith warriors stood firm at his back.

They will defeat the MacLeods, she promised herself, and whispered a prayer over it. *Drive them back into the water.*

But slowly, slowly and silently for the distance, the battle turned. The dark wave made up of MacLeod warriors pushed out from the water, lapped at the MacBeith forces, and drove them back. Moira quit her pacing. Everyone on the walls stared in dismay.

Rhian stopped breathing as she leaned forward out over the stones, the better to see. The strong line of MacBeith defenders, silenced by the distance, began to break up and form small, fierce pockets of resistance.

A strong hand came out and clutched at the back of Rhian's gown. Startled, she turned and stared into Farlan's brown eyes.

"Careful, mistress. Ye could fall."

Disregarding them, Moira called, "The battle has turned. The battle has turned! Prepare to defend the walls!"

The men on the ramparts scrambled, though there was little they could do so soon.

Moira juggled her weapons and turned to Farlan. "You stay here on the wall."

"Wha'?"

"I am going out. To fight wi' them."

"My love," Farlan said urgently, "ye canna!"

"I must." Moira fairly wept. "I canna stand here and watch them slaughtered."

"Moira." Farlan seized her shoulders. "One more sword will no' mak' a difference."

"It might."

"The men here will no' heed me," he argued.

Indeed, many of the men on the wall listened to the exchange, their expressions hard.

A cry went up. "Alasdair! He is down!"

"Nay." Moira threw herself at the wall. Farlan clutched at her. "Where? Where?"

"There, at the center," Farlan replied. "That is Rory who has him."

"Is he slain?" The measure of pain in Moira's voice betrayed her great affection for the big man, far more to her than a war chief.

Impossible to tell from so far. The morning sun had risen, and Rhian narrowed her eyes against the glare.

Another cry went up, still sharper. A small figure had thrown itself at Rory, sword drawn in challenge.

Rhian choked on a cry. "Saerla!"

Horror struck everyone on the wall silent. Rhian strained to see, but the MacBeith forces contracted around the place where Saerla was, blocking her vision.

"Oh, God," Moira whispered. "Please, God. Nay. Nay!"

Not Saerla. Not their wee sister, full of the mystical. Keeper of their light—

"I canna see," Moira wept. "I canna see! I am going out there—"

Farlan tried to hold her back. He had no hope. In the end, he went with her, leaving the defense in the hands of a senior member of the guard. Rhian was left terrified and forsaken. Alone.

They watched the two figures set out at a dead run. Moira possessed both speed and endurance. Farlan kept up with her, and they streaked toward the loch.

Everyone on the ramparts leaned over the wall. If Rhian had thought watching torturous before, this became a livid agony.

The crowd around Rory and Saerla had moved in tight. Battle had more or less ceased.

All at once, someone erupted from that tight knot. A man— Rhian could not at this distance identify him. Ewan, perhaps. He broke from the group of warriors and ran toward the keep. Toward Moira and Farlan.

They met less than halfway. The watchers on the walls stirred and muttered.

"They be talking," said the man next to Rhian. "Bargaining."

Battlefield negotiations were rare but not unheard of. If they failed, new bloodshed would break out. With Saerla at the center of it.

Rhian wanted to pray. She did not know quite for what to ask. *Saerla's safety.* The devout wish came from her. Only that.

The discussion among the three came to an abrupt end. They all ran toward the stronghold.

Rhian watched them pelt in, Moira with her plaited hair flying. She heard her sister shouting orders. Her own feet took her down the stairs from the wall.

Moira looked flushed, desperate, and determined. Her gaze met Rhian's briefly when she said, "He has Saerla. He wants to trade."

Everything within Rhian tensed. She knew what Moira would say next, even before she heard the words.

"Go get the prisoner. Rory is willing to trade Saerla for him."

Leith. Leith for Saerla.

"Nay," Rhian said, beyond desperate. "He is too sore hurt. No' ready to travel—"

"I do no' care." Moira seized Rhian's shoulders in both hands. "I do no' care if he dies as soon as MacLeod has him. He has Saerla, Rhian. Saerla!"

Rhian swallowed hard. There was naught she could say.

Several members of the guard stalked off toward Rhian's chamber. Farlan stepped forward.

"I will go. Try to explain to him—"

He moved off. Rhian stumbled after.

Leith. The other part of her, the man rooted to her heart. The father of her child. She must have a moment with him. She must—

But there would be no time. She knew that even as she followed Farlan's broad back. She understood the impulse that moved him, the same as her own. The guards would haul Leith out from her chamber, beat down the door if they had to, without regard for his condition. If he resisted, they would batter him ruthlessly.

The thought gave her feet wings. She outdistanced Farlan and the guards and arrived first at her chamber door.

"Leith?" She flattened herself against the boards. "Open. Lift the bar."

"Rhian?" Wha' is happening?"

The guards reached her then, nudged her aside, and pounded on the door. "Is it barred from within? Open!"

He did. He kept the bar in his left hand as a weapon, if a poor one. His gaze flew from Rhian's face to those of the guards and then to Farlan.

"What is it?"

"Do no' fight them, Leith," Farlan bade him. "Ye be going back home."

Chapter Forty-Six

HOME. BUT LEITH did not want to return home. At least not if Rhian remained here at MacBeith.

His gaze moved from the faces of the guards, filled with menace, to Farlan's, which urged caution. To Rhian's, where he beheld emotions such as he'd never seen.

Rhian rarely betrayed her feelings. She was a woman who concealed any inner turmoil beneath a composed and serene demeanor. Aye, he had seen her features alive with passion when she lay beneath him. Those circumstances were extreme.

As, it seemed, were these. Desperate agony stared at him from her eyes, and her lips had parted before words she could not say.

He heard them, though, in his mind.

He has Saerla.

He understood at once, and he felt the outrage and sorrow that filled her in equal measures, as if they were his own.

Rory had seized her sister. He would want to trade her for Leith.

Everything in him rose in wild protest. Because he did not want to leave her. Something inside him might well die if he did.

But he must do this. He would do this for her. Because Rhian loved her sister, and he loved Rhian.

'Twas as simple as that, in the end. Anything he could do for this woman, he would.

But he wanted—needed—a moment with her first. He wanted to kiss her. To make promises. To assure her of his love.

They would not have that. In front of these others, they could not so much as touch hands. To the guards, he was no more than her patient.

He looked away from her terrible agony, glanced at Farlan again, and nodded. "I will go."

Farlan took charge of him, hustling him from the chamber. He could feel Rhian as he stepped past her, feel her throughout his body, and he tried to come up with something he could think at her, to provide her comfort. There was nothing. This wound surpassed any he had ever borne.

She followed him and Farlan, and the guards came after.

As they went, Farlan spoke to him in a low tone. "Rory seized Saerla in the battle. He is willing to trade her only for ye. Once he has ye, both forces will withdraw. The war chief, Alasdair, is badly injured, so they want to end the fighting."

For now. Because the fight, as Leith well knew, would not truly end till Rory had his satisfaction.

"He badly wants ye back," Farlan said.

"I understand." The ache inside Leith had grown so intense, it shook him with each footstep. Worse, he could feel its echo in Rhian behind him. He could not endure this. She could not.

They met Moira at the gate. She appeared frantic. Her gaze swept both Leith and Farlan.

"Ye ha' him. Let us go. I will no' rest till we ha' her back in our hands."

Just like that. Just like that, he was to walk out, without so much as another word for the woman he loved more than his life.

"Wait." The cry came from behind him and spun him around. Rhian stood there, her eyes wide and burning with desperation. "Ye will tak' care o' yoursel', Leith MacLeod? Of—of that wound."

"I will, mistress. Thank ye for your care o' me." *Take care o' our bairn, who lies beneath your heart.*

I will.

"Come," said Moira, beyond impatient, and she seized him by the arm. He went out through the gate, an act that should offer relief and freedom, but did not, and into a beautiful day. He walked between the two of them, Moira and Farlan, with the guards coming after. But his heart remained behind.

⫸⫷

As soon as he laid eyes on Rory, he saw how unwell the man looked. Even more than himself, his cousin customarily boasted a profound vitality. It marked everything he did, from the performance of his duties to the planning of his campaigns. It went hand in hand with a steel-hard stubbornness that Leith suspected sustained him now.

As for Leith himself, he went sustained by another power. It uplifted him even as his own strength began to flag. He had not walked so far in many days, and all the endurance he'd built up in Rhian's arms swiftly waned. Yet he did not flag. He acted for her sake, even as each step away from her opened wider the wound inside.

Rory stood in a knot of MacLeod and MacBeith warriors, as indeed he must. Everyone there had his sword drawn and wore a dangerous expression. None would act, because Murgor, the MacLeod war chief, stood with Saerla in his clutches and his sword at her throat.

Rory himself did not hold her. Leith wondered if he could. Beneath several days of dark beard, Rory's skin had a pale, sweaty sheen that denoted pain. And new lines had appeared at the corners of his eyes.

Those eyes, though, still looked wickedly bright. They swept once, twice over Leith, measuring his condition before moving to Farlan and turning to ice.

The gulf between Rory and his former best friend, as Leith

well knew, was wider than the loch at Rory's back. And there was no hope of mending it.

"Leith?" Rory said, and it sounded ugly coming from his throat. "Ha' they mistreated ye?"

"I ha' been provided care." *Rhian's gentle hands smoothing the bandages across his arm. Her lips moving down his body, tasting and caressing.*

Could he live without that?

Moira aggressively came pushing up beside Farlan. She jutted her chin at her sister. "Let her go."

Leith heard no desperation in the command, but Saerla must have. For she looked at her sister with a hint of warning.

She appeared calm, for a woman resting in the hands of her enemies. But her chest rose and fell in short breaths.

"Leith," Rory said again, "step o'er to me."

Farlan let go of Leith. His grip had been one of support rather than restraint, and without it, Leith's legs wavered still more violently.

Rory, beholding it, stepped across, seized his arm, and drew him in. "Let her go."

Murgor released Saerla. Moira leaped for her and pulled her away behind Farlan.

"The exchange is made," Farlan said. "Let us withdraw fro' the field."

Rory's lips twisted in a sneer, and antagonistic fury flowed from him. As much as he'd once loved Farlan, he now hated him.

"Mistress MacBeith," he called to Moira, "ye canna win. Any force that places its trust in a traitor and allows women to fight is doomed from the start."

"Fulfill the agreement," Moira called back, "and withdraw fro' the field." She wanted to get her sister back to her stronghold, no doubt. And what of her wounded war chief? Leith could see Alasdair nowhere.

Fallen. Might he be dead?

"Or ha' ye no honor?" Moira added.

"I ha' more honor than to tak' a turncoat to my bosom." Rory's fingers bit into Leith's arm. "Come."

They waded into the waters of the loch to the nearest of the boats that waited there. Looking back, Leith saw Alasdair being helped up from the ground. Aye, he lived. Rhian would be glad.

Rhian.

His longing for her was a livid wound. One he did not know how to bear.

He scarcely remembered, later, the trip back home, the pull across the loch in one of the wee boats, or the tramp to Mac-Leod's stronghold. He did have a vague memory of Rory sneering into his face.

"Wha' be the matter wi' ye, man? Be ye hurt bad still?"

It is difficult to live without my heart, he wanted to say. But Rory's green gaze looked hard and merciless. And anyway, it was not the sort of thing one said to the MacLeod.

"Wha' ha' they done to ye?" Rory demanded again, once they entered the stronghold and were inside his study. Apparently he did not believe Leith's claim that he'd been treated well. "Poison? Torture?"

"Nay, none o' that." Leith said no more. For what beset him, he did not believe Rory could ever understand.

Chapter Forty-Seven

LEITH'S MA RUSHED to see him as soon as Rory left him alone in his quarters. She brought his sister, Aisleen, and he'd scarcely ever been so happy to see them. Ma, not a woman who customarily made a fuss, did so this time, running her hands up and down his arms before taking his face between her palms and kissing him on the forehead.

She looked like him, did his ma—the same fair hair and gray-blue eyes. Ainsley had been fair also. Da's hair had been darker, and Aisleen's carried a deeper hue, like red gold.

"We thought ye lost to us," Ma said as she embraced him, her voice choked by tears.

"Aye, brother," Aisleen agreed. "After so much time, we did fear the worst."

"Ye canna imagine how I worried," Ma went on.

He could. He'd known the whole time she would be sick with it.

"I was treated well, withal."

"Rory was beside himsel'," Aisleen said, sitting close beside Leith. "At least half o' it was from affection for ye. The rest—"

"The rest," Leith finished for her, "was aggravation at losing another man to MacBeith."

"Aye," both women agreed.

"Ye ken fine how Rory be." Ma's gaze met Leith's, dodging

no truths. She had helped to mother all three of them—Farlan being an orphan, and Rory motherless after his own ma had died. Being their mother, she'd learned their strengths and weaknesses. "It hurt him, losing Farlan, wounded him deep, though he does no' like to admit it."

"He'd sooner die," Aisleen put in.

Ma went on, "The prospect o' losing ye as well—I do no' think he could countenance it."

"He's a different man since Farlan left," Aisleen whispered with a glance to the door, as if afraid Rory would come in. "Short tempered and likely to fly into a rage."

"More than usual?" Leith asked, and they both nodded gravely. "Word came to me there at MacBeith that he'd been badly wounded in that last battle, the one that took place at MacBeith's gate. Arrow in the back."

"Aye, so," Ma confirmed. "He was carried back, and we thought at first we would lose him. I helped in tending him mysel'. 'Twas a bad time, him at death's door and me no' knowing what was happening to ye.

"But he rallied. Fought through the pain wi' sheer determination, I should say. He still has pain, though he does no' like to admit that either. It makes him impatient. Wi' himsel' and others."

Leith raised his eyebrows. A more impatient Rory, an angrier one. It made a formidable prospect.

"I will ha' to talk wi' him," he muttered. "Try to reason wi' him—over wha' to do about MacBeith."

"Wha' is to do about MacBeith?" Aisleen asked. "We fight them, do we no'?"

"We do no' ha' to fight them. We might, so I believe, strike a peace."

"Good luck wi' it," Ma said. "Since losing Farlan, he is more determined than ever to conquer the whole glen. How is Farlan? Is he happy there among strangers?"

"'Tis no' an easy path he has chosen. The clan has no' yet

accepted him."

"Poor lad."

"Yet he is happy wi' his Moira."

"One o' the old chief's daughters," Aisleen breathed. "Who would ha' thought?"

Who indeed? Could he tell these two, so dear to him, that he had also lost his heart to one of MacBeith's daughters? That the woman he adored carried his wee son? Ma's grandchild.

Nay, he could not. Not yet. They would think him mad and raving.

"And this wound o' yours? How bad is it?"

Leith met his mother's gaze again. "Bad. I ha' only just regained the ability to move this hand, and 'tis no' sound even yet. When first they brought me in as a captive, I was blinded from a blow to the head."

Both women exclaimed, "And ye there all alone!"

Leith swallowed hard. "My sight came back to me early on. There is a healer at MacBeith, a woman. She tended me. The other wound has been a struggle."

Aisleen asked, "Will ye be able to hold a sword, brother?"

"For a long while, I did no' think so. Now I ha' hope."

"We will tend ye ourselves," Ma declared. "Ye will be well and strong soon. The time at MacBeith will seem like an evil dream."

It already seemed like a dream, though not an evil one. Leith could scarcely believe all that had happened there. Except for the persistent tug of longing beneath his breastbone.

"For now ye need rest," Ma said. "Clean clothing and a good feed." Again she kissed him on the forehead, just as she had when he'd been a lad. "I am that glad, son, to ha' ye home."

Part of him rejoiced over it also. The rest of him struggled beneath the knowledge that the distance between him and Rhian felt far greater than the mere breadth of the glen.

RORY KEPT AWAY till nightfall, perhaps giving Leith's ma and Aisleen a chance to fuss over him before then. Ma called in the clan's best healer to consult over his wound and changed the dressing Rhian had last applied.

Another connection with her gone. But nay, what could be a stronger connection than the bairn they shared?

Rory arrived with the gloaming, admitting himself to Leith's bedchamber not long after Ma and Aisleen had left.

He looked exhausted. He had changed out of his battle clothing and wore a soft sark and a pair of leggings. He still moved with the same restrained power. But new lines showed clear in his face, and a hard bitterness filled his eyes.

It had been a long day for Rory, as for them all. And those lines could be the result of pain.

"How d'ye feel, Leith?" he asked as he drew up a stool beside the bed. He'd brought a flask, and glad Leith felt to see it.

"Better than I was," Leith replied. "And ye? Talk at MacBeith was ye took an arrow to the back."

Rory shrugged as if feeling the wound over again, and grimaced. "'Tis so. Nicked my lung, that arrow did. Better that than my heart. Though there are those who would insist I do no' possess one o' those."

"Ye do, though." Leith could attest to it. He recalled instances aplenty when Rory had stepped up to defend those weaker than himself, both human and animal. And he still remembered him weeping profoundly when his hound died.

Rory frequently disguised his softer feelings as anger. If the amount of anger he expressed proved any indication, he felt very deeply indeed.

Of late, though, he'd become more adept at disguising those feelings. He'd barely reacted when his father died. And his heartbreak over Farlan had been hidden behind more of that anger.

"In truth," he told Leith, "I thought I was goin' to die. For a day and a night, I did."

"Ah."

"Your ma was there for me. I will be forever grateful. In the end, I decided I could no' die. I ha' still far too much to accomplish."

"Glen Bronach."

Rory nodded somberly. "I want it. More than ever now."

Was this the old ambition, Leith wondered, or did the desire to have revenge against Moira—and through her, Farlan—play a part?

"I will ha' ye know, Rory, they were taking bets there at MacBeith whether ye were dead or not."

Rory's lips twisted. "Praying for it, no doubt."

"Aye. And me your sole heir, right there in their hands."

"I thought o' that. I did, while lyin' there struggling to breathe. I ha' no issue. And they held ye. 'Twas one o' the things that got me up again."

A will of iron, had Rory MacLeod.

Rory pulled the stopper on the flask and handed it to Leith. "Tell me wha' happened, from the beginning."

Leith took a long pull from the flask, and did.

He spoke of being tended briefly on the battlefield by a Mac-Beith healer, but did not tell her name. He spoke of his subsequent capture, how they'd clubbed him down and rendered him blind. That had resolved itself, again under the hands of the healer.

"Always had a head like rock," Rory muttered. "And I am grateful for it."

"As am I."

Leith went on, speaking of the wound in his arm, and his captivity. He left out a lot, including that the healer who'd tended him was one of MacBeith's daughters.

"And Farlan?" Rory asked. "Did ye see him?"

"Aye. He came to speak wi' me frequently."

A muscle jumped in Rory's cheek. He would not ask how his former friend fared. Too angry, and too stubborn.

"And that woman o' his—she still leads the clan? I can no' understand why they send their women into battle. 'Tis madness."

"They do no' send them as a matter o' course. As ye ken, Moira is MacBeith's daughter, and stepped into her slain brother's place. To be sure, on the field we never guessed she was a woman."

"And the other one?"

"Other one?"

Rory's gaze burned green. "The one we seized there, and traded back for ye. To be sure, I did no' ken she was a woman when we grabbed her. Just a whirling terror, trying to gut me. Not until I ha' a good look at her did I realize she was no' a man."

"Another o' MacBeith's daughters."

"Christ! Do they raise them to forget they be women?"

Nay, and nay. Leith thought of Rhian unfastening her bodice and drawing him to her breasts. Holding him inside her. All woman. The very description of femininity.

"Rory, we need to speak together."

"Is that no' what we are doing? But aye, ye will ha' a wealth o' information for me. Knowledge that traitor, Farlan, refused to turn over. We will talk. All night, if need be. And we will empty this flask. I am glad, Leith, to ha' ye home."

Chapter Forty-Eight

FOR A DAY and a night, Rhian deceived herself into believing she could withstand the ache of losing Leith. She kept busy during the day, looking after Saerla, tending the others who'd been wounded in the battle, and sitting in on a meeting of the council.

Alasdair's condition worried her. It worried everyone. He'd had to be carried from the field, something no one could recall having happened before. He was provided care first by one of the male healers. Rhian learned later he could be heard bellowing halfway across the settlement.

A bad wound to the gut, it was. Rhian knew from treating others how painful those were, and how hard to heal. Alasdair was a bull of a man, but even bulls could be taken down.

He was absent from the meeting of the council, and the council members appeared half frantic over it. They spoke little of the next steps to be taken as concerned MacLeod, and nothing of what would happen without Alasdair at the oars. At least they did not reintroduce the subject of removing Moira from the place of chief.

Rhian got almost no sleep that first night. She shied from the very idea of her bed where she'd been with Leith, and did little more than doze beside her fire. By the next day, her self-control and her endurance both began to erode. Her longing for Leith became an open wound, not unlike the ones she helped to tend.

She told herself over and over again she must bear it, even while doubting she could. She spent her loving energy on Saerla, who had a nasty cut to one arm, and who in turn studied her worriedly.

If Saerla said one word about it being best that Leith had gone, Rhian thought she would fly apart. But Saerla did not.

By nightfall of the following day, Rhian ached from head to toe as with a winter sickness. She began to fear her emotional turmoil would affect the child.

She went to visit Alasdair, installed in the rear room of the infirmary, fearing the worst. She found him fractious, which served to reassure her some.

It seemed strange to see the big man out of his leathers, and in a bed. His upper body lay bare of all but scars and bandages, and his abdomen was wrapped. His face wore a scowl.

"Alasdair, how d'ye feel?"

"Terrible, mistress. I canna believe one o' they MacLeod bastards took me down."

"'Twas a long while coming." In how many battles had he faced the MacLeods at his chief's side and since Da's death? If he took wounds in those fights, he mostly refused to speak of them. Alasdair, with his redoubtable energy, merely carried on.

No wonder he scowled so at being grounded now.

"Wha' says the healer about your wound?" She'd already spoken to the man, who had told her the wound was ugly but could have been worse.

"That I maun stay here in this bed if I want ever to carry a sword again on the field."

Ah, so that was what kept him in one place.

"Ha' ye been given a draught for the pain? If no', I can mix ye one."

"I am too angry to heed the pain. We maun tak' this respite to redouble our defenses. For he'll be back, never doubt it. Rory MacLeod will be back now that he has what he wants."

Leith. Leith was what Rory had wanted. Rhian tried not to flinch at the sounding of his name in her mind.

"Moira is seeing to the defenses, so ye've no need to worry about that. Alasdair, is there aught I can do for ye?"

"Calm these worries, mistress. The ones in my mind that will no' leave me alone."

Rhian wished that she could.

"For the life o' me, Mistress Rhian, I canna see how this will end. We win a battle, but it matters little, for that bastard will no' give up. Now he has his heir back again."

"Aye, so. It will do little good fretting over it," she told him, wishing she could follow her own advice. "Ye maun use your strength to heal."

"I canna seem to stop worryin'." Alasdair looked more troubled than she'd ever seen him. "Since Chief Iain's death, it has all gone wrong."

"Aye, so it has." She laid her hand over his.

"I should ha' defended him better in that fight. If that accursed Farlan had no' got in that blow, Chief Iain would still be here wi' us now. And all the rest o' it would no' ha' happened." He bared his teeth. "I swear, I hate everyone o' MacLeod blood."

Including the fragile life that fluttered beneath Rhian's breast?

"Alasdair, what happened to Da was no' your fault." It was not even Farlan's, a point much less easy to embrace. Men in battle fought one another. It was what a warrior did. She wondered if Moira had embraced that truth in loving Farlan. "You fought your best for him."

"Not well enough." The big man's gaze burned. "And I am no' doing well enough now, for his daughters."

"Ye are. Alasdair, there is such a thing as fate. As destiny."

He made a face.

"Saerla believes in it." And he believed in Saerla. "Moira too, I think."

"'Tis a fancy. No power chooses who lives and who dies. 'Tis all in the strength o' a man's—or woman's—arm." His gaze unexpectedly softened. "'Tis in your healing touch, as well. I will admit, I do no' ken why ye had to heal yon bastard Leith MacLeod. But perhaps 'twas best, for if he'd no' been alive to trade for Saerla, what then?"

"We might ha' lost her." Rhian had to swallow hard over that. "Alasdair, there has been so much loss."

Now his hand covered hers. "Too much."

"Aye." To her dismay, her eyes brimmed with tears. She blinked them away determinedly. "Perhaps 'tis time for the dying to end."

He snorted. "Ye tell Rory MacLeod that. He'll only be emboldened by getting yon Leith back."

Rhian rose to her feet from the side of the cot. "You focus on getting well, Alasdair. And if the pain becomes too great in the night as may be, call me and I will mix a draught. And I will tell no one that the mighty Alasdair MacBeith had recourse to a potion."

Unexpectedly, he grinned at her. "I just might do that."

Rhian went out from the healers' hut and sought the evening air, aching for a few moments alone. Out in the forecourt she found herself surrounded by yet another soft gloaming. Stars appeared overhead one by one, alongside a lopsided moon. The air smelled of wood smoke and wild thyme. *Home.*

She loved this place to the roots of her being. At one time, she'd been willing to swear she would die for it.

Now she wondered how she would survive a lifetime. Without him.

Like one testing the air, she framed a thought and sent it out. *My love?*

When they'd been lying together, close beside one another in her bed, they'd been given the gift of hearing the words in one another's minds.

But Leith was far from her now. She heard nothing in reply. Only a soft wind sighing over the land. Blowing down from the height where Da lay, where dwelt the clan's magic.

Deep magic, it was. It lay in those stones, raised so long ago. In the very soil of the glen, in the waters that flowed down the brae sides to the loch. It dwelt in them all, even in her, far more than she'd ever before suspected.

She twisted her fingers together and raised her face to the sky, drawing upon that magic.

Leith? My love. I canna bear it.

No reply came from the far-distant stronghold across the loch, the place where he must be. But the soft wind that caressed her cheek seemed to whisper to her.

Believe. Believe.

Chapter Forty-Nine

"WILL YE BE able to fight again, wi' that arm?" Rory aimed the question at Leith along with a narrowed stare. It was midday, and they had just come from the drilling field, where Leith had not taken part in the training. Neither had Rory, as it happened. Though he'd dressed in his leathers, he spent most the session directing the other men.

Now, back in Rory's chamber, which used to be Camraith's, he stripped off those leathers, affording Leith a look at the wound in his back.

The sight of it made Leith's stomach lurch and turn. Aye, they'd heard at MacBeith that Rory had been sorely injured. Even that he lay near to death. Leith had imagined naught like this.

Arrow wounds, as he knew, were dire things. The barbed head of an arrow went in much more easily than it came out again. This arrowhead had torn the flesh when it was extracted and opened up a huge wound just to the left of Rory's spine.

He now wore no bandaging upon it. The torn flesh looked raw, the scarring at its edges new and pink.

Leith swore bitterly, and Rory glanced over his shoulder.

"Christ Jesus, Rory, that looks bad."

Rory made a face. "Aye, so, ill luck had a part in it. The healer says the arrow took me at just the right—or wrong—angle, passed between two o' my ribs, and went in deep."

"How deep?"

"Deep enough, as I say, to nick the lung." Rory turned to face Leith, denying him further sight of the wound. "It took two o' them to dig it out again. The damned arrowhead turned and got caught on my ribs on its way out."

Leith's stomach did another slow roll. "I hope ye were senseless for most o' that."

Rory shook his head, a scowl wrinkling his brow. "I remember it all."

"Ye should no' be up on your feet."

"I ha' no the luxury o' bein' off them."

Ignoring that, Leith went on, "And for certain ye had no business launching another attack while still so torn up. How can ye stand the leathers against yer skin?"

Rory shrugged and drew a soft tunic on over his head. "I had nay time to wait. I needed to get ye back, did I no'? Ye being my heir and all."

"Aye, so." Dismay swamped Leith. He could not possibly tell his cousin, after such a sacrifice, that he had not wanted to return to MacLeod. Just as he could not share that MacBeith's daughter carried his child.

Rhian. Upon the thought of her, his head buzzed. It was as if he carried part of her inside him, even as she carried that part of him. Almost as if he could hear her voice.

"Ye ha' no answered me. Will ye be able to fight again?"

"I do no' ken." Leith flexed and opened the fingers of his right hand. "For a long while, I did no' think so. For a goodly time, I did no' think I would live. She clawed me back from the edge o' death."

"She?" Rory's green gaze sharpened.

"MacBeith's middle daughter. She's a healer."

"By God, how many wretched daughters did the man beget?"

"Three. There are three."

Rory gave him a look rife with suspicion. "If she saved ye, this woman, I hope ye do no' bear any soft feelings toward her."

"I am that grateful to her, aye."

Rory moved suddenly, approached the place where Leith sat, and pulled up a stool opposite him. "Leith, let us get one thing straight. There is no place in this for either gratitude or pity."

Or love?

"They ha' had a run o' luck, these accursed MacBeiths, and no mistake, the battles ha' gone their way. But the tide is turning now. That big man o' theirs, the war chief, was bad injured in that last battle."

"Ye suppose so?"

"I inflicted the wound mysel'. If he is taken out o' the picture, wi' what can they fight? I ha' ye back again, and day by day I regain my strength. I tell ye, cousin, the tide has turned."

"Mayhap." Leith held his gaze. "Mayhap no."

"Aye, so. We ha' the superior numbers, as always. Wi' their war chief down and wi' ye back at my side, we ha' only to tak' out their female chief. Wha' did ye say was her name?"

"Moira. Moira MacBeith."

"Aye. Farlan's lover."

That struck Leith silent. Rory followed a plan he'd harbored since boyhood. Had he also hatched a scheme for revenge against Farlan? He was a man who could pursue the two objectives at one time.

Rory might not want to admit he desired revenge. But Farlan had hurt him. What better than to hurt him in return? And what better way to hurt him than to take from him the woman he loved?

Woodenly, Leith said, "Ye want to kill Moira MacBeith?"

"Their chief, aye. It should no' prove difficult, wi'out her big defender at her side. And she but a woman."

"She fights well." Leith swallowed hard. "And wi' Farlan at her side."

Rory's gaze met Leith's. It glinted like steel. "Farlan and I trained together all our lives. I ken his every habit on the field. Every move."

"And he yours." The two of them had faced each other untold numbers of times while sparring. Never in deadly combat.

"Still…" Rory tossed his dark head. "I think I can tak' him."

"Rory, he is your best friend."

"*Was* my best friend." A bitter look flashed across Rory's face. "He made his choice. He chose her."

"He loves her. A man canna choose where he gifts his heart."

"Och, d'ye no' give me any o' that twaddle. A man is in charge o' his emotions. Always. Any man who will trade awa' his loyalty for the pillows o' a woman's thighs is no' a man."

"I am no' certain that is true."

Aggravated, Rory got to his feet. "Och, Leith, do no' ye begin wi' turning soft as well. Wha' do they do to men there at MacBeith? Is it some potion?"

Or magic. "I am sayin' only there is a strength in what Farlan feels for his lady."

"Pah!" Rory spat. "As soon as ye are ready to fight, Leith, or maybe sooner, we will launch another attack. And its sole objective will be to tak' the life o' this Moira MacBeith."

"He will ne'er forgive ye, Rory. Is that what ye want?"

Rory flashed another look, hard as iron. Leith heard what he did not say. *And I will never forgive him.*

"If ye attack her in battle," Leith went on, more upset than he could express, "he will stand for her. He will die for her, Rory."

"So?"

"So are ye prepared to kill Farlan as well?"

Rory did not answer.

"Man, he is like a brother to ye!"

"Everything has changed. Changed for all time. There is just one objective now. Finish my task. Accomplish my goal."

And get revenge against Farlan.

"At least," Rory said, squeezing Leith's good shoulder, "I ha' ye back at my side."

How could Leith tell Rory the truth? That just like Farlan, he'd lost his heart to one of MacBeith's daughters. That at least half his loyalty lay anchored to the other side of the glen.

He could not. Nor could he stand by and watch Rory make preparations to kill Rhian's sister.

"I think," he said slowly, "'twill be a while yet before I can lift a sword, to say naught o' training wi' it. We will ha' to bide our time."

"No' too long," Rory said, the fervent light shining in his eyes. "Ye maun recover before yon Alasdair does. Else I fear I'll ne'er get near enough to Moira MacBeith to put her to the sword."

Chapter Fifty

"RHIAN, YE MUST go and speak wi' Alasdair. I ha' just been to visit him, and he is bent on getting up and out o' his bed." Saerla gave Rhian a beseeching look. "I fear if he does, 'twill be the death o' him."

Rhian sighed and nodded. She had to agree. She'd spoken with the other healers just yesterday about Alasdair's condition, and they all warned against undue movement before his wound fully closed.

Five days had passed since the battle wherein Alasdair was wounded. Since Leith had left. She could not say they had passed so much as dragged by. She had barely slept, and felt as if she moved through her days in darkness. Indeed, the only thing that kept her moving was the desire to prevent her sisters finding out how deeply Leith's departure had affected her. The only thing that kept her eating and drinking was her concern for the welfare of her child.

At night she lay imagining Leith held her in the circle of his arm, and catching the flutter of life from within.

"Alasdair has ever been a stubborn man," she pointed out.

"Aye, so. But I swear I never guessed how stubborn till now. He has never been badly injured before, has he?"

"No' that I can recall. At least, not that he ever admitted."

Saerla wrinkled her nose. "He is no' a good patient."

That almost made Rhian smile. "I will go and see him, gladly." For all his scowls and grumbles, Alasdair was one of Rhian's favorite people. What would he say when he found out she carried Leith MacLeod's child? "But I am no' sure wha' I can say to make him obedient."

"I think obedient is beyond our reach. I am hoping for reasonable. He respects ye, Rhian. And ye bein' a healer, he may listen."

"Verra well. I will speak wi' him."

"I am going up on the rise later to say my prayers. D'ye want to come?"

Thinking on it, Rhian did not know whether she had the energy. "Mayhap, Saerla. Or mayhap ye be better going on your own."

"I thought it might do ye some good." Saerla turned upon Rhian those eyes that saw so much. "Since ye do no' seem yoursel', that is."

Rhian froze, and her stomach clenched. "I am fine."

"Even after the departure o' Leith MacLeod, wi' whom ye were sharing your bed?"

"Hush!" Rhian looked around, even though they were alone outside Saerla's chamber. "No one knows that did happen, save ye."

"You know. And he. Sister, ye ha' no' looked right since he got traded awa'. In return for *me*." Saerla tipped up her chin. "D'ye regret that?"

"How can ye even ask such a thing? I adore ye. And I would no' see ye in that monster Rory's hands."

Something dark stirred in Saerla's eyes. "He is a monster, is he no'?"

"Wi'out a saving grace to his name. I am certain he is no' done wi' us. But ha' ye Seen—"

Saerla's expression shut down. It was impossible to tell what she knew. What knowledge she'd been given. The spirits might have told her about the life that nestled beneath Rhian's heart.

Saerla lifted her chin higher and said nothing.

Rhian lowered her voice to a whisper. "Is Leith well? Can ye tell?"

"I ha' Seen naught o' him. But Rory MacLeod seeks to destroy us. And Leith has now returned to his side."

Rhian turned sick. Not a victim to morning malady, she nevertheless thought she might need recourse to a basin.

Would Leith move against them? Against her? Would he have a choice? But aye, men always had a choice.

She knew Leith MacLeod. She had been inside him, and he inside her. He was a man who would readily choose laughter and a path of light. Circumstances, though, might constrain him otherwise.

Dared she hope he might talk to his cousin? Persuade him from the murderous course he pursued?

Could *anyone* do that?

"Sister," Saerla said suddenly, gazing straight into Rhian's eyes, "Protect your heart, if ye can."

Good advice. But Rhian's heart was already lost.

"I will go see Alasdair." She put her hand on Saerla's arm. "Ye go up to your prayers alone." She had not the energy after all.

The settlement bustled today, folks rushing hither and yon about various tasks. Over in the far field, she could hear the men drilling, and wondered who led them. Bright sunlight lit the glen, and she paused a moment to gaze out over the wall in the direction of MacLeod.

The distant building of dark stone seemed clearer today, and closer. She fancied she could see men moving about there also. Then the wind blew her hair in her eyes and ruined the illusion.

She heard Alasdair before she saw him. As soon as she entered the infirmary, a bellow met her ears. She grimaced and hurried through to the room at the back.

Timor the healer stood beside the cot where Alasdair had been confined for the past five days, almost wrestling with his patient. Alasdair might be in a weakened state, but Timor was a man built on a frail frame, and Rhian hurried forward with a cry of dismay.

"Here, wha' is all this?"

Timor turned an aggravated face toward her. "He will no' stay still."

Alasdair, who appeared beyond aggravated, continued to roar. "Five days ha' I lain in this bed. 'Tis daylight out. I maun get up."

"I ha' *told* him"—Timor gritted his teeth—"if he arises and tears that wound open again, he will die."

Rhian raised her eyebrows. Timor did not usually use such words with his patients. But as Saerla had said, Alasdair was no ordinary patient. He was, in fact, not patient at all.

He growled and looked at Rhian. "That is no' true, is it, Mistress Rhian? I do no' feel ready to die."

Rhian crossed her arms over her chest. "'Tis true, though. Ye ha' been verra fortunate so far."

"Fortunate!"

"Most men perish from the sort o' wound ye took."

"Ah—bah!"

"'Tis just closed over now. If ye go getting up and tearing it open inside, all the poison in yer gut may spread through your body. It will kill ye."

He did not look happy about that. He believed her, however. Dismay and acceptance flared in his dark gaze.

Without another word, Timor left the room.

Unafraid of the patient, Rhian perched on the side of the cot.

"Ye maun not attack poor Timor, ye ken. He has worked hard to save ye."

"I did no' attack him. I shall go mad lying here, mistress, when there is work to be done. A clan to protect."

"I ken it is hard."

He raised his gaze to Rhian's. "Saerla came to see me. Somewhat is amiss wi' her. She would no' say what."

A chill chased its way down Rhian's spine. "I ken."

"D'ye think she has Seen somewhat?"

"She will no' say what."

"It maun be dire if she will no' tell even ye or Moira."

"Aye." And Saerla was bent this very day on saying more prayers. Seeking answers or foreknowledge?

Alasdair reached out and touched Rhian's hand. "Mistress, somewhat bad comes."

"Alasdair, we have had our share o' bad already."

"I ken. Ever since Himself died. But—well, I am no Seer, but 'tis as if I can feel it coming. Building. And ye ask me to lie here."

"I ken how frustrating that is."

"Ye do no'."

"But where would we be—where, Alasdair—if ye succumb to this injury?"

He lowered his voice. "That is wha' frightens me, mistress."

Alasdair? Frightened?

"'Twas yon Rory MacLeod who struck me during that battle. He kens fine I am injured, and will move against us while still I am unable to tak' the field. D'ye no' see I can no' leave all I love defenseless? I maun get up on my feet."

"I do see it, Alasdair. Ye ha' the heart o' a hero. Still, I would rather have ye alive and off your feet than dying on them."

"I swear, I will be fine."

"Willpower alone canna accomplish this. I wish it could."

"Who will lead the men if MacLeod attacks us again?"

"Perhaps Moira will herself."

"No' with that Farlan at her side! The men will ne'er countenance it. Nor will the council."

"Nay." Rhian did not suppose they would.

"Wha' if Moira marches out and MacLeod takes her down? Ha' ye thought o' that?"

Rhian had not. It was unimaginable.

"'Tis all I can think about. Lyin' here," Alasdair said wretchedly.

He loved her. He loved Moira still.

That knowledge made Rhian gentle when she said, "Ye maun believe, Alasdair. The battles ha' all gone our way so far. There must be some magic in it."

"I ha' told ye before, I do no' believe in magic. And has it no' occurred to ye, mistress, the battles may ha' gone our way because I was there?"

Chapter Fifty-One

DESPITE HER BONE-DEEP exhaustion, Rhian climbed the rise to the standing stones. She had intended not to go, and had told Saerla so, but something called her. She went just as the gloaming began to come down, bringing the close of another day. The wind had died, and she saw, when she reached the height, that a soft mist gathered among the stones, as it so often did.

When they were all young, the four of them, including Arran, had come up here frequently. Saerla used to say the mist was proof of the magic that dwelt at this place.

Ye can see it only sometimes. But 'tis here always.

Rhian did not spy her sister when she reached the height. Perhaps she'd missed Saerla at her prayers. If so, she would have to seek her out below. Because she needed to know what Saerla knew.

It had frightened her, what Alasdair said—that he sensed something big and terrible bearing down on them. He was not a fanciful man. Besides, she too sensed it.

Slowly, she walked toward the mist and felt the ancient magic descend upon her. So quiet here amid the steeped knowledge of the ages and the sleeping dead. She paused at Da's cairn and laid her hand on one of the stones.

She wished she could speak to him for even one moment. Unburden her heart as she had so often in the past. Gaze into his kind blue eyes and feel the strength of him that always bore her up.

Perhaps she could still speak to him.

"Da, I am so weary. Tired to my verra soul. I do no' ken how to go on wi'out him."

Not so much as a bird settling for the night made answer. But the mist continued to roll out from the stones as if reaching for her.

She caressed the stone with her fingers and whispered, "I carry your grandchild. Your first. But I canna see a future for him."

Saerla stepped forward out from the stones. She seemed to materialize from the mist itself, and looked so otherworldly, Rhian caught her breath.

"Sister?"

Was that Saerla, or merely an image of her? A memory. Because the woman with the flowing red-gold hair and dreamy gaze did not glance at Rhian or acknowledge her presence.

"Saerla?"

Rhian took her hand from the stone, still warm from the day's sun, and went to her sister. Flesh and blood, aye. And caught fast in some wonderment.

A Vision?

Not sure what to do, she very hesitantly touched Saerla's cheek and watched her sister come out of the trance, as if awakening.

Saerla's knees gave out, and she stumbled. Rhian led her to Da's cairn, and they sat with their backs against the warm stones.

The mist continued to flow out from the stone circle as if following the young woman whose hands trembled in Rhian's.

"Saerla, wha' ha' ye Seen?"

"I canna tell. I canna tell!"

Could not, or would not? Whatever it was, it had frightened Saerla badly.

"You can tell me."

"Strife. Darkness. The very fabric o' us torn asunder." Only Saerla's lips moved. The mist swirled in her eyes.

"War? Are ye saying we face outright war wi' MacLeod?" Against all likelihood, Rhian had hoped otherwise. The desperate love in her heart wanted peace.

"Aye. But worse. Worse than that."

What could be worse? To Rhian's mind, war appeared a terrible gulf, with Leith on one side and her on the other. And their child here with her.

The unborn heir to MacLeod.

"Will he attack us again? Rory MacLeod?"

"Rory MacLeod," Saerla repeated woodenly.

"When? How much time do we have?" If Alasdair learned of this, she would never keep him in his bed. And aye, if he went to battle, he would quite likely die.

"Soon." The word, sibilant from Saerla's lips, lifted the tiny hairs all over Rhian's body. "Soon."

"Ye maun tell Moira. She maun prepare."

The three of them, MacBeith's daughters, must be together. They were always stronger so. And yet, and yet…

She could not stay here and continue to try to live without her heart.

The knowledge came to her all of a piece, filtered through her like the soft kiss of the mist that now surrounded them. Perhaps it came from the mist. Mayhap this was how it felt to receive a Vision.

She could not live without Leith MacLeod. She would wither and die, and the child within her. If he could not come to her, she must go to him.

But it was impossible. *Impossible.* She could not leave this place that was part and parcel of her, blood and bone. She could not leave her sisters.

Saerla looked at her as if she heard those thoughts. Gladness and sorrow moved together in her eyes before she reached out and captured Rhian's face between her hands.

"Why did ye no' tell me? Why did ye no' tell me ye carry Leith MacLeod's bairn?"

"Och!" Rhian caught her breath. All her agony rose inside her as she stared into Saerla's face. "I could no'."

All at once, she began to weep. Saerla gathered her close into the shelter of her arms and let Rhian sob against her shoulder. It felt almost as if Ma's arms encircled her in warmth and love.

"There. There now, let it all out."

They remained so, with their backs against the stones, while the mist swirled around them. Rhian wept until she could weep no more.

Only then did she draw away and mop at her face with the hem of her dress. "I could tell no one. No one except him."

"He knows?"

"Aye. He left me knowing."

A brief silence fell before Saerla said, "If the child be a boy, that means ye carry the heir to MacLeod."

"The child is a boy."

"By God, Rhian!"

"I ken."

"Ye will ha' to tell Moira."

"If 'tis known, if 'tis known I carry a MacLeod child, 'twill stir hatred. The bairn will be hated. As will I."

"Ye need not tell everyone, not yet. But Moira maun know. And Farlan."

"If the council find out, they may wish to use the child in a bid for power, the way they wanted to use Leith."

"Aye, 'tis a measure o' power, holding MacLeod's heir."

Rhian looked at Saerla and blinked away tears. "That is why I think I canna stay here."

The words fell like the droplets of the mist, settling soft and separate.

"What?"

"I canna allow this child to become a pawn in the struggle that should no' be. Besides, I do no' think I can live wi'out him,

Saerla."

"Him?"

"Leith. I canna live wi'out Leith MacLeod. I maun go to him."

Saerla gasped. Rhian could feel the protest rise inside her. "But sister, ye canna leave. We are the three sisters MacBeith. Iain's daughters! Stronger always together."

"Aye, I ken." Rhian began to weep again. She had more tears after all.

"Ye canna go—go there! To live among strangers. Alone." Horror filled Saerla's face.

"Not alone. Wi' him. The father o' my child."

"Alone! Ye ha' no idea. We ha' ne'er been so alone."

Rhian tried to imagine it, the bonds between her and her sisters stretching over that distance that encompassed both land and emotion. Would those bonds break?

"This," Saerla whispered, "this must be the terrible darkness I Saw. The event too awful to imagine."

"I love him, Saerla."

"As Moira loves Farlan."

"Aye, and as Farlan loves Moira. He gave up everything for her. Can I do any less?"

"This is awful. It is deep and wide. But I will no' dissuade ye, will I?"

Rhian shook her head.

"Then wha' can I do but stand wi' ye?"

Chapter Fifty-Two

LEITH COULD NOT keep still. His body told him he needed to rest, as did Rory's healers. But keeping to his bedchamber felt far too much like being confined back at MacBeith, and it allowed his thoughts to beset him.

Thoughts likely to drive him mad.

Rory wanted him to grow hearty and strong, to regain the use of his arm so he could march out to battle. Wage an attack in which Rory's main objective would be to slay Moira. Rhian's adored sister. Farlan's precious love.

He was not sure whether, if he delayed, Rory would march out without him. Pushed for time, Rory wanted to launch his attack before Alasdair could once more take the field.

Leith could not imagine how to dissuade him. He knew only that he must.

So he paced the settlement, even though it drained what strength he managed to harbor. He spoke to his fellow warriors, all happy to see him returned, and all curious about what had happened to him at MacBeith.

He dared not say. Unbearable pain, and unimaginable joy also. Lying in Rhian's arms, tasting her lips and her skin. Being inside her. When he thought about it, his body tightened, and the bonds between them also. He felt both wretched and more fortunate than he'd ever imagined being. Because if only for a time, he'd had that. His merciful angel in his arms.

The weather proved soft and kind, a particular irony. White clouds sailed down the glen on a sea of blue, the color lighter than Rhian's eyes, and peered at their reflections in the loch. The warm scents of summer filled the air, thyme from the hills and the peaty smell of the water.

It came to him—it would be the easiest of things to walk out across the green sward, cross the loch, and return to MacBeith. Once the thought occurred, he could not banish it.

If he chose to go, could Rory stop him? He remembered that terrible scene with Farlan only weeks ago—Rory's face black with rage as he denounced his best friend. As he stripped him of even the right to wear his own tartan, and sent him, nearly naked, to the woman he loved.

Leith knew how Farlan had suffered for that, and how Rory had.

Rory would never let that happen again.

Besides, Leith was Rory's heir, at least for the time being. How could Rory let him go?

So he paced and pondered and thought about impossibilities. At night he lay aching, and tried to imagine Rhian there with him. He recalled when they had lain so close, so connected, that they could catch one another's thoughts, and tried to catch them again. But the distance proved too great.

Surely, surely she thought of him as he thought of her. With his child inside her, surely she did. Did the child grow well? What best might he do for his son, and his son's mother?

He wanted to tell his own mother the truth, confess how he'd fallen in love at MacBeith, with the old chief's daughter. How he'd left the better part of his heart behind. He wanted to tell his sister, but he felt reluctant to involve her in his tangle.

He tramped the grounds to tire himself out, and worked his hand when no one could see. He'd never been a man suited to strategy or weighty problems. Now he dared not speak a word or take a wrong action.

"I am ill-suited for this," he muttered to himself as he walked out to watch the men drilling in the bright morning sunlight.

Rory was there and at practice, as he should not be, with that wound in his back. How did he endure it?

The scowl on Rory's face denoted he did not endure without pain. If there was a more stubborn man in all Scotland than Rory MacLeod, Leith did not know his name.

The men worked nearly silently, with none of the customary banter or teasing insults, which in itself was telling. Rory had been in a permanent bad mood since Leith had returned. No one wanted to cross him.

Leith stood to one side, arms crossed upon his chest, watching the men work and sweat.

But his gaze wandered up and away. Across the loch and through the distances, till it found the stronghold situated halfway up the rise on the far side of the glen. Visible in the clear air, MacBeith's keep looked almost like a place of dreams.

A sword point dug into the turf beside him and made him jump.

"There," a hard voice said. "Take it up."

Leith eyed the weapon. Rory's sword, with the copper-inlaid pommel, still aquiver from the power of Rory's thrust.

"I will no' use your sword." And he had lost his own, leaving it somewhere on the bloodied field the night of his capture. When the angel had found him.

He focused on the face of Rory, who stood beside him, aggression in his every line. It came to Leith that his friend did not look well. Beneath the sweat of exertion, his face had turned sickly pale, and those new lines, the ones that had appeared since Farlan left, bit deep.

Rory missed his friend. And he thrust that pain away from him by force, just like the pain in his back.

"Then fetch another," he growled, no mercy at all in his eyes. "There are plenty in the armory. I ha' the smiths working day and night."

Aye, Leith had heard the clanging.

"Either way, fetch a sword and get to work. There is no use pampering yoursel'."

Ruefully, Leith flexed the fingers of his right hand. Doing so still caused pain up near his shoulder. But could he say so to Rory, after watching him work with that hole in his back?

"I've nae strength yet, cousin."

"Ye'll no' build strength standing there like a great lump. Fetch a sword, damn ye."

Leith thought about it. He could, aye, walk over to the side, where he saw a number of spare weapons, and pick up a sword, any sword. Or he could try to reason with his cousin. Staring into that militant gaze, he knew the wiser course.

"Rory, man, gi' yoursel' a few days to recover. Ye and me both."

"I do no' ha' a few days. How long d'ye think before that war chief o' theirs is on his feet?"

"I do no' ken, not knowing how badly he is injured." But from all he'd seen of Alasdair, it would not take him long to be back training.

"Get to work," Rory growled, and stalked back to the fray, pain in his every movement.

Not often did Leith defy his cousin. Neither he nor Farlan ever had, growing up. Rory made the rules he and Farlan followed into mayhem and mischief.

But Leith had been a boy then. Now he—just like Farlan—was a man. A man who loved.

He did not hesitate as he turned his back on the training field and walked away.

HE HAD NO need to seek Rory out later to deliver the words that danced through his head. Instead, Rory found him sitting in the corner of the nearly deserted warriors' hall with an empty mug in front of him.

It had grown late. The only thing that kept Leith from his bed was the thought of endless hours lying there alone.

Rory stalked in and thumped a flagon of ale down on the table. "So here ye are."

"Aye." Leith looked up at Rory, trying to measure his mood—dark and ugly, from what he could see.

Rory toed out the bench opposite Leith and sat down. "Why did ye walk out on training? Ye ken fine we never do that."

Aye, for Rory, training was akin to sacred. In the past Leith had always gone along with that, a regimen that no doubt accounted for half his bulk of muscle.

No more.

"I will no' pick up a sword against MacBeith."

Rory stared at him. In that moment, completely nonplussed, he might have been struck dumb. Thoughts moved in his eyes—shock, honest surprise, and then anger.

The anger restored the power of speech. "What?"

"I say, I will no' make war on MacBeith, no' again."

Disbelief joined the anger. Anger won. "Ye will. If I order ye. As yer chief."

Aye, so. That was Rory all over. An order given out of an unswerving belief in entitlement. No shades between right and wrong for him.

Open defiance, as Leith well knew, would not work. An appeal to old affections might, only Farlan had already burned any such bridges.

"Man," he said softly, "there maun be a better way. Better than continuing to kill each other. Ye be sore wounded, as am I. As is MacBeith's war chief. 'Tis the right time to speak for peace."

"Peace." Rory repeated it, and all other emotion fled before his disgust. "Will MacBeith surrender to me, then? For 'tis the only way they will achieve peace."

"Nay. But listen. Wi' Farlan there close to their chief and me here beside ye—Well, we spoke o' it when I was there. Farlan and I did. Of forging a treaty for the good o' all."

"Ye. And Farlan." Rory's lip curled. "All cozy there, were ye?"

"He remains my good friend."

"He remains a *traitor*. There maun be some poison that resides in that accursed place. I would say 'twas dark magic, did I no' spit upon such fancies."

"Rory." Leith reached out and touched his cousin's arm. "There be a woman there, at MacBeith. The healer of whom I told ye." *She carries my child.* But he would not add that. He could not, given what now blazed in Rory's eyes.

Rory scraped back his bench and got to his feet. "A woman! Another o' the old chief's daughters, ye said. Aye, and will ye turn traitor to be wi' her also, as Farlan has done? All for the sake o' a *woman*?"

"Rory, I love her. I want—need—to be wi' her. If that requires achieving a peace—"

Leith thought his cousin would choke on his anger.

Low and angry, Rory said, "I canna cast ye off as I did Farlan. Ye be my blood. But ye will forget this woman, aye? Ye will drop these childish fancies, and ye will march out to face Clan MacBeith at my side."

A dark tide of despair rose to engulf Leith. "And if I will no'?"

"Then ye'll be prisoner here, cousin, even as ye were at Mac-Beith, because I will not—*will not*—stand by and watch the one nearest me to turn his back on me again."

Chapter Fifty-Three

"MOIRA, I NEED a word wi' ye. Please."

Rhian had not slept all the night. Instead, she'd lain with her arms wrapped around her belly, cradling the precious life that lay within and pondering what Saerla had said to her up on the rise.

She'd arisen early and come to Moira's door. So early that now, when Moira opened it, Rhian could once more see Farlan still abed, his chest bare and his brown hair in a tangle.

Indeed, Moira wore no more than a chemise, rucked around her thighs and no doubt hastily donned.

Moira blinked at her. "Sister, can it no' wait?"

"Nay, I fear it canna."

Moira opened the door wider and motioned Rhian in. Farlan began to scramble up from the bed. Rhian wondered wildly if he were naked beneath the blankets.

"I will go," he said.

"Nay, Farlan, pray do no'. This concerns ye also. At least, it concerns your friend, Leith."

Farlan, looking startled, settled back against the bolsters.

Moira peered at Rhian. "Sister, ye do no' look well. What is it?"

Rhian closed the chamber door behind her and leaned against it. "I am carrying Leith MacLeod's child."

"What?"

Rhian watched as all the color drained from Moira's face.

"But how—how?"

"My love," Farlan whispered, "I believe there is only one way." He looked at Rhian kindly. "Leith?"

"I love him." She pronounced it in a gasp. "As I ne'er thought to love any man."

"Christ Jesus!" Moira backed to a bench and collapsed upon it.

"Our feelings for one another grew while I helped to care for him. After he was moved to my chamber—I did no' spend those first nights wi' Saerla but in my own bed. Wi' him."

"But, but," Moira sputtered, "that was mere days ago. How can ye possibly ken ye carry his child?"

"I just do. I felt it almost at once. The bairn is male."

"Heir to MacLeod," Farlan murmured.

Rhian moved her gaze back to him. "Aye."

"Och, God! Sweet, merciful heaven! Rhian, how could ye let this happen? Ye, o' all women. Sane. And careful."

"Moira," Farlan said. "Were ye no' sane and careful—once?" Their eyes met, and something in Moira's face eased.

"Aye. Aye. But I do no' carry your child. Can ye imagine wha' the council will say?" She switched her gaze back to Rhian. "Does anyone else know?"

"Only Saerla, and Leith himsel'."

"Leith knows?"

"Aye. I told him at once."

Farlan muttered, "It maun ha' killed him being sent awa'."

Rhian removed her palms from the door behind her and twisted them together. "'Tis killing both o' us. I ha' no' slept. I fear for the welfare o' the child."

Moira glanced at Farlan again. "The council cannot be told. If they know Rhian carries the heir to MacLeod, they may seek to hold her and thus the child hostage."

"'Twill become all too evident soon enough," he replied.

"Nay," Rhian said, breathless. "It will no'. Because I plan to leave MacBeith. Soon, before I begin to show.”

Moira’s mouth opened and closed again. Sympathy flooded Farlan’s eyes. Aye, if anyone were to understand, it would be him.

“Ye mean to go to Leith.”

“I do.”

“Nay.” Moira forced the word between her parted lips. She stumbled to her feet. “Nay! Ye canna leave us.”

Rhian looked at her sister with regret. She blinked back tears. “I must.”

“Ye canna go there! To live among strangers. We will manage this somehow. I will face the council down. We will protect the child, the three o’ us, with Farlan and Alasdair—”

“Sister, ye do no’ understand. I canna live wi’out Leith. I ha’ tried, these past days and nights.”

“But Rhian, we canna live wi’out ye! Ye be the very heart o’ this place, since Ma died. Ye be the best o’ us.”

“Saerla is the best o’ us, and ye be our strength. Wha’ ha’ I ever done but kindled a few fires?”

“’Tis the fire,” Moira pronounced, “that keeps us alive. Rhian—nay. It is meant to be the three o’ us.”

“And we shall remain three. Naught can sever the love between us. I shall merely be *there*, instead o’ here.”

“Can ye truly leave your home?” Moira challenged her. “The hills? The stones up on the rise? Arran’s grave and Da’s cairn?”

“I will carry it all inside me, just like this child.”

Moira began to weep, though Rhian doubted she noticed her own tears, since they flowed unchecked down her cheeks. “When? When will this terrible thing take place?”

“As soon as I can pack up my belongings.”

Moira looked wildly at Farlan. “Talk to her! Talk her out o’ it.”

“I am the last man, love, to talk her out o’ it.”

“Will Rory MacLeod accept her? Will he allow here there, bein’ who she is?”

Farlan thought about it. "He will no' harm a woman, though I doubt much he will be happy wi' the situation. Rhian, this is a difficult path ye choose. Ye will ha' nary a friend there at MacLeod—save Leith."

Rhian lifted her chin. "I did no' choose the path. It chose me."

"Destiny," Farlan said to Moira. "Can we gainsay it?"

"I will gainsay aught that takes Rhian from me. I am losing my sister!" It came in a wail, and Moira pulled Rhian hard into her arms in a fierce hug. "Sister, say ye will change your mind."

"I canna." Rhian drew away—not far—and dabbed her eyes. "Mayhap wi' me there, I can do some good. Work for peace."

A scratch at the door interrupted them. Saerla slipped in and threw herself into a three-way embrace.

For many long moments they remained so, arms hard around each other and red heads touching. Rhian could feel the strength of it, and the pain.

"She is leaving us, Saerla!" Moira cried. "Leaving us for Mac-Leod."

"Aye. Aye, I ken."

The three of them, born but five years apart from eldest to youngest, had been together most their lives—all Saerla's life. Losing that seemed unimaginable.

But would Rhian truly lose them?

Looking into her sisters' faces, she said again, "We are still three. I will merely be there, and ye here."

"How d'ye mean to go?" Moira asked. "Ye canna go alone."

Farlan arose from the bed, wrapping the blanket around his hips as he did so. "I will tak' her." His gaze, warm with compassion, touched Rhian's face.

"But Farlan, will Rory want to see ye?"

"I do no' care if he does or if he does no'. I will ferry my sister across the loch and see her safe in Leith's hands."

Because he understood, Rhian thought. He alone comprehended the magnitude of what she surrendered. And what she embraced.

He had faced his destiny with courage. Could she do less?

"Thank ye," she told Farlan with true gratitude. "I will be safe in your company."

He nodded. "In yer own time, Rhian. Gather wha' ye do no' wish to leave behind and say farewell to wha' ye must."

"I dare no' say any farewells, other than I ha' done."

Moira said, "Ye maun say farewell to Alasdair."

"And have him try to talk me out o' this? Nay. I will carry wha' I truly need to tak' wi' me, in my heart."

Farlan nodded. "Let me but dress m'sel'. I will meet ye at the gate."

Rhian cast a look into each of her sisters' faces—Moira, stark and full of pain, Saerla, broken.

She would travel across the loch, aye, to find her love. She would also leave love behind.

Chapter Fifty-Four

RHIAN'S LEGS TREMBLED beneath her as she stood on the green turf overlooking the glen. Another bonny morning it was, with beauty spreading out from her on all sides. The gentle wash of morning light flooding golden from the east. The shadows of the hills slipping away westward. Behind her, to the south, the rise and the stronghold—her home—where lay all the safety she'd ever known. Away northward, MacLeod's keep in the distance.

It seemed such a very great distance after all.

Even as she contemplated that, Farlan took his place at her side. He wore his gray kilt and cloak—a reminder of all he'd given up—and enough weapons to outfit a small army. He had tied back his mop of brown hair, and his level gaze met Rhian's.

"Rhian, be ye certain o' this?"

She could still change her mind. Or could she? Moira had already been up on the walls with a word to let the guard there know what transpired. Those guards now hung far out over the battlements, watching. That, though, was not the only reason she could not turn around and go back inside. Because if she did, what of her longing? What of the unbearable tug that drew her relentlessly to the man she loved?

She could scarcely bear to go. She could not bear to stay.

"I am certain," she told Farlan.

But och, she felt sick with it. Sick with terror. Her heart beat so hard it shook her whole body. And aye, her legs quivered so she did not know if they could hold her up.

Moira walked out from the gate and pulled Rhian hard into her arms. "Ye need not go."

"That is just it, sister. I must."

Saerla, stepping out softly, embraced her next. Her scent enfolded Rhian like the very breath of magic. "Be safe."

Rhian nodded, not trusting herself to speak.

Farlan took her arm. His hand felt strong and steady. "One step," he whispered. "Then twa."

One step. The very turf felt uneven beneath her foot, as if she would tip and fall. Or maybe float away.

Two steps.

I am coming, my love. I am coming because I canna bear to live awa' from ye.

Did he hear? No response came across the distance. Only the light finding and surrounding her as she and Farlan walked out, him half supporting her, and carrying her pack.

What of her fire? What of the hearth she had tended in her father's home since Ma's death? Who would keep that now?

Almost—almost that thought made her turn back. The fire was the heart of her being. How could she abandon it? How, and still remain the woman she was?

Her step faltered, and Farlan looked at her. The depth of kindness in his gaze touched her clear through.

"Ye can still turn back."

"Nay, I canna. He—he awaits me."

"Leith is a blessed man, far more than he ever knew."

They exchanged very few words during the balance of the journey. Rhian did not look back, and the tears that blurred her vision and choked her throat slowly cleared. Longing sprang up in their wake. She would see him soon, be with him and answer the terrible yearning.

Farlan murmured solicitously when they reached the loch and he settled her in the tiny boat. He rowed them across with clean, strong strokes, and she wondered what he felt. Going home. Not going home.

"D'ye miss it? D'ye miss MacLeod?" she asked him while he helped her out on the other side. Foreign soil.

He shook his head without hesitation. "Moira is—Well, she is my place o' belonging now."

"I hope that happens for me."

"Aye, Rhian, so do I."

They had already caught the attention of the MacLeod watchmen, and a number of them set out at a run to intercept them. Farlan remained outwardly calm and kept a steady pace. They could see the figures, though, scrambling and heading toward them.

"Will they challenge us?" Rhian asked in a whisper. "Attack us?"

"A lone warrior and a woman? Nay, though I doubt Rory will welcome my presence here again. Ah, now—they ha' recognized me and sent for him. Here he comes."

Terror gripped Rhian by the throat and invaded her mind, raw and bright. If they did come under attack, Farlan would fight to defend her. Outnumbered, he would die. Perhaps they both would.

She would die for the sake of love.

There'd been a time she would never have believed it, that she could trade her safety, trade her known existence, for what she considered a fanciful emotion. That had been before Leith.

She could see a man who must be Rory. He had taken the place at the head of the others, pelting toward them. A big man with long black hair that flew behind him, shining in the sun. Heavily armed.

She wanted to draw back then, but Farlan just kept walking. His hand hovered over the hilt of his sword, but he kept on steadily. God bless him.

She stole a look up into his face—smooth and apparently calm. "Thank ye. Thank ye for this. If I do no' ha' a chance to say—"

"Here he comes. Do no' be afraid. He will be angry and will likely shout."

Rhian fixed her narrowed gaze on the black-haired man who did indeed appear angry. A train of other armed men came after him. including—

All the breath left her body. Her feet seemed to leave the turf. She floated rather than walked.

Leith came behind Rory at a jog, his gaze fixed upon her.

And suddenly nothing else mattered. Pulled forward by the anchor beneath her heart, she let go of Farlan's arm and ran forward. Ran to Leith, until an arm came out to block her way like an iron bar extended. "Stay!"

A furious Rory it was who halted her passage. He possessed an enraged face that contained a pair of blazing green eyes and enough ire to halt an army.

Rhian stopped. She could do nothing else. So, this was the Chief MacLeod.

"Who in Satan's realm are ye?"

"Do no' touch her. Do no' touch her!" The bellow sounded just as Leith barreled into Rory and knocked him aside. His hands came up and closed on Rhian's arms.

Her world fell immediately into place, all the pieces coming together one after the other, the ache beneath her heart blooming into a blaze of sheer rightness.

How could she have been such a fool as to mourn for her fire? She carried it within her. It burned for him.

Leith's eyes, gray blue like the sky above his head, embraced her. In them lay amazement, incredulous wonder, and gratitude as deep as the loch. In his touch on her arms lay all the comfort she would ever need.

Beside them, Rory sputtered curses. His brilliant gaze swept over Rhian and Leith before he turned on Farlan with a growl.

"Ye are no' welcome here, traitor."

Farlan made a placating gesture. "I will no' stay. I come only to deliver Mistress MacBeith safely where she belongs."

"Mistress MacBeith?" Rory turned on Rhian and Leith. His gaze swept over his cousin with inestimable fury. "So this be another o' MacBeith's accursed daughters?"

"I am." From somewhere—perhaps from the strength of what flowed to her from Leith—Rhian found the courage to speak.

Rory sneered. "Ye are no' welcome here either."

Leith stepped forward. Rhian could feel him trembling, every muscle aquiver, not with weakness but with the force of his determination.

"She stays. She stays, Rory, as she chooses. Else I walk awa' wi' her now. Wi' her and Farlan."

Rory looked like he'd been struck. Color came and went in his face, leaving it pale, and the desire for murder stood in his eyes. They flicked to Rhian, and for an instant she was sure he would knock Leith down, and possibly her also.

"Ye expect me to allow her into my keep—an enemy?"

"I do. And I intend to wed wi' her, if she'll ha' me."

Those gathered went dead silent, each one right down to the guards freezing in place. At that moment it seemed the very air of Glen Bronach stilled to listen, as if the fate of the future hung in the balance.

Rory quivered with rage, and the look in his eyes turned savage. He thrust his face into Leith's as he growled, "O'er my dead body."

He stalked off then, anger in every line of him. Leith gazed into Rhian's face. "Do ye? D'ye mean to stay wi' me?"

"I do."

"Will ye wed wi' me?"

"I will."

"Och, God. 'Tis a miracle." He closed his eyes in fervent gratitude, only to open them and look at Farlan. "How can I thank ye?"

"No need. Be happy," Farlan whispered before he brushed his

fingers across Rhian's arm and looked at Leith. "Both o' ye."

He walked away, and Rhian watched him go. Moira would be glad, so glad to have him back.

She turned and gazed into the face of the man she loved.

Who promptly sank to his knees in the turf.

They still had an audience. Rory had gone, aye, but members of the guard lingered out of curiosity or caution.

Leith disregarded them. Taking both Rhian's hands in his, he gazed into her eyes.

"Merciful lady, I do no' deserve ye. And I do no' ken quite what magic has brought ye here to me. But I will strive every day o' my life, with all that is in me, to mak' ye happy and prove worthy o' this gift ye bring to me."

Tears clogged Rhian's throat. She could not speak.

"Rhian MacBeith, d'ye swear ye will be mine forever and always?"

"I am already yours, Leith MacLeod. And the gift lies between us."

He got to his feet and bent his head over her hands. "So it does, merciful angel. So it does."

Hand in hand, with Rhian carrying the future, they walked away from Rhian's past and toward MacLeod's stronghold.

Epilog

LEITH SHIFTED IN the warmth of the bed, half dazed by wonder at having Rhian once more in his arms. From the moment the alarm had been given and he'd run out to behold her walking toward him across the green turf with Farlan, he'd suspected he moved in a dream.

But aye, she lay with him here in his bed. In his arms. He could smell the fragrance of herbs coming off her hair—by God, he loved her mop of wild hair. He could still taste her on his tongue. And aye, he had only recently been inside her.

Where he belonged.

Now they lay naked. Sated in body and spirit. He ran his hand—his left hand, for that still served him better than the other—over the satin of her skin and across her belly.

Into her ear he whispered, "Is he well, my son?"

"Very well indeed." She purred like a cat when contented, did his Rhian.

His touch on her belly grew protective. "I will do all I can for him. And for ye."

She swiveled in his grasp, and her lips slid across his in a fleeting caress. The heat inside him, so recently banked, flared to life. "Ye will ha' to tell Rory about him before I begin to show."

"Aye, I will."

She shivered slightly. "He is an intimidating sort o' man."

"I will face him down for ye. 'Twill be a new experience for him, aye, but I will. I would do anything for ye."

"Work for peace?"

"Work for peace." Leith repeated it like a vow.

She moved softly in the bed until she lay atop him. He gloried in the movement and in the sight of her face, beautiful in the morning light. Their first night together here at MacLeod was done. First of many, so he prayed.

Twining his fingers into her hair, he gazed at her earnestly.

In his head he asked, *Will ye be all right here among strangers?*

So long as I am with ye.

"Then I need naught else," he told her aloud. "You, me, our child.

She dimpled. "Perhaps some laughter. It comes to me that laughter has been too much lacking from my life. I ha' been a serious sort o' woman, withal."

"I will be your laughter."

"And I will be your fire."

"The fire in my hearth." He saw her gaze kindle and picked up the heat of it throughout his body.

Kiss me, oh kiss me, she begged silently. And he did.

The End

About the Author

Laura Strickland delights in time traveling to the past and weaving deliciously romantic stories for her readers. Her first love has always been Scottish Historical Romance, and her work has garnered her several awards including a RONE. At home in Western New York, she's been privileged to mother a number of very special rescue dogs. Her lifelong interest in Celtic history, magic, and music, along with her mantra of *Lore, Legend, Love* are all reflected in her writing.

Visit Laura at www.laurastricklandbooks.com

www.ingramcontent.com/pod-product-compliance
Lightning Source LLC
Chambersburg PA
CBHW070525310726

48976CB00002BA/541

9 781961 275881